Possession

Book Three

The Middleton Series

Lisa Lang Blakeney

Writergirl Press

LISA LANG BLAKENEY

Love reading novels featuring hot alpha men who fall for smart women?
Then join <u>MY VIP MAILING LIST</u> at https://LisaLangBlakeney.
com/VIP and get a FREE book just for joining!

Copyright © 2025 Lisa Lang Blakeney.
All rights reserved.
Published by: Writergirl Press

FOLLOW ME

Follow me on Facebook
Join my Fan Group
Follow me on Amazon
Follow me on Bookbub
Follow me on Instagram

License Note

This book is a work of fiction. Any similarity to real events, people, or places is entirely coincidental. All rights reserved. This book may not be reproduced or distributed in any format without the permission of the author, except in the case of brief quotations used for review.

The author acknowledges the trademarked status of products referred to in this book and acknowledges that trademarks have been used without permission.

This book contains mature content, including graphic sex. Please do not continue reading if you are under the age of 18 or if this type of content is disturbing to you.

Books By Lisa

****Discounted Book Bundles****
Ultimate Masterson Book Bundle
Ultimate King Brothers Book Bundle
Ultimate Nighthawks Book Bundle
Ultimate Alpha Book One Bundle

The Masterson Series
Devour this addictive series about the possessive bad boy,
Roman Masterson, who falls hard and fast for the girl he's
promised his family to protect.
Masterson
Masterson Unleashed
Masterson In Love
Masterson Made
Joseph Loves Juliette

Masterson Next Generation Series
The crazy hot fruit doesn't fall far from the tree. Dive into
this second generation of Masterson men!
Knox - Knox & Gigi

Bronx - Bronx & Karma
Seven - coming soon

The King Brothers Series

Dive into this series of interconnected standalones featuring 3 alpha hot brothers and the women they lay claim to without apology.
Claimed - Camden & Jade
Indebted - Cutter & Sloan
Broken - Stone & Tiny
Promised - All King Brothers

The Nighthawk Series

Sexy, smart sports romances set in the professional world of football. All standalones.
Saint - Saint & Sabrina
Wolf - Cooper & Ursula
Diesel - Mason & Olivia
Jett - Jett & Adrienne
Rush - Rush & Mia
Freak - Freak & Willow
Brick - Brick & Kaya
Dak - Dak & Katrina

Valencia Ice Mafia Series

Hot hockey romances set on the college campus of Valencia City University.
Neo - Neo & Violet
Shane - Shane & Kennedy
Bass - Coming Soon

The Middleton Series
(Club Blue Whiskey)

Dark, age-gap, romantic suspense trilogy, set in the underbelly of Los Angeles featuring dangerous billionaire Hunter Middleton and the object of his obsession, Megan.

Obsession

Submission

Possession

Introduction

All He'll Surrender To Is Her...

POSSESSION is the heart-stopping finale of Hunter and Megan's story—raw, real, and packed with the kind of love that conquers everything.

There's nothing I wouldn't do for Megan. She's the one thing in my life I got right, even when the rest of the world tried to tear us apart. I've fought the demons of my past and eliminated some of hers, and now she's back where she belongs—in my arms, carrying my child, building our forever.

But peace doesn't come easy for men like me. The ghosts of what we've endured still linger, threatening to pull us under. Only this time, I'm not letting go. Megan and I didn't come this far to lose now.

We've earned this love.

We've bled for it.

And now, nothing will stop me from giving her the life she deserves.

She's mine.

Chapter 1

Where Is She?

HUNTER

I pace the length of our penthouse, my mind racing as fast as my steps. It's been hours since Megan left the apartment to clear her head after our argument, and something feels off. The air is thick with unease, and my gut twists tighter with each passing minute. I glance at my Rolex again, cursing under my breath.

Where the fuck is she?

"I'm just going for a walk," she had said. But regardless of the circumstances, Megan never takes this long for a walk. I've called her phone repeatedly, each time greeted by the mocking drone of her voicemail. My calls to Parker, waiting downstairs, go unanswered, too.

Dread envelops me.

But I try to reassure myself. Maybe she just needs time to cool off, to process the whirlwind of changes I basically threw at her without warning. It's my fault. I did the thing I always do. For God's sake, why would I buy her house without letting her pick it out? And while that's a good reason for her to shut me out, deep down, I know something isn't right.

This isn't like her.

Not Megan.

I stride over to the window, peering down at the street below, hoping to catch a glimpse of her returning. But the street is just a flow of anonymous faces, none of them Megan's. The city seems to have swallowed her whole.

The unease I feel morphs into a sharp spike of fear. Megan is pregnant and vulnerable. The memories of everything we've just been through over the last few months send a cold shiver down my spine. I thought it was finally over, but has someone targeted her again because of me?

My jaw clenches at the thought.

My pacing quickens. I reach for my phone again, dialing Lars. As usual, he answers on the first ring. I should have called him an hour ago.

"Boss."

"Have you spoken to Parker?"

"I thought he was with you."

"I can't reach him."

"What's going on, Hunter? You don't sound right."

"It's Megan. She hasn't come back. I can't find her or Parker."

"Do you know for sure that they're together?"

"I don't know anything for sure."

There's a beat of silence, then Lars' voice, tense, says, "I'm on it. I'll check the security feeds, and see if I can spot her. She can't be far."

I end the call and start to pace again, my mind a torrent of worst-case scenarios. If someone has taken her...

My phone buzzes. It's Lars. I answer immediately.

"Hunter, you need to see this." His voice is grim.

My stomach drops.

"What is it?"

"Just come down to the security room."

I'm out the door in seconds, taking the stairs two at a time, my heart pounding in my chest. As I burst into the security room, Lars is in front of a bank of monitors, his expression dark.

He points to a screen showing the lobby from earlier. The security man I hired to man the front desk of the building is knocked out from behind. His attacker out of view. Lars switches to another camera angle to see if we can see more but the next frame shows Megan.

"Pause it," I instruct Lars sharply.

He pauses the footage and zooms in on her face. Tears are streaming down her cheeks, no doubt ones that I put there.

Ten minutes later there's screen footage of Megan, her body language tense, upset. Then the screen shows a large black Audi pulling up front, and a tall, imposing-looking man getting out. The man and Megan have a brief exchange, their conversation clearly upsetting her more than she already was, and then...

My breath catches as I watch the man grab Megan, the struggle, her being forced into the car. The screen is a silent witness to my worst fears coming true.

"She's been taken," Lars says, his voice barely above a whisper.

The love of my life.

My unborn child.

Both are at risk.

Anger and fear collide within me, an explosive mix. "Who the fuck are they?" I demand, my voice a roar.

"I don't know, but I'll find out."

My years of experience searching for criminals click in. I rattle off a checklist of things we need to do to find my woman.

"Get the plate numbers off of that Audi. Take screenshots of the man arguing with her and run them through identification software. And then–"

"We'll get her back, Hunter," Lars tries reassuring me.

"Where is Parker!"

Parker should still be parked in front of the building, waiting for me. Protecting my fiance. Where was he when she was snatched from right under my nose?

"I don't have the answers yet."

"You don't think that's odd?"

"Boss, I know you're worried, but Parker wouldn't be a part of hurting Megan."

I pace back and forth, running a hand through my hair in frustration. "How could they get to her so easily?"

"They must have been watching the building for some time," Lars says. "They knew our patterns, when and how to hit our security."

"What patterns? Megan and I fought. She wouldn't have been down here if we didn't have one."

"You can't blame yourself for that. They just would have waited to grab her another time."

"Dammit." I clench my fists at my sides. If only I had been more vigilant and more prepared.

"We'll find her," Lars reassures me. "That's my niece or nephew she's carrying. Bringing her home safe is the only option."

"Right," I reply, but the knot of fear in my stomach remains.

We continue scouring the footage for any clues or leads

until Lars' phone rings. He answers quickly and listens intently before hanging up and turning to me.

"That was one of our sources within the network," he says gravely. "He confirmed who took Megan."

"Who?"

"The Fabres."

Naomi's family.

Why didn't I think of them before?

"Where is Naomi?"

"They have her too."

"Did he say why they took Megan?" I demand to know. "It makes no sense. I thought his daughter was his only priority."

"We aren't sure of his intentions. He hasn't attempted to make contact," Lars responds. "But our informant did give us a location."

"Yeah? Let's go." I grab my coat and rush out of the security room with Lars close behind me.

"Boss, it's a little more complicated than that," he says, running behind me. "It's not an exact location. She's on the move."

"Where, Lars?"

"They're on the highway, headed toward New Orleans, I think, and they're at least an hour ahead of us."

Fuck!!!

All I can see is the image of Megan being taken, playing over and over in my mind. This is my fault. The Fabres are dangerous.

So, I bargain with God.

Years ago, I asked him to spare my family from the house fire, and for years, I didn't think he listened. I thought they were dead. Lost to me. But then a miracle happened —

and my sister Lena walked right back into my life. If he did that once, he can help me again.

God, if you bring her back to me, I will be more careful. I will love her unconditionally. I will respect her. I will protect my family with my life. I won't let her down again.

"I need to find her, Lars," I say, my voice barely recognizable even to my own ears. "And when I do, I'm going to bring that motherfucking family of gangsters to their knees."

Chapter 2

Is Something Off?

HUNTER

"Why are you driving like somebody's ninety-year-old grandma?"

"I'm trying to get us to the airport in one piece, Hunter," Lars grumbles as we bob and weave through traffic a bit too slowly for my taste.

The two of us are headed to LAX airport to catch the next flight to New Orleans or to catch Fabre taking the next flight to New Orleans. There's a second security detail following us in another car as well, just in case we face any trouble when we get there. At this point, I don't know anything for sure, totally relying on instinct and a single Red Bull for nourishment.

"Hey," Vaughn answers my phone call.

"I'm not even sure if this is the right play," I say to him when he picks up on the first ring, my doubts swirling around my brain, making me question every decision I'm making.

We don't know what Fabre is planning or if he's even

headed to New Orleans, but it's the only logical answer I've come up with. He came here to get his daughter and return her home. So where else could he be headed?

"It's the play that makes sense," Vaughn replies.

"They could be at a smaller airport so they can fly out undetected. That would be the smarter way to go."

"We've been over this, Hunt."

"But you haven't seen Naomi or Megan's names come up in any flight list out of LAX, and I don't give a shit who Fabre is, there's no way he can get those girls on a major US flight without identification."

"He'd have to pull a lot of strings to pull off a private flight without me knowing. I know it sounds counterintuitive but it's easier for them to get out at LAX."

"It would take some balls to just take my woman and fly out of a major airport."

"I think we've already established that Mr. Fabre has got balls the size of tennis balls. He knows exactly who you are and still took Megan in front of her house. He's arrogant and thinks he's invincible. Which is why I think he'd do exactly what we think most people wouldn't do."

I don't really like how much sense Vaughn is making. I don't need common sense right now. I just need answers.

"What about reporting her missing?" I suggest.

"Hunt, you know that's not what we do. They're only going to get in our way."

We've always kept our business in-house no matter what but desperate times call for desperate measures. I'll even depend on police support if it means that I get Megan back, but maybe only after we've exhausted all our resources.

"Fine," I grumble. "I'll call you back."

I catch Lars looking at me cautiously in the car's

rearview mirror. He's worried that I'm losing my shit but he has other things to concern himself with like where the hell Parker is.

"Have you heard from Parker?" I ask him.

"No," Lars says solemnly. It's obvious that he's worried about his partner and friend but fuck Parker. If he was doing his damn job, Megan would be in the penthouse in our bed next to me where she belongs.

"How long has it been since you've talked to him?"

"I don't know, maybe a few hours. The last time I saw him was with you."

"Was he acting strange? Did he say anything that made you think something was off?"

"That kid is always acting strange," Lars mocks. "But to answer your question, nothing was off."

"If he isn't dead already, I'm going to kill him," I say with a hard edge.

"He could be in some real trouble, Hunter." And I can feel that *just like Megan* are the words he withholds from the rest of his statement.

But I know Lars is right. Disappearing without a word is not something Parker's ever done. For all we know they have Megan and Parker. But I'm just so consumed with rage and fear that I can't see straight. I want to blame somebody when there isn't any one person at fault but myself.

When we arrive at the airport, Lars double parks at the departure area, knowing full well the car will be towed by some predatory towing company but we can deal with that later. We both quickly exit the vehicle and I run to the closest airline agent, cutting in front of a line of angry travelers.

"Hey, you can't just cut the line like that!"

"Who the hell do you think you are?"

The agent purses her lips at me when I don't budge out of the way.

"Sir, there's a line."

"This is an emergency," I tell her, trying my damndest to hold on to the last bit of restraint I have. "A woman has been kidnapped and brought against her will to this airport. I need to know how many flights are headed to New Orleans today."

"Sir, you have to wait your turn."

"Did you not hear me? A woman's life is at stake?"

"Would you like me to call LAX police to help you, sir?"

A random man tries tapping me on the shoulder, probably in an attempt to punch me in the face for my intrusion but I can hear Lars taking care of it behind me so I continue with my pursuit of information.

"I need to know the flights."

She exhales in clear frustration with me and points to the electronic board a few feet away. "You can check the board for all outgoing flights right over there, sir."

"The board doesn't show every flight leaving today, only upcoming ones, and I need them all," I retort, slightly raising my voice. Then I take a breath. "Just give me what I need and I'll move out of the way so you can help the rest of these people."

I can tell I've flustered the woman who rapidly blinks a few times and then furiously types at the keyboard of her computer.

"There are five more departures with three different airlines. I don't have the capability of printing them out so here."

She jots down each flight and airline on a small piece of paper and hurriedly hands me the note.

"Thank you."

The good news is that the departure times are spread out enough that we should be able to catch each one before they leave. The bad news is that LAX is a huge airport and the gates for these flights are spread out. We'll have to split up.

"You take these two gates," I tell Lars. "And I'll check these three. The other team can keep an eye on the entrances and exits just in case he changes his plans. Keep your phone on. Leave no stone unturned. She may be in a restaurant or a bathroom or–"

"I'm on it, Hunter. Don't worry. We'll find her."

I never took much notice of just how many people travel through the airport on any given day but now I see. Searching for Megan among the throngs of people sitting in departure areas and eateries is like looking for a needle in a haystack—especially when every woman I see suddenly looks like her.

"Excuse me, have you seen this woman?" I show every single person I come across one of my favorite pictures of Megan on my cell phone. It's one taken in the morning light and she's working on one of her paintings in the apartment. I called her name and she turned around, somewhat startled, but smiling...and I took the shot.

I check in with Lars and the second security team thirty minutes later and feel defeated when they tell me what I already know. They haven't had any luck locating Megan and suddenly my rage morphs into a moment of sudden clarity.

I call Vaughn.

"We did exactly what he wanted us to do," I tell him. "We're spinning our wheels."

"How so?"

"They're not here Vaughn. I don't feel her."

"You don't *feel* her? What am I supposed to do with that kind of logic, Hunter?"

"Fabre knew we would come here looking for them. Think about it. Taking Megan was not in the plan. She just happened to be downstairs when they got Naomi."

"Yeah, and?"

"And if it was us and we had to suddenly change the plan, what would we do?"

There's a long pause and then Vaughn responds, "We'd drive."

Exactly.

"I'll get Lars. You pull the teams. We need to get on the road. We've wasted too much time in here."

I check the time.

If Fabre stayed in that damn car with the girls and hit the highway, they have two hours on us.

"They'll have to pee at some point, especially because Megan's pregnant. They'll stop and burn up valuable time. If we haul ass we can catch up to them. It's a long fucking way to Louisiana from here."

The thought that he's dragging my pregnant fiancee across the country, pregnant, and probably scared is almost too much to bear. Trying to catch up when he has a two-hour head start is not productive.

But I know what is.

"No," I say in a deadly calm voice. "We're going to fly to Louisiana and meet that motherfucker with a welcome party of our own. Book us a private jet in Burbank."

"On it."

"And Vaughn?"

"Yeah, Hunt?"

"Don't skimp on the ammo."

It's about to be war.

Chapter 3

Who Is This Girl?

MEGAN

I've been through a lot of pain in my life, both physically and mentally but if I don't get out of this car soon, I'm going to break. My is pounding like there's a swarm of bees inside my head. And I'm so nauseous, I feel like I want to die. I'm sure part of it is the new life growing inside of me but another part is that I'm locked inside a moving piece of steel and fiberglass with people that I literally hate including now, Naomi.

I stare daggers into her beady little eyes hoping she can feel every bit of the malice I'm projecting her way. While I realize that she couldn't physically protect me from this abduction, she didn't do much to stop it either. She's just sitting solemnly in her seat, staring out the window, like a child who's been scolded and is now trying their very best to "behave" for Daddy.

"You look a little green around the gills, Miss Taylor," her slimy father notices, his pot belly threatening to pop the buttons of his collared shirt. "Eddie has a small can of ginger ale in the front if you'd like. We always keep a stash."

Creepy-ass Eddie gives me a grin in the rearview mirror, flashing one of his gold-capped canine teeth.

"Ginger ale isn't going to cure what ails me."

"Trust me, I know what morning sickness looks like. My dear Patricia, God rest her soul, suffered from it with each pregnancy, especially with my sweet Josephine." He pats Naomi on her knee.

"There's more of you?" I ask, looking directly at her, never knowing that Naomi had siblings.

"Didn't she tell you?" Her father gloats. "She has two big brothers."

I try not to react and am annoyed that I'm surprised by his revelation at all. Of course, she has brothers. There are probably a million other things that I don't know about my friend. What on earth has Naomi got me into?

Suddenly I think about Hunter.

God, I miss him.

I'd give anything to be enveloped in his strong arms right now.

I can't imagine what he must be thinking. I didn't leave our place on good terms. I was emotional. Angry. He probably thinks I've walked out on him or maybe he thinks I'm an ungrateful brat and am never coming back. Is he even looking for me?

My emotions shift.

He should be.

Part of this is his fault.

He knew Naomi was lying to me and kept it from me way longer than he should have. Maybe I wouldn't be in this predicament if he'd just told me the truth. At best, I could have helped her come up with a plan to leave town and duck her father. At worst, I could have kicked her out for lying to me for almost two years.

Pfft, who am I fooling?

I would have never kicked her out.

"What are your brother's names?" I ask her as she sinks further into her seat from what I hope is shame.

She looks at me with a blank stare. "The less you know the better, Megan."

"Don't be ridiculous. Megan is practically family now. Her brothers' names are Leo and Claude," her father gushes with pride. "We named them after family members just like Josephine. We can trace half of our roots back to France, you know."

"How nice for you," I deadpan.

All of a sudden I wretch when Eddie swerves the car. I glare at him in the mirror and he snickers. The asshole did it on purpose.

"Ginger ale, please." Naomi's father snaps his fingers twice and Eddie hands him a can of Canada Dry which he then offers me.

"Drink."

I clean the top of the can with the band of my sleeve and open the soda taking two very small sips.

"So what is the plan, Mr. Fabre?" I ask him. "Too much longer in this car and I'm going to vomit on everyone in here."

"I'm afraid you'll have to bear with it a bit longer. You don't have any identification on you which makes plane travel practically impossible in today's post 9-11 world. Back in the day, I could have maneuvered something but the times are a-changing, Miss Taylor."

"Why do I have to come with you at all?"

"To Josephine's wedding? Why wouldn't you come?"

Because a day ago I didn't even know she had a fiancé.

"I'll send a gift. Please let me go home." I try appealing to whatever humanity he may possess. "This pregnancy means everything to me."

He sighs almost apologetically. "All I wanted was to come get my daughter but there you were, ripe for the taking, so I took."

"For what? Bringing me along has already made things difficult for you. I'm a pregnant art student with barely two nickels to rub together. How could I possibly be of any benefit to you?"

"Now, Megan, you and I both know that isn't true," he scoffs. "Your Mr. Middleton might give me the keys to the entire city of Los Angeles if he thought it meant getting you back. You are of great benefit to me."

"We were nothing but good to your daughter and this is how you treat us? You left her out here in Los Angeles without a dime."

"I didn't leave her anywhere penniless!" For the first time today, Naomi's father lets his sense of control slip. "That was my daughter's own doing. Josephine, you have my permission to speak so you can address this accusation your friend has disrespected me with."

Naomi turns to me, her face suddenly stern. "My father didn't know where I was. If he did, he would have made sure I was taken care of. He's a good man."

"Are you serious, right now? Your daddy didn't know where you were because that's the way you wanted it, Naomi. You're a hairstylist and a makeup artist, not a house-wife. Your dream is to style Beyonce and Taylor Swift at the Grammy Awards. Not this!"

I'm trying to shake Naomi out of the stupor she's in. Who is this girl and what has she done with my vibrant, loud mouth friend? It's like she's some sort of Stepford Wife who easily falls in line when her controlling father is around.

"Josephine doesn't paint faces or fuss with hair for a living. She's a Fabre and she will take her rightful place in the family and make us all proud just like all the people who came before her."

This is insane.

And this man is literally insane.

Tears fall down my face and Naomi looks away, clearly pained by my show of emotion.

I take a deep breath and try to get myself together. Being emotional about this is not getting me anywhere. If I'm going to help myself out of this situation, I'm going to have to think smarter.

"I need to eat something," I say with resolve. "And not a snack. I need some real food. That's part of why I'm so nauseous."

"You heard the lady, Eddie. Let's take a detour at the next rest stop."

"This would have been so much easier if we could have flown home," Eddie mutters in protest.

Home.

So we're definitely going to Louisiana.

"It's a good thing that your convenience doesn't matter then," Naomi's father chastises him and I throw back one of Eddie's snide smiles at him.

Then I repeat to myself what they just said and gasp. Are we driving all the way to Louisiana for an arranged wedding between my duplicitous best friend and her mobster fiance?

Oh. Hell. No.

Chapter 4

He's Coming For Me

MEGAN

It's a good thing that one of Mr. Fabre's love languages seems to be food because we do indeed stop at the next rest area on the highway.

"Get Miss Taylor whatever she wants, Eddie. She's eating for two. My daughter and I are going to stretch our legs. Oh, and get me a coffee with creme and get Naomi a burger or something."

"I don't want a burger," Naomi objects. It's the first thing she's said in over thirty minutes.

"You haven't eaten in hours, beloved. Eddie will make sure it's something you like."

I have to turn away because I can't stand to watch the weird as fuck dynamic between Naomi and her father. The more I watch them, the less angry I am with her and the more pity I feel.

Her father is so passive-aggressive that every word he speaks seems to suck the air out of a room and light out of the sky.

"Hurry up," Eddie the creep commands, nudging me hard with his hand.

"Get your hands off me!" I protest.

"Just move your big ass."

The nerve of him.

I've got a great ass.

This is probably the only stop we're going to make for the next few hours and I didn't ask for it to simply grab a slice of pizza. I need to figure out a way to escape my captors or at the very least...get word to Hunter.

"You get the coffee and I'll stand in line for my pizza," I tell Eddie as we walk inside.

"I think you're confused. You don't give the orders around here, not to mention you have no money to pay for anything. We need to stay together so I can pay."

"Then give me some cash so I can pay."

Eddie cocks his head to the side already naturally suspicious of me. "Fuck, no."

I have no choice but to stand in the long pizza line with Eddie the asshole breathing down my neck until I think of another plan.

"Hey, I need to go pee. Can you get me a slice of margarita pizza and a side salad while I go?"

"Do I look like I work for you?"

"I'm pregnant and I need to pee. Now do you want to get out of line and come watch me or do you want to get the damn food so we can get back on the road?"

"Where's the bathroom?" He replies reluctantly scanning the area. I do the same, looking for a police officer, but I don't see any.

"How the hell should I know? I don't even know where we are. I'm just going to look for the signs."

"You've got five minutes."

"You clearly don't have a girlfriend. I'm going to need more time than that."

"Ten minutes. Any longer than that and I'm coming in that fucking bathroom and pulling you out by the hair."

"Aww, what woman broke your heart, Eddie?" I taunt, assuming he isn't going to put his hands on me in front of witnesses. "You don't like us very much, do you?"

"I don't like you." His fist clenches. I've pissed him off.

Is it weird to take offense that Mr. Fabre's henchman doesn't like me? I mean one of my superpowers at the Blue Whiskey is that everyone likes me. That's why I was able to effectively manage the place at my age and with minimal experience. What the hell did I do to him?

It doesn't take me long to find the sign for the restroom and I make a beeline straight for it knowing that Eddie has his eyes fixed on me, at least until I'm out of his line of sight. Once in the bathroom, I get to work.

"Excuse me, can I use your phone? My battery died and I have an emergency," I ask the first woman I run into.

"Oh, I'm sorry I left my cell in the car."

"Okay, thank you anyway."

I ask another woman who looks about my age knowing she'd never part ways with her cell like the older woman, but she acts like her house is on fire and rushes out of the bathroom apologizing along the way.

I'm getting frustrated that no one seems to want to help me and tears sting my eyes as I wash my hands for the fifth time.

My time is running out.

"Excuse me, I overheard you saying you need to use a phone." A woman with a warm smile and a single, salt and pepper braid down her back approaches me.

"Yes!" I say brightly. "Yes, I do."

"Here you go. You can make your call while I use the toilet."

"Thank you so much!"

The woman unlocks her phone using her thumbprint and hands it over to me.

Suddenly it hits me that I've never actually pressed ten actual numbers to call Hunter–ever. I've always had his number stored in my phone and I just pressed his name.

Fuck!

What should I do?

I decide to go to the web browser application on the woman's phone and search for The Blue Whiskey. The club hosts some nefarious people on any given Saturday night but thank God it's still searchable in Google.

The Blue Whiskey

310-555-7822

I press the linked phone number and decide to continue with the call inside a stall just in case Eddie decides to actually make good on his threat and come inside the bathroom.

"Blue Whiskey," a woman's voice answers the phone after the first ring.

"Vita?"

Vita is a server who started a few months ago and I'd know her voice anywhere because she's from Texas and has a distinct accent.

"Yes, who's this?"

"It's Megan."

"Oh, hey Megan."

Her response is quite casual and I figure that Vita has no clue that I've been taken.

"Um, is Hunter there?"

"No, he's not."

"How about Lena?"

"Is everything okay, Megan?"

I almost burst into tears but quickly regain my composure.

"What about Lars or Vaughn or Christian or–"

"Oh, wait, I think Christian is here."

"Put him on please, Vita."

"Okay."

I hear a stall door open and then the woman's voice who lent me the phone soon after.

"Excuse me, are you still here?" she says out loud. The two of us never have exchanged names.

"Yes, I'm in here," I reply. "Can I just have another minute though?"

"Uh, sure."

Finally, Christian picks up the phone.

"Megan?"

"Hi, Christian!"

"Are you okay?"

"No, I'm not okay. Naomi's dad made me get in the car with them basically at gunpoint and we've been driving for hours."

"We know."

"You know?"

"There are cameras positioned all around the perimeter of your apartment building. But why are you calling here? Hunter is going to burn this city down if you don't contact him."

"Believe it or not I don't know his number by heart and I'm using someone else's phone. Listen, I don't have a lot of time and I can't make another phone call. You're going to have to reach him for me."

"Megan, where exactly are you?"

"I'm at a rest stop in Arizona."

"Do you know what part of Arizona?"

"No."

"Can you run?"

"No, a man is waiting very impatiently for me to finish in this bathroom."

"Don't leave that bathroom and tell someone in there to go get the police."

"I thought about that but Christian but I haven't seen anyone out there. Plus, even if there is someone, I'm pregnant and I'm scared. I think this guy Eddie would hurt me and other people if he caught me talking to an officer. I just need you to tell Hunter that I'm fine, that I'm sorry, and that Mr. Fabre is hell-bent on taking me to New Orleans with them."

Then I start to cry.

"Don't cry, Megan," Christian says. "Just play along and keep calm if you can't get away from them."

"I'm just getting so tired, Christian."

"We're going to get you back." His voice wavers with emotion. "I promise you. Hunter knows you've been taken. He knows it's Fabre. And he's ten steps ahead of him. We'll bring you home soon, okay?"

Suddenly, I hear a thump on the bathroom stall door. I must have pissed off the owner of the phone, that is until I hear someone shriek, "You can't be in here, dude!"

"Wipe your ass and get out of there now!" Eddie's voice booms over everyone else.

I abruptly end the call with Christian and toss the phone into the sanitary napkin waste bin, then flush the toilet for effect.

"You're making a scene," I say as I nonchalantly open the door.

"What the fuck were you doing in there?"

He looks inside the stall behind me.

"Taking a shit."

The Good Samaritan whose phone I borrowed stares at the two of us with fear in her eyes and luckily says nothing as I quickly wash my hands and walk out of the bathroom with Eddie on my heels. I hope she discovers where I've hidden her phone.

"Where's my food?" I ask him, noticing that he's empty-handed.

"I told you what would happen if you took too long."

"Well, I'm still hungry and I'm not sure that Mr. Fabre would approve of you starving a pregnant woman because you have trust issues with women."

"You don't know anything about what Fabre would approve of. If his precious daughter wasn't here, we would have left your ass in an alleyway somewhere a long time ago."

A chill runs down my spine.

Because I'm leaning towards actually believing him.

"Well, his precious daughter *is* here and I'm her bestie, so?" I shrug my shoulders and smile.

"Just get your food and shut the fuck up."

I smile triumphantly.

Not just because I've successfully irritated the hell out of Eddie but because I've made contact with someone back home and things are looking up.

Hunter is coming for me.

Chapter 5

I've Got To Take It

MEGAN

The drive to the next city is a blur of anxiety, nausea, and silent prayers. On this leg of the trip, Naomi is sitting up front and I'm sitting next to Naomi's father in the backseat, my mind racing with plans of escape. After going over my brief conversation with Christian in my head, and understanding that Hunter may have a solid plan to rescue me, it's pretty clear that Christian was suggesting I should figure out a way to rescue myself.

We finally pull into the parking lot of a dingy motel on the outskirts of the city. The neon sign flickers, casting an eerie glow on the cracked pavement.

"This is our stop for the night," Mr. Fabre announces as if we're on some twisted family road trip.

"I thought you were wealthy," I say to him, turning my nose up at the dingy location especially because of how unsafe it looks.

"I know you're used to penthouse living, Miss Taylor,

but these accommodations are going to have to do for now. Josephine can tell you, I'm known to love the finer things in life but the first place your fiancé is going to look for you is at the closest Four Seasons Hotel. Eddie, get the girls squared away," he orders dismissively. "I have some calls to make before I settle in for the night."

"Yes, boss."

Eddie's grip on my arm is tight as we shuffle into the motel room. It's small, with two beds and a lingering smell of cigarettes.

"Why don't you ever manhandle Naomi like this?" I fuss.

"You and Josephine will share a bed," he ignores the question, throwing a pointed look my way. "And I'll sleep in the other one."

"I can't sleep with you in here."

"Sleep or don't sleep but shut your mouth. I'm tired of hearing it."

I nod, trying to mask my fear, because sometimes Eddie looks at me as if he's just biding his time until he can get me alone and hurt me. Naomi lays on top of our bed and curls herself into a quiet ball while I look for the remote control and find anything on television that will numb me to my present circumstances.

A text alert illuminates Eddie's phone and he excuses himself to handle a problem at the front desk with the credit card he used to pay for the rooms.

"I'll be back in a few minutes. Don't answer the door for anyone but me or Mr. Fabre. You understand?"

I nod silently.

"Josephine?" He calls out to Naomi.

"Yeah," she mutters.

"You heard me, right?"

"Yep."

My heart pounds when Eddie walks out the door. This is what Christian meant. A chance to make a run for it.

I land on a channel showing an episode of some sort of reality show that I don't recognize and tell Naomi, "I'm going to take a shower."

The fact that I have no clean clothes to change into should have made Naomi raise an eyebrow, but she barely moves. In fact, all she does is grunt an inaudible response as I enter the bathroom and stare at myself in the mirror above the vanity.

I look like shit.

God knows I really should take a shower.

If anyone was paying attention, they'd see that I'm clearly in distress. My eyes are sunken in, my hair is practically sticking on top of my head, and I feel like I have days worth of dirt on my skin.

But I don't have time for that.

This is my moment to escape.

I've got to take it.

I wait until my nerves settle, lock the door, turn on the shower, and then quietly open the bathroom window. Luckily, it faces the side of the hotel and not the front where we're parked. The opening is small, but I manage to squeeze my hips through, my breath catching as I land on the ground outside. I feel like Tom Cruise in a *Mission Impossible* movie.

I don't have a plan beyond getting out of the motel room, but I don't look back as I start running, my feet pounding against the pavement. I can hear shouts behind me, not really sure if it's Eddie or Mr. Fabre's voices, but I don't dare to glance back. I just run, fueled by desperation and the thought of freedom.

I'm a few blocks away when I hear the screech of tires. I duck into an alley, my heart in my throat. Footsteps echo behind me, getting closer. I'm cornered, with nowhere to run.

Suddenly, a hand grabs my arm, pulling me into the shadows. I'm about to scream bloody murder when a familiar voice hushes me. "Hey, it's me, Parker."

I throw my arms around Parker's neck and relief floods through me, followed by an onslaught of tears.

How did he find me?

What's going to happen now?

And where's Hunter?

But before I can ask him anything, Parker's expression hardens. "We need to move. Now."

We dart through several narrow streets, Parker leading the way, me stumbling behind. I can barely keep up, my mind racing with questions. Finally, we reach a black sedan I recognize, parked in front of a small strip mall and Parker opens the passenger door for me.

"This is one of Hunter's cars," I say. "Did you follow me here from LA?"

I'm so confused.

Has Parker been the plan to rescue me all along?

"Get in," he simply orders.

As we speed away, I turn to him, searching for answers in his eyes. But before I can speak, his cell phone rings. He answers, his face turning pale as he listens.

"What's wrong?" I ask, my heart sinking. "Is it Hunter?"

Parker's jaw clenches as he ends the call.

"No," he says, his voice barely a whisper.

"What's going on, Parker? You're acting strange. What aren't you telling me?"

"Nothing."

He drives with an intense focus.

Never asking me if I'm okay.

Never looking me directly in the eye.

Not giving me any fucking answers about Hunter.

"What's going on?" I ask again, fed up with his weird silent treatment. "Give me your phone now and let me call Hunter."

"Have I ever told you about my Mama, Megan?" he asks out of the blue.

Parker and Lars have been fixtures in my life ever since I met Hunter but I wouldn't say that I know much about their personal lives, only the things that Hunter may randomly share with me about them.

"Well...no."

"She worked her way up from a cafeteria worker to an executive assistant in the administration department in Cooper LA hospital."

Uh, okay.

He continues. "If she had grown up with different opportunities, I'm sure she would have been a nurse or even a doctor though. My mom's real smart and a hard worker."

I still don't get it.

What's the point of this story?

"Why are you telling me about your mom, Parker?" I feel uneasy. "Are you going to let me use your phone or not?"

"I'm sorry, Megan. You know I've always liked you a lot."

"Why are you sorry?" My stomach rolls and I have to take a few deep breaths to stop myself from gagging. "You just rescued me from Naomi's crazy daddy. Why would you apologize for that?"

"My mama is sick, Megan. Heart issues. She's a patient

in the same hospital she worked in for most of her life. But that greedy ass place doesn't care about that. If she doesn't pay her growing tab, they're ready to send her to the teaching hospital across town."

I stay quiet.

"And I can't have that."

"And so what does that mean?"

"I dropped Hunter off the other day. I was sitting outside waiting like I often do to take him anywhere else he may want to go. That's when Fabre approached me."

Oh no.

"He knew about my mother," he continues. "And he knew about my financial situation. Hunter pays me fairly but I've spent a lot of the money on bullshit. I'm not a saver."

Please God, no.

"Fabre offered to pay me more money than I've ever seen in my life at one time to simply take a drive and not answer my phone for an hour. That's it."

"Parker!" I cry. "What have you done? Hunter would have given you the money to pay your Mom's hospital bill."

His forehead creases.

"It never crossed my mind that Fabre wanted to snatch you, Megan. I swear. I thought he was going to take Naomi and just didn't want any problems when he did."

"So you were fine with throwing my friend under the bus? You've been around her a million times, Parker."

"When it comes to saving my mother's life, I'll throw anybody under the bus."

"So if you drove away and didn't answer your phone, how did you find me all the way here?"

"Everything happened faster than I guess he planned. I was just about to drive off when you approached his car, and I saw the other guy forcibly put you inside. That's when I realized just how badly I fucked up."

"Why didn't you help me? Why didn't you immediately tell Hunter or even Lars? Do you give a shit at all about me, Parker? I thought we were friends?"

"We *are* friends which is why I came here to West bubble fuck Arizona, to try and figure out the best way to handle this."

"Okay, great. Why not just call Hunter and tell him everything so we can put an end to this?" I demand.

"That's the complicated part, Megan. I initially followed y'all here to figure out a way to bring you home and not get myself killed in the process. But I've had some time to think. It was one thing to sell out Naomi but now that you're involved, and especially because you're pregnant, Hunter is never going to forgive me."

"His first inclination may be to fire you but I can help you get your job back once you come clean."

"Fire me? No, college girl, Hunter Middleton will put me six feet under in a place where no one will find me."

"Hunter is not a cold-blooded killer."

"Where do you think your daddy is?" Parker scoffs. "Do you honestly think Hunter put him in some sort of relocation program for abusive fathers?"

I've tried not to put much thought into what became of my father, his wife, and my half-sister. Whatever their fate, I'd already decided that ignorance was bliss.

"Hunter will not kill you, Parker. This was just a huge misunderstanding."

"This was not a misunderstanding. It was a betrayal."

"The one thing Hunter will want is me back in one piece. So maybe if you're the one to return me, he'll be more forgiving." I try talking some sense into Parker. "I'll talk to him for you. I'll explain the situation. He'll listen to me. Just let me call him. I need to hear his voice and tell him that me and the baby are okay."

Parker turns his head and gives me a blank stare that makes me question whether I've ever been a good evaluator of character.

"I'm sorry, Megan, but it's decided. I'm not taking you back."

Chapter 6

I Have To Find Her

HUNTER

The metal shovel weighs heavily in my hands as I use it to penetrate the dry top layer of earth underneath my boots.

"I can do it, boss," Lars offers.

"No, it's my job to do," I tell him because it's the truth.

I haven't cried in probably twenty years, I'm not even sure that I did back then, but there's absolutely nothing I can do to stop the tears from running down my face.

I'm a fuck up.

A failure.

I had one job, to protect the woman I love, and I couldn't even get that right.

"We'll be here all day if you keep up like this, and we aren't even sure if she's here. Give me the shovel."

The conflict rages inside of me.

On one hand, I pray that she's not buried in this desolate area, on the side of the road, as if she's just a piece of trash. As if she isn't my entire world. But then, on the other hand, a little piece of me is dying inside with every minute that passes, and I don't know where she is.

I have to find her.

After handing Lars the shovel and basically collapsing in an area of brush, I rest my head in my hands and begin sobbing like a child.

I am a total wreck.

What the fuck am I going to do without her?

A sudden harsh sound jars me awake in the passenger seat of the truck and for a brief moment, I don't know where I am. My eyes open against a glass window and all I see in front of me is a stretch of unfamiliar highway.

"Lars?" I say in a sleepy voice as I try to get my bearings. "What the fuck did you give me?" I ask accusingly, not understanding why I feel so groggy but also very glad it was a nightmare.

Megan is not dead, I repeat to myself. *Megan is not dead.*

"You haven't slept in days. You need the rest."

"That's not what I asked you."

"I just dropped a bit of tincture in your drink."

"What kind of tincture?"

"A THC mixture."

"You put weed in my cranberry juice? How long have I been out? I should shove your head through that fucking window."

"If you do that, then you'll never figure out where we're headed, and that would be a goddamn shame."

"I already know where we're going. The airport."

I check my phone to see if I've got any messages from

the club or anything from Megan. I'm desperate for any news at all as I continue to vacillate between wanting to choke the life out of every human being who isn't Megan or crumbling into a puddle of hopeless mush.

"Negative."

"What?"

"We're not going to New Orleans because she isn't there."

"Stop the fucking car, Lars."

Lars swings our heavy black SUV over on the shoulder of the road and it's only now that I notice the worry lines etched across his face as well.

"I didn't want to tell you until I knew for sure, but I had Vaughn check all the trackers on the cars."

"Okay?"

"A tracker is moving in Arizona."

I don't do any business in Arizona, so there's only one reason why one of my cars would be there.

I don't want to even say it.

But the truth is staring both of us in the faces.

"Is it Parker?"

"It's the same sedan he always drives, the one he used to drop you off at the apartment," Lars says somberly. "I don't want to jump to any conclusions as to why, but Parker is in Arizona, but for some reason, I think it may have something to do with Megan."

"He's in *my* car but not picking up his phone?"

"I know it seems suspicious, but Parker's a good kid. Maybe he saw Megan getting abducted and is following them on his own."

"Like fucking Batman, Lars? Yeah, I don't think so. She called the club and spoke to Christian, scared as fuck, confirming that Fabre has her."

"I said that he may be following them, not that he's saved her yet."

I call Vaughn annoyed with Lars's farfetched theories.

"Hey."

"Lars told me about the tracker."

"I wondered what was taking you so long to call me about it."

I give Lars the side eye.

"Someone got the bright idea to drug me."

Lars looks away from me in what I hope is remorse, but knowing him, he feels nothing of the sort.

"The good news is that the tracker has stopped moving for about an hour now. It looks like Parker made a stop to eat. It's the only thing close by in the location the tracker is beaming from. If you haul ass, you should be able to catch up to him."

"Lars, how long have you been driving?"

"All night, boss. We're close."

"Are we even in Arizona?"

I look up at the green highway signs and don't recognize any of the exit names or route numbers. All I see are mountains in shades of burnt sienna and rust. We could still be in California, or it could well be Arizona. I have no idea.

"We are."

"Fabre hasn't called with any sort of terms?" I ask Vaughn.

"Nothing."

I tap my foot, frustrated with this whole scenario.

"How's Lena?"

"She's holding up okay. Obviously, she's worried about Megan and you, but she's been coming to work and keeping busy."

"You're keeping an eye on her?"

Vaughn pauses for a moment, then answers, "Uh, Christian is making sure she gets to and from work safely."

I turn my head to look back for the other security team, but I don't see Jim or the car.

"Where's Jim and Cecil?" I ask out loud, expecting an answer from whichever of them can tell me.

"They had to take a break. They were both wiped. But they're not too far behind us."

"I don't pay them to take breaks. My pregnant fiancee is missing!"

I pound my fist against the dashboard to emphasize my point.

"Whatever we find when we get to Arizona, the two of us can handle until they get there," Lars says assuredly. "We've done it before."

"Stay strong, Hunt," Vaughn says through the speaker on the phone, almost forgetting he was on the line. "You're going to find her."

"She's in trouble, Vaughn. I can feel it."

I reflect back on the pieces of my nightmare that I can remember. At first, I took it literally and thought it was her signaling me from her grave, but maybe it was just a vibration of her distress she was transmitting.

"Is the tracker still transmitting from the same location?" Lars asks out loud so Vaughn can hear.

"Still there. And based on your location, you're only ten minutes away!"

"He could have dumped the car, remembering there's a tracker," I say, praying for the opposite to be true but preparing myself for the worst.

"We'll find out in five minutes, my friend," Lars says with determination, pushing his foot heavier on the gas pedal to get us there faster.

I take a deep breath and visualize Megan's sweet face in my mind's eye. The way her face looks at peace when she's sleeping. The secret kisses I gave her abdomen, hoping that the baby growing inside of her would feel my presence.

In five minutes I'm going to know more than I did five minutes ago, baby, and then I'm going to find you.

Don't give up on me.

I'm coming.

A sense of relief washes over me when Lars and I see the blue sign for the upcoming rest stop. We're moving at an ungodly speed over the entrance ramp and into the parking lot. I remind myself to make a mental note to upgrade our tracker system. If I had the more advanced model, I'd be able to pinpoint the exact location of my car in an application on my phone. Unfortunately, we're going to have to do this the old-fashioned way.

"I'll go in the building and check the restaurants and the bathroom," I say checking to make sure my gun is locked and loaded. "You look for the car."

Lars stares disapprovingly as I place my gun in the waistband of my slacks.

"What?" I snap at him.

"Be careful and keep a low profile. The goal is to get information. We don't know what happened yet."

I don't have time to get into a war of words with Lars. While I understand that he feels some sort of responsibility for Parker because he's the one on my team who spends the most time with him, I don't give a shit about any of that.

All I want is Megan back.

And with all of my years of experience in the Los Angeles underworld, my gut is telling me that Parker is not running towards something but running away.

I move with stealthiness through the small rest area

scanning the open space from left to right. It reminds me of my days when I was new to the organization, and it was my job to do the grunt work.

Parker has a distinctive walk, and I'd know it anywhere, but I don't see anyone with his same gait. I approach a woman with aged skin and long silver hair who's crouched in a small spot in between two stores selling a variety of Native American pottery. I notice that she's watching everyone coming and going in a very deliberate way.

"Excuse me, but I'm looking for this man. Have you seen him in here today?"

The woman looks at my phone and then back up at me. "Why are you looking for him?"

"My wife is missing and I think he may have some idea on where to find her."

"Oh, that's grave indeed."

"It is."

"How long have you been married?"

"Technically, she's my fiancee," I admit, feeling badly that I've stretched the truth for some reason. Maybe because the woman reminds me of someone's grandmother.

"Let me see the photo again." She stands. "My eyes aren't what they used to be."

"Of course."

After a moment, I watch as her eyes squint and shift to the left corner of the room.

"Pretty sure your guy was over at Coffee Junction about fifteen minutes ago," she says.

"Thank you," I say gratefully, handing her a crisp twenty-dollar bill. "This is for your time."

It takes everything for me not to run over to the small eatery. I don't want to draw any attention to myself just in case he considers scurrying out of here if he sees me.

My eyes bulge at my discovery once I grow closer.

What in the actual fuck?

Not only is Parker sitting at a bistro table sipping on a goddamn latte, but Megan, *my Megan,* is sitting across from him as if she doesn't have a care in the world.

I plunk myself down on a free chair at the table, startling them both. It's not like Parker to be so off his game. He should have seen me coming if he was paying any attention to his surroundings. Instead, all of his concentration seems to be centered on my fiancee. The woman I thought was in dire straits under Fabre's thumb. The center of my world.

"Well, isn't this fucking cozy."

Chapter 7

Can You Put That Away?

MEGAN

My brain and heart are at war with each other.

My Hunter-starved heart is bursting with joy that he is physically in front of me after what felt like a lifetime being apart, but my brain is confused as to why he looks like he wants to kill someone... particularly me. But even with his scary ass Glock spinning in the center of the bistro table, my heart wins this battle, and I jump to my feet and wrap my arms around him.

"Thank God you found me!"

As he holds me with one arm around my waist, the taut hardness of Hunter's body relaxes just a smidge as I try my damndest to lose myself in his embrace.

"Are you okay?" he whispers with words that sound somehow broken instead of jubilant.

"Yes...yes, I'm alright."

"Are you here with him?" he asks, sounding somewhat bewildered.

"No, not exactly."

I know that Parker has royally fucked himself, but before Hunter arrived, I was talking him into taking me home instead of back to Naomi's father. One more bite of his burrito, and I think I would have been successful.

"I know what you're thinking," Parker says in a tone full of fright.

"What am I thinking, Parker?" he bites back, positioning me behind his broad back, a place that I wish I could nestle for longer than this tense moment will allow.

"You're thinking that I've had some part in what's happened to Megan."

"My fiancee was taken, and now she's with you, eating bad Mexican food, at a pit stop in Arizona. It doesn't take rocket science to figure out what's going on. One plus one equals motherfucking two," he retorts cooly.

"Can you put that away, boss?" Parker asks, referring to the gun on the table.

"Oh, didn't you hear? You are no longer under my employment. You stole my car. You stole my woman. The name is Mr. Middleton to you."

"I didn't take her!" he pleads. "I saved her from Fabre."

Okay, that's not exactly what happened.

"Then why didn't you pick up your phone one single time when we called?"

"Boss—"

"You're always on that damn phone."

"I had to toss it."

"I bet you did. Get up."

Hunter reaches for his gun, so I squeeze him harder around his waist.

"It's okay, Megan." He pats my hand softly. "We're just

going out to the car," he assures me. "And Parker, if you run, I will fuck you up."

"I'm not going to run," Parker sighs defeatedly.

"Then get up and walk toward the exit. When we get through the doors, turn to your left."

It's only a matter of moments until we see Lars and another security team that usually works at the club. The look on Lars's face when he spots me next to Hunter is priceless. I imagine it's the type of look a loving father would give his long-lost child.

I offer him a smile in return.

"You found her," Lars says to Hunter as he approaches.

"It wasn't hard," Hunter quips. "She was having lunch with our boy Parker here."

Lars rakes his eyes over Parker with the complete opposite look he gave me. It's one full of disappointment and pretty much disgust. It's obvious that both Hunter and Lars believe that Parker is guilty of something, which he is, but for a pretty good reason in my opinion. I see it's going to be up to me to help him, but when dealing with Hunter, the timing always matters, and this is not the time to try and save Parker's ass.

Hunter turns to me, my face between his two strong hands, and it's at this very moment that I see just how much our separation has cost him. His eyes are sunken in and are missing their usual silvery-grey glow. The frown lines on his forehead have deepened, and he hasn't shaved at all.

"Lars and I need to talk to Parker for a moment before we get back on the road. I need to understand how much danger you're still in."

"I'm not sure he can tell you anything, Hunter."

"I don't want you to worry about any of this. You've

already been through enough. I'm just asking you to sit in the truck with the other team while we talk to him."

"I don't want to be separated from you again," I say, almost panicked.

His face looks pained by my reaction. "Of course, that was thoughtless of me."

"Can't you talk to him later? I just want to get home."

Lars leads Parker a few feet away to give the two of us some privacy. After a moment of staring me intensely in the eyes, Hunter finally asks the question I think he's been wanting to ask since he found me.

"Megan…is there anything you're not telling me?" he asks hesitantly and dare I say almost fearfully as if he's afraid of my answer.

The nerve of him.

But I'm exhausted.

And dirty.

And I don't feel like getting into this with him in a parking lot in west bubble fuck Arizona.

"Like what?"

"I'm not accusing you of anything; I'm just saying that I wasn't expecting to find you here with Parker."

"And so? I didn't expect to get kidnapped in front of my house either!"

His eyes narrow.

"Why are you being so defensive?"

"I'm just trying to understand if you're just being curious or accusatory right now. I was being held against my will by some New Orleans gangster and his creepy henchman. Are you happy to see me or not?"

"Of course, I'm happy," he says through gritted teeth. "I'm offended by the suggestion that I wouldn't be."

"And I'm offended that you think that I have some secret agenda going on with Parker."

"I never said that."

"You didn't have to."

Suddenly, his eyes drop to the ground.

"I had a nightmare that I lost you." His voice cracks. "I've had a lot of them since you were taken."

I raise my hand to the side of his face.

"But you found me."

His eyes land on my lips and his mouth soon follows, and we share a languid kiss that quickly reminds us both of what's most important.

"I can't stomach that this happened at all," he admits, our foreheads touching. "It's my job to protect you and our baby. If I can't do that, then what the fuck am I doing at all? What does that say about my ability to be a husband and a father? This is why I want to move us to the house I found and–"

"Stop," I tell him firmly, placing a hand on his chest. "Talking about that house and *your* plans for *our* life is part of what got us here in the first place. I don't want to talk about it. I want to get in that truck, drive to the nearest airport, and fly home– period."

I've taken a firm stance in many conversations with Hunter before, but this is probably the first time that I've said my piece and could care less about the ramifications of my words.

"Forgive me," he says. "You're right. Let's get you home where you belong, and I'll deal with Parker and Fabre later."

Ugh, for a split second, I forgot about the fact that Hunter is not going to let any of this go without some sort of serious retaliation, and even with all of her lies and obvious shortcomings, I don't want Naomi to be a casualty of war.

But that's a problem for tomorrow.

Today, I just want to get back into my bed and sink into my fiance's embrace, momentarily blocking out the world and the carnage that's ahead of us.

Chapter 8

Only The Facts Please

HUNTER

The weight of my Glock feels heavier in my hand than it usually does as I hold it close to Parker's temple. Obviously, I know why. Parker is a friend. Correction– *was* a friend.

"So this is what goes on down here?" Parker scoffs, his eye already swollen and purple from the interrogation I've started in the basement of The Blue Whiskey.

"You don't want to do this," he pleads.

Lars stares at him, arms crossed in front of him, with the quiet judgment of a disappointed big brother. From the other side of the room, I can feel Vaughn watching me, worry oozing from his pores. I haven't been myself. I'm running on vodka and rage, and I'm not in the right mind to make a smart decision.

But I don't give a shit.

Not when it comes to Megan.

"You're right, Parker. I don't want to do this but yet here

we are." I lower my gun but keep it at my side as I pace in front of him. "Now, let's go over it again."

"I've told you a hundred times."

I lift my gun again, pointing it straight at his balls.

"Are you being a smart ass?"

"Tell the story until it makes sense," Lars says, speaking for the first time since we've been down here. "You're leaving something out."

Parker's head drops.

We've been beating his ass for thirty minutes, but it turns out that all we actually needed was a bit of condemnation from a very disillusioned Lars.

"I dropped you off. I stayed in the car like you asked me to do. I was playing on my phone, texting a woman I met a few weeks ago."

"Too much backstory," I say, sick of his bullshitting.

"Okay," he huffs. "That's when I spotted the car. Fabre's car. He was having some sort of argument with Naomi outside of the car, and then she finally got in. He didn't make her, and neither did the goon with him. She got in on her own. I know she's Megan's girl, but I didn't think anything of it. "

He takes a painful breath, probably because I kicked him in the ribs for ten minutes.

"Continue," I say, not giving a shit about the pain he's in.

"It might have been five minutes later when I noticed Megan. She came out of the apartment and didn't have a handbag like she usually does. I figured she was going for a walk or something."

"And you didn't keep eyes on her?" I ask in an accusatory fashion.

"Whatever she was doing was none of my business. The

apartment is her home and she had a sad expression on her face. I guessed that you two had some sort of an argument, and she needed a beat."

"Is that right? You know my fiancee that well that you can sense when she needs a beat?"

Parker looks up at me with a fiery determination in his expression. "You had me follow her for months so yeah I think I know her."

I smack him against the side of his head with the butt of my gun, and he howls in pain.

"I can finish this," Vaughn interjects, knowing that he's only interfering because he thinks I'm about to kill Parker.

I'm not.

I don't take life and death lightly.

And whatever role Parker's played in all of this, I know that the real person I have beef with is Naomi's father.

I raise two fingers, signaling that I want Vaughn to back off. I've got this.

"What happened next?" I ask him. "And stick to only the facts."

"It's hard to get all of the facts straight when there's blood dripping down my neck."

Before I can respond, Lars places a hand on the arm that's holding the gun and steps forward. Parker's hands are zip-tied behind his back so Lars takes a small handkerchief out of his back pocket and dabs the side of Parker's face.

"Thank you, Lars."

"Parker, this is not a joke." Suddenly the Eastern European accent that Lars always works so hard to mask peeks through. "You've worked here long enough to know how badly this can end for you."

"I'm trying."

"No, you are not. Something is holding you back. What

is it? Tell us everything, no matter what it is, and I am sure that Boss will be lenient."

I clear my throat, letting Lars know that he's making promises that he can't keep, but Vaughn taps the back of my heel with his foot, wanting me to allow Lars to continue working his magic on the kid.

"Something happened before Megan ever came outside."

"Go ahead."

"After Naomi got into the car, Fabre's man spotted me." Parker sighs heavily with reluctance, clearly not wanting to tell this part of the story. "They must have asked Naomi who I was, or maybe they just knew by the look of the car, and Fabre approached me."

"This was your first time talking to Fabre?" Lars asks.

"Yes."

"You never met him before? Talked to him before?"

"No."

"And what did he want?"

"He identified who he was. He told me he was Naomi's father and that he was here visiting. He asked me if Boss was home so he could thank him for looking out for her."

"And?"

"I knew immediately when he said that something was off about the guy. I knew a thank you wasn't exactly what he wanted to give. I told him that Boss wasn't home."

"Wait–" Vaughn interrupts. "Why would he think that you knew who Naomi or Hunter were at all? How could he know that if you've never met?"

"Exactly," I mutter, taking a seat across the room and letting my guys pick Parker's lies apart, statement by statement.

"I might have forgotten to mention that he knew who I

was. When he came over, he called me by name. He called me Parker. I thought that maybe Naomi told him who I was but that wasn't the case because it didn't take him long to bring up my mother."

"Your mother?" Lars questions.

I didn't even know Parker had a mother. Well, I mean, I guess we all have one, but he's never mentioned her. What the hell does she have to do with any of this?

"She's sick. Really sick."

I stand up. "I've never even heard about this mother of yours, and you're trying to tell me that Fabre knows who she is?" I say.

"Yes, I don't know how. I guess the dude does his homework. It isn't hard to find if you care to look. We have the same last name, live in the same city, and her address is one of the old places I've lived that you can pull up on any credit report."

I turn to look at Vaughn, and he gives a slight shrug of his shoulders. It's his job to vet all my employees, but it's not his job to remember every single detail about their lives. If he ran across the address or the name of Parker's mother in his search, it's probably sitting in a file somewhere on his computer. And even if he did, the fact that someone has a mother is not cause for a red flag.

"Okay, so she's sick," Lars says. "And Fabre knew this?"

"Yes, he knew she was sick, and she knew she was broke. She doesn't have enough money to even continue care in the same hospital she worked for her whole life. So he offered me a king's ransom to leave the area for an hour."

I am fucking livid.

"Do I not pay you enough for your loyalty?" I roar, charging forward and bitch slapping him like the traitor he is.

"It's for my mother!" He cries.

"Did it even dawn on you to tell us the truth about your situation and ask for help?" Lars asks.

"No, it didn't. The boss is not warm and fuzzy. Do you think he would give a shit about my sick mother? All he cares about is *her*. Look around, Lars. He doesn't care about us. We're just a means to an end. It'll be a miracle if I make it out of here alive and you know it. I'm only here because Megan begged me not to take her back to Fabre because she believed that Boss could be reasoned with."

I'm so incensed by his admission that I can't see straight.

"So you found her and were going to take her back to Fabre?"

Megan didn't tell me any of this. To be fair, I didn't want to push her to explain anything after all that she's been through, but this...is untenable.

Why is she protecting this piece of filth?

Can I trust anyone around me?

"I didn't know he was going to take her. He gave no indication that he was going to hurt Megan. How was I even supposed to know that she'd come downstairs alone? That's not her usual MO."

"If you were supposed to disappear for an hour, then how did you know she was taken? How did you end up in Arizona following them?" Vaughn asks with the calm demeanor of a police detective.

"A part of me knew that whatever he had planned wasn't going to involve just talking, although I wanted to believe the best, so I stuck around. I parked around the corner and walked back on foot, staying out of sight."

"Your story doesn't make any sense," I say, shaking my head in disbelief. "None of it."

Lars's body language mirrors my own. Neither of us

believes this story. Parker's not stupid, and there are holes in it. He's probably been working with Fabre for a long time, just biding his time.

"If y'all are not ready to shoot this liar yet, then I've had enough for today. I have a club to run."

"Hunter–" Vaughn tries calming me down.

"Maybe Parker needs a moment in silence and several moments away from his *dying mother* to consider what's truth and what's fiction," I continue.

Everyone knows what this means.

We'll leave Parker tied up down here in total darkness, with no food, no nothing until he decides to tell us what we need to know...the complete truth.

And I don't care how long it takes and who may disagree with my methods.

Even Megan.

Chapter 9

Trust Goes Both Ways

MEGAN

The faint smell of fabric softener feels comforting against my skin as I snuggle under the sheets of the king-sized bed I share with Hunter. The problem is, he hasn't been near it since we've returned from Arizona. I think he's been consumed with uncovering whatever he thinks that Parker knows or maybe he's just still furious with me for walking out of the apartment that day. After all, if I hadn't stormed out, I wouldn't have been taken by Naomi's father that day.

I've been asleep for hours now and with the drapes closed I'm not even sure what time of day it is but whatever time it is, I know that I can no longer rest (hide) in here forever. It's time to have the conversation that both of us have been avoiding but before I do that, there's a knock at the door.

"Lena." I open the door and smile, happy to see a friendly face.

"Were you sleeping?" She stares at the hair on my head sticking straight up in the air.

"Not at all," I tell her. "I was just getting my day started."

"Your day?" She grins.

"What time is it?"

"About eight."

"PM?" I ask incredulously.

"Yes, ma'am."

Lena pats a few of my curls down and strides inside the apartment.

"Your brother isn't here," I tell her.

"I came to see you, obviously."

"I'm fine."

"Are you?" She lightly grips my shoulder. "You've been through a traumatic experience."

"My whole life has been traumatic, Lena," I say dismissively.

"Except for meeting my brother, right? No trauma there."

"Even my first meeting with Hunter was...eventful," I recall that fateful night at Table 21. "I guess I attract drama."

Lena's kind eyes narrow. "What's going on with you two, Megan?"

Her eyes avert from mine, a dead giveaway that she probably was sent here on a fact-finding mission.

"Did Hunter send you here to check on me, Lena?"

"I may have spoken to him earlier, but he didn't send me here. Would it have been a problem if he had?"

"Nope, no problem."

"I stopped by to give you a hug." She reaches out to embrace me. "And to suggest that maybe you should go see your doctor and make sure things are okay with the baby. I could go with you."

There's a gentleness to Lena's tone that suddenly makes my eyes water. I haven't expressed much, if any, emotion about my abduction since Hunter found me. Not in the car. Not on the private plane he chartered to fly us out of Arizona. And not since I've been home.

I guess I've been numb.

"It's okay to cry," Lena assures me, rubbing my back as I openly sob in her arms. "You're safe now."

"I'm sorry. I think it's the hormones."

"Don't apologize to me." She pats my back. "It's all right."

Both of us turn our heads when we hear the tone of the keypad unlocking on the front door.

"What's going on here?" Hunter asks, his eyes focused on the tears running down from my own.

"I'll let you two talk," Lena says in a hushed voice and I almost want to stop her because my chest feels tight, and heavier now that he's in the room.

Hunter leans over, giving Lena a peck on the cheek. "I'll call you later."

"Sure."

"You need anything?"

"No, I'm good. Just take care of our girl here."

"Always."

"You're up, I see," Hunter says as he carefully places his leather backpack down and pulls off his shoes.

"Can't sleep forever."

"Were you able to get a decent rest?"

"Yeah, it was good being back in my own bed."

"Our bed," he corrects me.

"Yes, our bed."

"Are you glad to be home, Megan?" He turns to ask with a serious look on his face.

"What the hell kind of question is that? Of course, I'm glad."

"Then why are you crying?"

"Sometimes people express emotion when they've been through something traumatic."

"I found you laughing and eating a burrito with your driver. You didn't seem that torn up to me."

I wipe my face with the backs of my hands, pissed that I allowed myself to be this vulnerable. He doesn't deserve my tears.

"You've misconstrued this entire situation. Parker wasn't the one who took me."

"He didn't bring you home either."

"You didn't give him a chance. He was going to."

"It didn't look that way to me."

"Well, how did it fucking look?" I stand in front of him now, hands on my hips, staring fiercely into his steely gray eyes.

"Watch your mouth, Megan."

"No, you watch your mouth! I don't appreciate what you're insinuating. You think I planned to run away with Parker because he's closer to my age than you are?"

Hunter glares at me. "That was a fucked up thing to say."

"Why? It's true."

He steps an inch closer.

"Why do you keep bringing him into this?"

"I'm not! You are. The fact that you didn't find me lying

dead somewhere in a ditch and safe with Parker is blinding you. You're focused on the wrong person right now."

"Then who should I be focused on?"

"Me, asshole!"

"You? I am focused on you! This is what being focused on nothing but you looks like. Look at me. I mean really look at me, Megan. I tell you that I've bought you a house, and you storm out of here like I committed some sort of a crime, then someone snatches you right from the front door of our home, and you think, what? That I'm thinking about anything else but finding you? Protecting you? You're all I can think about every single moment of the fucking day. My life has been turned upside down since the day we met. My work is shit. My club is practically running itself. I don't even recognize myself anymore. And you think I need to focus more on you?"

Hunter's breathing is labored, almost violent. I can hear his heart pounding from where I'm standing, but I can also hear my own after the hundreds of tiny cuts his cruel words have just made into it.

"Forgive me for ruining your oh-so-perfect life. I'm glad we cleared that up before we made a huge mistake."

"And what mistake would that be?" He lifts my chin with two of his fingers.

"Well, you don't think we're getting married now, do you?"

"You're carrying my child."

"This is not the Gilded Age. I can raise a baby on my own."

"Not my baby."

"Watch me."

"Megan, you've misunderstood the situation. You can't just bail every time we disagree. That's not how this works.

We're committed to each other, and we're bringing another human being into the world based on that commitment."

"I will not marry and raise a child with a man who doesn't trust me."

"Trust goes both ways, and I never said I thought you were fucking Parker, but you are holding back something from me. That I know."

"What do you want to know!" I exclaim, angry tears streaming down my face. "For fuck's sake, let's just get it over with."

"Did Parker hurt you?"

"No! Never."

"Was he there in Arizona to help you?"

My eyes immediately drop.

"Not exactly."

Hunter runs a few paper towels underneath some warm water from the kitchen faucet and uses them to tenderly wipe my face clean.

"Then why?"

We sit on the couch, and I calm down long enough to explain how I wiggled out of the motel bathroom window, away from Mr. Fabre's henchman, and ran into Parker during my escape. I tell him the deal Parker supposedly made with Mr. Fabre and how it momentarily impaired his judgment.

"He was never going to take me back to them. He was going to call you and tell you where to come and get me. He was just mustering up the courage to do it when you miraculously walked inside that rest stop."

"This could have ended much differently," Hunter says with a tinge of regret in his voice.

"What do you mean?"

"All he had to do was tell me that he needed the money."

"He didn't know he could ask you that. He's your driver, not your friend."

"He could have asked Lars."

"I don't think it was a thought-out plan. I think he saw an opportunity and, in the heat of the moment, said yes. He didn't know that I was going to be involved."

"But, Megan, he knew I would be."

I pause for a moment to consider Hunter's words and I have no logical response to them. Anything else I say at this point would be an excuse, so I simply say, "Just forgive him."

"It's too late."

"What does that mean?"

"It means we're past the point of forgiveness."

My chest tightens.

"What have you done, Hunter?"

He pulls me gently into his arms, nuzzling his face into the side of my neck.

"God, I've missed your smell. I couldn't breathe when I thought there was a chance that I'd lost you forever."

I close my eyes, reveling in his touch.

"Please don't do anything you'll regret, Hunter."

His hand gently eases under my sleep shirt, tracing the length of my spine with his fingers.

"That's the thing, baby, when it comes to you and ensuring your safety, there's nothing I could do that I'd ever regret."

Chapter 10

I Don't Fucking Share

MEGAN

"Yesss, right there."

Hunter's strong arms are completely underneath me, cradling my ass and hips as my legs languidly drape over his shoulders.

He is eating me out with a careful touch, making sure not to press too hard with his tongue or mistakingly graze me with his teeth. Like everything since I've been home, his handling of me is with kid gloves.

I don't mind it.

It still feels good.

But this isn't how Hunter makes love to me. He's holding back, like *really* back. Almost as if he's scared to break me.

I arch my back as the pleasure of my impending orgasm winds down my spine and settles softly between my legs.

"God, yes," I hiss.

It's not a cataclysmic orgasm, but still one that leaves me

lightheaded as Hunter massages my inner thighs, making sure to draw out my release.

When he gives me a brief kiss on my left thigh to mark the end of our lovemaking, that's when I know it's time for me to speak up.

"What are you doing?" I ask as he walks over to use our ensuite bathroom.

"Peeing."

"Why?"

"Because I have to pee?" he says casually.

"You're not done."

He peeks his head out of the bathroom door to look at me. "You came, didn't you?"

"But you didn't come, and we didn't have sex."

"I've got a meeting back at the club. I'm sorry."

I pull the covers up to my chin, my knees bent.

"Maybe we need to talk to someone," I suggest.

"Talk to who, Megan?" he asks as the water runs.

"A therapist."

"What the hell would we do that for?"

"Something is wrong."

He storms out of the bathroom.

"Because I didn't fuck you for an hour?"

"Because you didn't fuck me at all! Is it because I'm pregnant, or is it something else?"

"I know it's hard to believe, but I'm not a porn star. I can't just turn it on when you say jump."

"Who are you? Where the fuck is my fiance?"

"He's right here!"

We stare at each other, both of us breathing heavily after our exchange. Hunter is standing in all of his naked glory, looking like a Roman god. Even at this moment, when

I'm so mad at him, all I want is to fall in his arms and make love to him for the rest of the night.

For the rest of our lives.

"I need you to start being honest with me."

"When have I ever lied to you, Megan? If anything, I'm too honest with you."

"Where is Parker?"

Hunter's jaw ticks as he moves forward to the bed.

"What did you say?"

"If you're so honest, where is Parker?"

"Ask the question you actually want to know."

"I just did."

Hunter takes another few steps, and now he's right beside me, standing by my side of the bed. He grabs my chin and lifts it to meet his gaze. I sit strong and try not to blink, daring him to make the next move.

He studies me closely no doubt trying to ascertain what my motives are in bringing up a topic he thought we squashed yesterday.

Without another word, he climbs on the bed in front of me and sits on his knees.

"I can't fuck you if I'm not hard," he says cooly. "Put your hands behind your back and suck me off like a good wife then maybe I'll give you what you want."

This isn't how I wanted it between us, but his crude words turn me on nonetheless, and I follow his directive, bending at the waist and lowering my mouth to his lengthening dick.

The first taste is salty and delicious.

I've been craving him for days.

My center of gravity is kind of off now that I have a little human growing inside of me, but my skills would put a porn star to shame. And no matter how mad he is right now, I know he's enjoying this.

"Stop," he orders with a cool bluntness. So I stop. Then, I raise myself to meet his eyes again. "I'm hard now."

"I see that."

"Get on."

"Get on?" I parrot back his unromantic suggestion.

"Do you want this or not?"

"Not if you're going to act like a bitch about it."

Suddenly, his left hand wraps around my throat, and his thumb gently rests on the notch at the base of my throat. Then his right one slides between my legs, where he inserts two fingers inside my pussy and rests his thumb at the top of my clit.

A strange moan hovers in the air.

I think it came from me.

When he presses down on the notch of my neck with one thumb simultaneously with the other one on my clit, I almost cry. "Hunter!"

His face is still hard.

"Are you ready to do what you're told?"

"Yes," I mew.

He removes the hand from my pussy but keeps the other around my throat, guiding me closer to his lap. I rest my upper arms on his shoulders, cradling the back of his head in my hands as I begin the slow, delicious descent down his dick.

I'm warm and wet, but it's still a tight fit as I ride Hunter with sensual precision. I close my eyes, relishing every stroke I take from him as I rock my hips back and forth, up and down.

When I feel more pressure at the base of my throat, my eyes pop open to meet his steely grey ones.

"Do you love me, Megan?"

"Of course."

"Only me."

"Only you."

My hips grind down on him faster.

"This is my pussy," he growls.

"Yes!" I say, getting closer to my next orgasm.

"And I don't fucking share."

God, yes!

This is what I've been craving for so long from him. This is exactly what we needed. Things might have been off for us for a while, even before I was kidnapped, but when we're together like this–that's when I know that everything is right.

"Hunter!" I yell as every muscle in my body, especially my core, contracts and sends blood rushing to my head in the most perfect orgasmic tsunami.

I think I hear him grunt a release, too, but it's hard to tell with this ringing in my ears. I know for sure as I feel him release himself in small pulses inside me.

My heart is finally calming to a normal rate as he holds me in his arms, petting my hair. I mirror the act and start playing in his too.

"I forgive you, Megan," he says in a soft voice.

Huh?

I lean back to look at him.

"Forgive me for what?"

"For whatever happened with Parker. You're my one weakness, baby. I realize that now. I accept that now. And I can forgive you for anything. I will always love you no matter what. Even if the baby wasn't mine, I'd still love you."

What in the actual fuck?

I can't scramble off of Hunter's lap fast enough.

"Even if the baby isn't yours?" I spit back at him. "You think I'm carrying another man's child, Hunter?"

"I didn't say that. I meant that even if it was, I'd still love you."

"Well, that's some fucked up shit for you then because that sounds nutballs!"

I look for my largest duffle bag and start stuffing it with whatever I find first in my dresser drawers.

"This is the thing," I tell him as I pack. "You're supposed to be so much wiser than me, so worldly, got your shit together and all of that but you know what you really are? You're a man who has the emotional intelligence of a child. It's obvious you've never been in love before because you don't know what the hell to do with it!"

"Sit down, Megan. We're not going to have a repeat of what happened last time. You're not just going to storm out of here because you heard something you didn't like and–"

"And what? Do you think I got myself kidnapped on purpose? This is all my fault now? I've never been in more danger than the moment I stepped foot in your godforsaken club, and I've had enough. I'm out. I quit!"

I find a clean sweatsuit in my closet and put it on.

"You've misunderstood."

"I think I understand you perfectly for the first time ever."

"There's no leaving me. There's no quitting us. You are mine, and I am yours, and instead of running from every disagreement we have, you're going to have to learn how to stand and fight."

"No, I think you've misunderstood, Mr. Middleton. I've been standing and fighting for myself my entire life. You met my family, right? That's not how I'm trying to spend the rest of my life. I want a soft life. I want peace. I want happiness. Dammit, I deserve it. And clearly, I'm not going to get any of that with you."

"I'm not just going to let you leave, not after everything that's happened. Your safety is–"

"Oh, be quiet. I'm going back downstairs to my apartment. You'll know where I am. You'll know that I'm safe. But I need some immediate distance from you."

I tug at my engagement ring.

My fingers have started to swell because of the pregnancy, and it's tough to get it off, but after turning it a few times, I'm able to manage.

I place it on the dresser.

My beautiful ring.

I think about the moment he gave it to me. The moment he asked the question, I'd never imagined I'd be so lucky to hear. It was such a beautiful time in our lives and it's all changed so drastically...so fast.

"The engagement is off," I say somberly.

I lift the duffle and head to the elevator.

"Taking off the ring means nothing," he says calmly, following me to the living room. "You are still my wife in every way that matters."

I turn to him, tears streaming down my face.

"Why would you want a wife who's carrying another guy's baby?"

Then, as if on cue, the elevator doors open, and I walk inside. I can't turn around as the doors close because I know if I do, I'll run back inside.

I drop the duffle.

And collapse against one of the elevator walls.

I know in my heart that this is a turning point for us and I should stand my ground. I can't be with someone who doesn't trust me. There's no future in that. Not a good one anyway. But I also know that my heart is literally breaking.

Chapter 11

I'll Pay You Double

HUNTER

A man I knew from my days as an underling in the organization carefully approaches my Mercedes Benz truck, a gun carried somewhat discreetly on his hip under his leather blazer.

I lower my window slowly down, aviator shades on my face to hide the little sleep I've been getting since Megan moved out.

"Hey, Jack."

"Hunter."

"It's been a long time."

"It really has. Thank you for meeting me here instead of the club."

"No problem."

I invite him to sit in the back seat of the truck alongside me so we can chat privately.

"So, how can I help you?"

"I have a situation that could use some of your magical mediation skills. You know how I like to stay low, not make any waves. I have a small boutique business with a very particular clientele."

"Sure, I get that."

Jack has moved up since the early days of us running the streets as well. He runs guns but only specific ones to a very exclusive clientele.

"Over the last two weeks, there's been a new faction poaching some of my clients. Promising them more at better prices."

"Capitalism," I shrug.

"No, they're not sanctioned by the organization to make these kinds of moves. They're trying to put me out of business and before I start a war, I want to try and have a sit down. Maybe they don't understand how things work here."

"Who are they?"

"The Fabre Family. They're out of New Orleans."

Fuck.

"I'm not interested in any sort of mediation situation with those people, Jack. I'm sorry."

Jack's disappointment is palpable. I understand that he's been waiting well over a week for this meeting with me. I don't make it easy for people I don't have a relationship with to contact me. If I did, I'd get calls from every Tom, Dick and Harry. This isn't the outcome he was hoping for.

"I'll pay you ten percent extra your normal rate."

"It's not the money."

"Fifteen."

"Jack, you're not listening."

My new driver, Brian, raises his eyes to glance at us through the rearview mirror when the tone of my voice changes. A good sign that he's paying attention in case anything goes sideways.

He grows more frustrated. "Hunter, it's no secret that

the Fabres are making a move out here. They flew across the damn country and took your woman right from under your nose to prove a point. I shouldn't have to beg you to handle this for me. You should be jumping at the chance."

"Respectfully, Jack, you're in no position to tell me what I should or shouldn't be doing when it comes to my business. I'm worth ten times what you are and built it up from the dirt. Everything you have is what the organization has allowed you to have."

"I'm not disputing that. All I'm saying is that there's a code that we all follow and the Fabres are not. I'm just asking for someone to step in and explain it to them."

"I don't know that those people can be taught anything."

Jack sighs heavily. "What can I do to convince you to take me on as a client?"

"I'll tell you this, attempting to shame me into the job was not a good fucking way to start."

A call from Vaughn comes through my phone, but I press decline. I know what he wants and I'm not in the mood to talk. That's the problem when your friends work for you. They always think that everything is up for discussion.

"I'll pay you double," he says in an apologetic tone. "To compensate you for the disrespect, which by the way was not intentional."

Before he even got inside the car, I fully intended to pass on the offer but once he brought up Fabre's name, I had to consider it.

Not that I needed this guy to tell me but I have unfinished business with Fabre, not to mention that no matter what I think about his liar of a daughter, a part of me knows that if I save her from being handed over in marriage like she's a piece of meat, Megan will forgive me.

Fuck me.

I need to take the job.

"The way I work is half the fee as a deposit and the other half once I set the meeting."

"Mmm, but what if the meeting goes south?"

My phone buzzes again.

"Do you need to get that?" Jack asks.

I press the decline button.

"It's not my job to settle your business," I tell him. "It's my job to set the meeting."

"I think for double the fee you could at least guarantee the safety of an old friend."

"You're a big boy. You can guarantee your own safety, plus you're pushing it, Jack. You're lucky I'm even entertaining this. Protecting your business is not in my self-interest."

"But preventing a war is, and you know it's not just going to end with me. Fabre is coming for all of us."

"I don't run guns."

"Yeah, but he seems like the kind of guy looking to run everything, not just one thing."

"I will arrange the meet, and I'll make sure you leave it breathing, but that's my final offer."

Jack extends his hand. "Deal."

"Payment is in cash," I tell him before I commit to the handshake.

"Any idea on how long this meet will take?"

"It will take however long it's going to take, Jack."

"When did you become such a hardass, Hunter?"

"I've always been a hardass."

"Ain't that the truth," Jack jeers. "So where should I

bring the money? Should we arrange another meet like this?"

"You don't have the cash on you?"

"I don't roll like you, man. I need a minute to get that kind of money together."

"You don't have a minute. Come to the club tomorrow at noon with the cash and I'll get started. Arrive even one minute after twelve and the deal is off."

"Damn, Hunt, okay. Why are you so uptight?"

"Get out of my car, Jack."

After Jack leaves, Brian finally tears himself away from whatever he was doing on his cell phone. "Where to next, boss?"

"Beverly Hills."

I want to buy something obnoxiously expensive for Megan. I know it's not going to get her to move back to where she belongs, but it's a show of good faith. A gesture from me, at least trying to say I'm sorry.

"Sure."

I give Vaughn a call back since he's called me three times in the last hour. It could be important, although I doubt it.

"It's about time," he yells.

"Excuse me?"

"When I call you, you should pick up."

"Is Megan okay?" My chest tightens.

"This isn't about Megan. As far as I know, she's perfectly fine."

"Then what's so urgent? I'm working."

"Christian and I have made an executive decision."

"Oh yeah? And what's that?"

"We're letting Parker go."

"The fuck you are."

"He's not the reason that your life has gone to shit, and Megan's left the apartment. You fucked that up all on your own."

"And what the hell would either of you know about what's going on between me and my fiancee?"

"You've been sulking for a week. We both know she's back in her old apartment because you accused her of carrying Parker's baby."

"I'm not having this conversation with you. Keep Parker exactly where he is. His accommodations are better than a fucking Four Seasons penthouse."

"Hunter...it's been too long."

"I put a bed down there, and he's eating three square meals a day. What else do you want? You want me to braid his hair, too?"

"Megan has been snooping around and asking questions. Do you want her to find out that you still have Parker in the basement of the club? Do you think she'll ever forgive you and move back into your place once she finds out that you're holding her friend hostage?"

"He is not *her* friend! He was my employee who sold me out for a hospital bill."

"Hunter, in this situation, you're the boss, but you're also my friend, and I'm telling you this can't continue. The kid made one bad decision."

"A decision that got Megan and my baby kidnapped!"

"You're angry. I get it. If I still loved my ex half as much as you love Megan, I'd probably be the same way. But I'm telling you what nobody else around you will say. This is not the first time Megan has gotten hurt on your watch, and you're mad at yourself, so you're taking it out on him."

"Vaughn—"

"Listen to me, you hardheaded son of a bitch, the snatch

was random. Megan was simply in the wrong place at the wrong time, and you know it. Fabre was only here for the daughter."

"Everybody has a soft spot for this traitor," I mutter.

"What's the endgame, Hunt? If you don't want Christian and me to make the call, then you make it. You either need to kill Parker or let him go. What's it going to be?"

"You don't make the fucking demands. I do!" I roar.

"One thing you've always been is careful. That's what makes you who you are. Parker has a mother in a hospital somewhere who's going to call the police if she doesn't hear from him or the morgue soon."

I sit in silence for a moment and dwell on the fact that I know that Vaughn's right. I just hate that he is. I have connections in the force, but I also have plenty of enemies. Enemies who have known me since I was a teenager and who have been trying to pin a felony charge on me for years.

"Are you at the club?"

"Yeah."

"Go down there and put him on the phone."

After a few minutes or so, Parker's scratchy voice is on the other end of the line.

"Boss?"

"When will you stop calling me that? You're sitting in the hole of the club."

"But you can't be that mad at me. I just had a medium rare rib eye steak and a loaded baked potato."

Fucking Vaughn.

"Let me be crystal clear, Parker. You no longer work for me, and you never will again, but I won't leave you empty-handed. I'll pay for your mother's care as long as she needs it and for you to relocate."

"You want me to move?"

"Out of California for good."

"But my mom."

"She can go, too."

"But all her doctors are here."

This guy is unbelievable.

"Parker, I'm giving you a pass. Something I never give to people who betray me. I understand you didn't realize the gravity of what your betrayal would mean, but that doesn't negate that it led to someone I love being hurt."

"Can I talk to Megan before I leave? I need to apologize."

"The best apology you can give her is to do exactly what I tell you to do. Leave town and stay out of her orbit. Now put Vaughn back on the phone."

"Thanks, Mr. Middleton."

When Vaughn gets back on the phone, I give him a directive. "Pay for the mother's care and let him go. Don't let anyone see you do it, especially Lena."

"Anything else?"

"Find him somewhere to go. I want him out of California in the next 48 hours."

"A place where we have eyes?"

"Yeah."

"Hunt, I know it doesn't feel like it right now, but this is the right call."

"Your approval was not needed or asked for, asshole."

The last thing I hear is Vaughn's audible laughter as he hangs up.

God, he gets on my nerves.

"Any particular store, Mr. Middleton?" Brian asks from the front. "We're here."

I open the location feature on my phone under Megan's

contact to see where she is. It's something I do several times a day to help me curb the urge to call her. It helps me maintain my sanity since she demanded I take the security detail off of her. While normally I would have ignored that ridiculous request, I'm doing what I can to keep the rest of her pregnancy stress-free.

But once my beloved delivers our little bundle of joy.

All bets are off.

Chapter 12

Life Is Too Short

MEGAN

I would laugh if it wasn't so pitiful.

Every day, there's a different tragedy. Today, I dropped my fork on the floor, and because of the Frankenstein-sized baby growing inside of me, I couldn't reach it.

"I'm eating a salmon salad, for God's sake!" I yell at the universe. "I'm hungry, dammit."

And now come the tears.

My hormones are raging like a California wildfire, and I'm sure that no one is more sick of me than I am of myself. I'm two seconds away from eating this salad with my fingers when there's a sudden knock at the door.

"Who is it?" I shout.

"It's Lena."

"Why are you knocking on the door? You live here," I grouse.

"I'm so sorry, Megan, but I think I may have left my key in my bedroom."

"Well, you're going to have to wait. It takes me damn near an hour to get on my feet these days."

"I'm not in a rush," she chuckles. "I'll just sit here. I wish all the apartments had an elevator open up into the living room like the penthouse has. Then all we'd have to remember is a code."

I lean my palms heavily on the breakfast table and push myself to a stand. The moment I get on my feet, the pressure of the baby on my bladder makes me desperately want to pee, but it's a shorter distance to head to the front door first.

"Almost there."

"Ooh, I think the baby's grown since I saw you this morning," Lena says with a smile as I let her inside our apartment. She rubs my stomach, something that's become somewhat of a daily ritual now that I've moved back in here.

"Were you crying?" She asks, concern etched on her forehead.

"Yep."

"Aww, what's wrong? Are you missing my brother by chance?"

"Uh, not at all. I dropped my fork, and I couldn't bend over to pick it up," I say as I walk towards the bathroom.

Lena picks up the fork and washes it in the sink for me. "Problem solved."

After using the bathroom I return to find that Lena has brought home some Caribbean food and has reset the table.

"Is that curry?" I ask, my eyes widening.

"I made some for lunch."

"You're making curry chicken at the club?"

"I'm working on a recipe for a small puff pastry filled with curry, sort of like a turnover but lighter."

"What would we charge for them?"

"We could serve two maybe and charge twenty bucks."

"Twenty-five," I say, savoring my first bite of the scrumptious chicken. "Anything with puff pastry is going to be good. They can pay twenty-five."

"I'll recommend your pricing to the acting manager."

"Who is?"

"That would be Gage."

I nod my head in approval. "He's a good choice. He understands the clientele, he's good with the staff, and your brother trusts him. Honestly, he's a way better choice for manager of the club than me."

"That's not true."

"I've lost all credibility with the staff, and you know it. I'm pregnant with the boss's child. I'm exactly who they think I am."

"If I were to think like that, then the only reason why I'm leading the kitchen is because I'm his sister."

"Well, there is some truth to that."

"Thanks a lot! How quickly you forget that Billy recruited me on his own back when I was Lacy and not Lena."

"Mm, that's right. Forgive me. It's this baby brain I have."

"Speaking of that," Lena gets up and grabs us both some cool bottles of water from the fridge.

"Speaking of what, baby brain?"

"Speaking of the baby you're having."

"I don't want to talk about Hunter, Lena. I thought I explained that the topic is off limits."

"I don't want to necessarily discuss your relationship. I just want some advice in dealing with him."

"Advice about what?"

I take a long swallow of the water, regretting it almost instantly because I know it's only going to send me back to the bathroom in about thirty minutes.

"I think I may have a little crush on someone he knows."

"Christian," I scoff. "Do you really think nobody knows?"

"Has Hunter said anything to you about it?" she asks with a deep-seated look of worry in her eyes.

"There's been a lot going on, Lena. The last thing that Hunter and I have discussed is your love life."

Ugh, that came out meaner than I intended.

"I'm sorry. You're right." She stands and clears her dishes, clearly hurt. I feel bad that I've made her feel as if she needs to leave.

"I'm sorry. I'm in such a shitty mood lately. I apologize. Nobody tells you at the obstetrician's office how pregnancy can and will affect your mood. Please sit back down. Tell me more about Christian."

"It's silly really. I'm talking about one of my brother's friends as if anything could ever happen between us."

"Why do you say that?"

"He thinks of me as a little sister, and then there's the whole Hunter factor. Even if I thought Christian liked me a little, Hunter would never allow it to happen."

"You and I are practically the same age, and so are Hunter and Christian. What's the difference?"

"You know there's a difference. I'm his best friend's little sister. I wouldn't be worth the risk."

"Then what are we talking about the possibility for? If that's how you feel about yourself, then why bring it up?"

"Megan, you're being so mean! I bring you home a delicious dinner and ask for your advice and this is what you say to me?"

"Listen, girl, I'm pregnant. I broke off my engagement. And I was kidnapped by my best friend's father. I have zero fucks to give about anything but this baby growing inside me. If you are attracted to Christian, tell him. If he reciprocates those feelings, explore them. If Hunter has some shit to say about it, fuck him. Life is too short not to live it how you want."

"And you want to live your life raising this baby on your own without Hunter?"

"Hell no! This is not what I wanted at all, Lena. I love your dumb ass brother, but I will not be controlled by his inability to trust anyone or anything but himself."

"He's had a hard life, Megan."

"Who hasn't!"

"He said and perhaps did some things in a moment of fear, and fear is not an emotion he is used to navigating. He doesn't have many emotional attachments, but you are one of them, maybe the only one, and it frightens him."

"Well–"

"If you don't forgive him, I'm afraid of what he'll do next. This whole thing with Naomi's father is far from over. You know that. And I'm afraid of the decisions he'll make if you are not around. You know what he's capable of. Look at poor Parker."

With everything going on between Hunter and me, not to mention this uncomfortable period of my pregnancy, I haven't thought about Parker in days.

"What's wrong with Parker?"

Lena's face turns a shade of pale grey.

"I shouldn't have said that."

Her reaction reminds me of the argument between

Hunter and me. It only escalated when I brought up Parker's name. Maybe his guilt over something is why he started acting irrationally.

"Is he dead, Lena?" I ask the painful question, the one I should have had strength enough to ask Hunter myself.

"Dead? Oh no."

"Then what's wrong with him? Where is he?"

"I shouldn't have mentioned it. I'm not supposed to know."

"Know what!" Lena takes a moment to consider what she's going to do as I stare her directly in the eyes. "And don't lie to me."

"Hunter has been holding him in the basement of the club since you returned."

"Like a hostage?" I whisper.

Lena's eyes drop to the ground.

"Please don't say anything. I'll get in so much trouble. If he finds out I know, he'll want to know *how* I know."

"Christian?"

"He confides in me sometimes. Please, Megan, you can't say anything," Lena pleads with watery eyes.

"So I'm just supposed to let Parker die in a dungeon somewhere while people drink and dance above his head every night?"

"He's not dying."

"If Parker dies in that basement, I promise that Hunter will never see me or this baby ever again!"

"Calm down. I will get you proof that he's fine. Trust me," she pleads.

I've never seen Lena try this hard to be so convincing about something. She's worried sick that I'm going to blow up her spot. This thing with Christian is more serious for her than I thought. It's clear to me now that what he thinks matters to her.

And that's the beginning of the end.

Been there, done that.

But I take some pity on her.

"You've got 24 hours to get me proof, or I'm waddling in that club myself ."

Chapter 13

Time For An Ugly Cry

LENA

"Gage, I just checked the fridge and the freezer, and I'm missing a few t-bone steaks and a large pack of chicken wings."

"That's odd," he responds, wiping down the main bar top.

"Uh, yeah. Someone is stealing food."

Gage keeps his eyes low on the white cloth in his hand as he cleans in meticulous circles, and that's how I know he's keeping something from me. But what? And why?

"If there's someone who needs help you can just tell me. I worked in a soup kitchen for over a year. I get it."

"I don't know anyone dealing with food insecurity here at the club, but I'll be sure to keep an eye out."

"Gage."

He lifts his head. "Yes, Lena?"

"Are you lying to me?"

His hand stops moving.

"You're upset about this missing food, aren't you?"

"I just feel like some secret dinners are being made."

"Secret dinners?" he scoffs. "That sounds ominous. I'm sure it's just a delivery error. I'll check the order log when I'm finished over here."

"That bar couldn't get any cleaner if you tried."

"I have a certain standard." He smiles.

"Are you trying to take Megan's job from her?"

"Now you and I both know that Megan is about to own this place once she marries Hunter."

"And?"

"She won't need this job."

"Are you saying she should be a good little wife and stay at home, do as she's told, and let the men handle the business?"

Gage leans on his forearms, which I guess I never noticed were that lean and muscular, and offers up a questionable smile that I don't trust.

"I see that you're breaking out of the whole shy little sister thing, and now you're sticking up for your future sister-in-law? It's cute."

"You should watch how you talk to me. Like you said, I am the boss's little sister."

"Definitely cute," he says, standing straight up again and reaching for a bottle of whiskey. "You want some before our shift starts?" he offers me a shot.

"No, thank you. I don't cook drunk."

"One shot will not get you drunk; in my opinion, everyone cooks better tipsy."

"Not me.

Then it hits me.

Gage is the key to this whole thing. He knows everything about everyone but always stays under the radar. If anyone knows what's going on with Parker, I'm convinced that he does.

"Fuck it," I tell him. "Pour me one."

I take the shot of amber liquid and sip it slowly.

"Are you sipping a shot?" he chuckles.

"You're questioning the drinking skills of someone under the age of twenty-one?"

"Right, I keep forgetting that."

"Yeah, like you're the only person who doesn't constantly remind me of that."

"You're very mature for your age. It's easy to forget you're not quite legal yet."

I sip the rest of the whiskey and clank the glass down on the bar, uncomfortable with what I think was just a compliment from Gage. It's now or never.

"If I asked you something, would you tell me the truth?"

"Depends."

"It depends? What kind of an answer is that?"

"A truthful one." He winks playfully.

"Okay," I take a nervous breath. "I need to know if Parker is okay?"

"What would I know about Parker?"

"You know about everything that goes on around here."

"He doesn't work here anymore."

"Gage, I know," I whisper, pivoting my head around to make sure that no one else is within earshot of us.

"You know what?"

Gage pours himself another shot but places my empty shot glass in the bar sink.

"I know where my missing supplies are going."

"Then why did you bother asking me about them?"

"Because you know where they're going too. I just

wanted to see if you would be man enough to tell me the truth."

"Funny, that's the second time you've questioned my manhood today, Lena. Yeah, you're definitely turning over a new leaf, and I have to admit...I like it."

My neck flushes, which completely confuses me. I'm attracted to Christian, not Gage.

I need to stay focused.

"We just want to make sure he's okay."

"We?"

I hesitate to reply, but I've come this far, and I promised Megan I'd get her some answers.

"Me and Megan."

Gage raises what feels like a judgemental eyebrow. "I hope that you find him so you two can...focus on other things. More productive things."

"So you refuse to confirm for me what I already know?"

"I promise that you don't know anything that you think you know, and you're getting yourself all worked up for nothing."

"Who's getting worked up for nothing?" a familiar voice says from the shadows, and my stomach churns. It's difficult to tell what time of day it is inside the windowless walls of the club which is why neither of us saw Christian approach.

"Nothing," I stutter, not understanding why I'm so damn nervous.

"Gage?" Christian addresses him.

"It seems that our Lena is looking for some missing steaks and chicken parts."

"Our Lena?" Christian looks between the two of us with a perturbed look on his face. I can already tell what he's thinking, and I swallow thickly.

"Just a figure of speech," Gage replies after noticing my discomfort. "I just figured she's like the unofficial little sister of everyone at the club."

"Not everyone," Christian says flatly. "Lena, can I talk to you for a moment?"

"Um, sure." I'm almost certain that he overheard our conversation, and he's pissed. "I'll catch up with you later, Gage."

Gage raises an arm to wave me off silently, and I follow Christian to Hunter's private office on the second floor of the club–like a lamb to the slaughter.

Before I can explain myself, though, he starts barking out orders.

"Close the door."

His abruptness takes me aback for a moment. Christian is usually so calm, and so sweet, but right now–not so much.

"What's wrong?"

"Why are you grilling Gage about the missing food?"

"Because I'm the head cook now and it's his job to order supplies and mine to keep track of it."

"That's not why, and we both know it."

"Christian–"

"Listen, Lena, I fucked up and told you a few things that I shouldn't have. That's on me. But I need you to let them go. You can't start snooping around the club like you're some private detective."

"Just tell me everything about Parker, and I won't have to."

"What? Hell, no!" He takes a few steps closer to me. "No, Lena. Leave it alone. Your brother won't like it."

"Hunter isn't thinking straight. I'm just trying to save his relationship. Megan will never forgive him if he permanently hurts Parker, and those two are about to bring a baby into the world."

"Parker deserves whatever he gets. You don't bite the hand that feeds you. You just don't."

"Parker saved her from Naomi's dad, though."

"You're twisting the story a little. That's not exactly what happened."

"All I know is no matter what part he may have played in her abduction initially, if Parker hadn't found her when he did, Megan would be the one in a basement somewhere in Lousiana."

When I get upset, I sometimes cry. Not an ugly kind of cry but my eyes tend to water up which is exactly what I'm doing right now.

When Christian reaches a hand up toward my face, using his thumb to rub a tear away, my eyes close from the soothing feel of his skin touching mine.

"Calm down; I don't like to see you upset like this."

"I don't like it either."

Without even thinking, I wrap my arms around his waist and hug Christian. My head rests on his chest, and I smell sandalwood and hints of musk. But once his body grows instantly taut, I realize I've made a huge mistake.

"I'm sorry," I apologize as I try to create a reasonable amount of distance between us again. "I shouldn't just go around hugging random people," I laugh awkwardly.

"I'm just some random person to you?" he says in a lower voice than usual as he grips my upper arms, keeping me in place.

I blink twice.

And my tongue feels as if it's grown three times its size.

"No," I say in a mousy voice that I barely recognize. "No, you're not."

"Don't ever apologize for hugging me, Lena."

"Um, okay."

"Ever."

"Okay."

"And Lena?"

"Yes?"

"If Megan wants to find out anything about Parker, she should call her fiance and ask him directly. You need to stay completely out of it. The last thing I'd want to see is for you to become collateral damage because those two can't get their shit together."

"Do you think Hunter would cut me out of his life or something?"

The thought of that frightens me. We've just found each other.

"I'd never let that happen but there would be consequences. I'm hoping that we'd never have to cross that bridge."

"It's nice to know that I'd have another big brother willing to take Hunter's place if he ever did." I smile. "Thanks for always being there for me Christian. You've been a great friend."

"A friend?"

"We are friends, aren't we?" I ask questioning whether he's been taking care of me because Hunter ordered him to or because he genuinely cares for my well-being.

A conflicted look I don't completely understand the meaning of crosses Christian's face and my heart sinks. One of my biggest flaws is that I've always misinterpreted people's true intentions. It's a skill I'm sure you learn if you grow up in a normal way and not alone and frightened like I did.

Of course, this man doesn't give a single *real* shit about

me. Why would he? He's just doing whatever Hunter's told him to do.

"We are," he says plainly and his eyes give him away.

I am nothing but an assignment.

Or perhaps a favor for his friend.

None of this is real.

And I need to remember that.

"I've got food to prep so I'm going to head off now," I tell him desperately trying to mask my hurt feelings with a superficial smile.

"And the thing with Megan?"

"Stepping away and minding my business." I throw my hands up.

Once I make it back downstairs, I dip into a side hallway before I enter the kitchen, and for the first time in a long time, maybe years... I have an ugly cry.

Chapter 14

First Things First

MEGAN

If I watch another episode of a woman falling all over herself, embarrassing herself, to get a rose from a man with the hopes of screwing him in a hot tub I'm going to vomit.

It's my own fault.

This is what happens when you quit your job, dump your fiancé, and basically blow up your entire life in one moment. You end up bored as hell on the sofa eating shit to keep the baby walrus growing inside of me happy.

That's it.

I have to get out of this apartment.

I promised I'd give Lena 24 hours to find out what she could about Parker, but her search and find mission came up short. She didn't say much but that she reached a dead end.

She's a sweet girl who is trying to find her way in this new life that she's found herself in with Hunter as her brother, but I'm done sitting passively as things happen around me.

Those days are over.

I will not be pushed around in my relationship just because he thinks he can, or that he should, or that he's older than me and knows better. I have a voice and it's time that I use it.

First things first.

I want to know the truth about Parker and make sure he's not floating at the bottom of the Pacific Ocean somewhere.

Sure, the guy lost his way for a brief moment in time but he quickly course corrected himself. Truth be told, I don't think he was ever going to turn me over to Mr. Fabre. I don't think he has it in him.

I ease myself up from the couch and look out the window. It's much easier to see what's going on in my neighborhood when you're on the seventh floor instead of the Penthouse suite. It doesn't take a genius to realize that regardless of the status of my relationship with Hunter, he's assigned a security detail outside the building. The black town car is a dead giveaway. But I don't care. They can watch me. I'm headed straight to the club, anyway.

I'm not sure what I expected when I strolled in the Blue Whiskey. It hasn't been that long since I quit. The world hasn't imploded. Everything is as it always is. The only difference is that Gage is the one giving the orders instead of me. A small part of me wishes he wasn't so good at my job, but that wouldn't only be wishful thinking.

"Megan!" Gage greets me animatedly.

"Hi."

"Have you come to put me out of my misery?" He jests.

"No, way." I rub my stomach. "I have a bigger job on my hands."

"That's true." He smiles. "Are you looking for Lena or Hunter because Hunter isn't here right now?"

Perfect.

I don't feel like dealing with him today.

"I was looking for Lena."

She's in the kitchen, seasoning some wings I think.

"Great, thanks."

Lena isn't pleased to see me when I walk into the kitchen area.

"What are you doing here?" she asks, worry etched on her forehead.

"Hey, roomie," I greet her with sarcasm. "Nice to see you too."

"We just saw each other a few hours ago when I left for work."

"You know why I'm here."

"Megan–"

"You have nothing to worry about. I won't bring your name in it at all."

"We live together. We're friends. He'll know."

I'm not sure if the *he* she's referring to is Hunter or Christian, but it doesn't matter. The person I should have gone to straight from the beginning won't divulge anything.

"I promise you. You're safe." I walk over and give her a brief hug. "I'll see you later at home, okay?"

"Where are you going? I don't think Hunter is even here right now."

"I'm definitely not here to chat with him."

Although secretly I miss the man like crazy, or at least the man he was when we first met.

"Are you sure you know what you're doing, Megan?"

"I'm sure. I'm not here to make a scene just to get answers."

"That sounds like the same thing to me."

"It's not," I chuckle. "Trust me."

I hate that Hunter's secrets have created this uncomfortable wedge between Lena and me. I shouldn't even be living in the same apartment with her. His apartment. But I have nowhere else to go and I'm not going to put our baby in harm's way just to prove some sort of point. I don't even think he'd let me go that far. Knowing that man, he'd lock me up in the same damn basement where Parker is before he allowed me to just disappear with his baby.

I head to the second floor and find Vaughn in Hunter's office. His eyes light up when he sees me. No doubt thinking that I've come to patch things up with his bestie.

Not even close.

"Hey there, new mama."

"Hey, Vaughn."

"Were you looking for Hunt?"

"No, I was hoping to find Lars."

"Lars?"

"Yeah, is he here?"

"Well, usually he's with Hunter since...well since the driver position is vacant."

"You said usually."

"Hunt didn't need him today."

"So he's alone?" I immediately worry about Hunter's safety. "Is he out on business?"

"Things have calmed down now that we have the Jonathan situation neutralized. He's okay on his own."

"Then why do I have two guys in polyester suits and a town car tailing me around town?"

"That's different, Megan." He gives me a knowing look as if it was silly of me to even ask the question.

"Where can I find Lars?" I skip to the point.

"I'll call him for you. Have a seat and make yourself comfortable. Can I get anything for you? Water? A snack?"

My spidey senses are tingling.

What is Vaughn hiding?

"No, I'm good."

Vaughn gives Lars a call on his cell phone and five minutes later, he magically arrives.

"Megan?"

"Hi, Lars." I smile cautiously.

"You wanted to see me?" He rolls down the sleeves of his Western-styled denim shirt and snaps the cuffs back in place.

Vaughn watches us both intently.

"Can we take a walk outside, maybe?" I ask Lars.

Lars looks at Vaughn for a quick moment, then back to me. "Sure, are you okay?"

"I'm fine. I just wanted to talk to you about something."

"Okay, sure."

Vaughn's eyes narrow as we leave the office. I know that he's going to call Hunter as soon as I step over the threshold of the office, so I have to keep my interrogation of Lars brief and to the point. I start my inquisition as we walk down the club's steps to the main floor.

"First, I want to start by thanking you for all your help in trying to find me, Lars."

"No thanks needed, Megan. It was my job, but it was also my pleasure that you were found safe."

"Lars, I realize that you work for Hunter, but I'd also like to think that we've forged our own friendship amid what is *just work* for you."

"It sounds like you want to ask me something, Megan."

Lars is a no-nonsense sort of man. I've always appreciated that about him, so I get to the point.

"I know that whatever you feel about me, you feel ten times more of that for Parker. So I'm asking, do you know where he is?"

Lars pauses for a moment, no doubt deciding how much of the "truth" he's going to tell me. We've walked through the kitchen and into the back alley of the club now, which is perfectly safe and private at this time of day.

"Yes, I know where he is."

My chest tightens as I get closer to the truth.

"Is he being held against his will in this club?" I ask.

Lars's face hardens. "Do you think I would ever tell you that, Megan?"

"I know that you're not a liar."

"No, I'm not, but I also don't answer to you. You're my boss's girlfriend, *not* my boss."

"Humph," I scoff. "Your non-answer tells me everything I need to know," I say with a steely glare. "Parker trusted you."

"You don't know anything," he says thickly and I think I hear a hint of his Danish accent which he has managed to mask most of the time.

Suddenly the metal door to the kitchen swings open, and Hunter emerges dressed in a monochromatic tailored black suit, shirt, and tie. He got here quicker than I expected and damn he looks fucking delicious.

"Megan," he greets me, staring me down with those deeply cold grey eyes and my thighs tremble.

"Hey," is all I manage to say.

"Is there a reason why you've brought Lars out here in the alley to chat?"

Hunter looks between us both and it dawns on me that I may have just gotten Lars into some trouble.

"I made him come out here to ask him if he knows where Parker is?"

"Still looking for him, are you?" he retorts through gritted teeth.

"May I be excused?" Lars asks. "I need to finish up something."

"Certainly, Lars," Hunter replies. "I apologize for this." He makes a hand gesture in my direction.

"Apologize for what?" I respond, offended by the insinuation that I'm making a scene.

Once Lars goes back inside the club, Hunter walks down the steps and strides toward me.

"I apologized for your behavior."

"My behavior!"

Hunter runs his hand down the side of my face. I shudder at the feel of his textured fingertips across my skin.

Shit, I wasn't expecting that.

"You're so beautiful, Megan. I've never seen a more incandescent pregnant woman. You fucking glow."

"Hunter–"

"It's disappointed me how you've put the welfare of that traitor ahead of our life together."

"That's not what's happening here."

"What will you do when you find out what you came here for?"

"What do you mean?"

"What's your next move? What are you going to do with the information?"

"It depends on what the information is."

"Is that right?"

His fingertips trail down my face, the side of my neck, and leisurely skim the bones of my clavicle.

I won't stop him though.

I've missed his touch and it feels too good. I forgot just how intense it can be between us.

He leans in and brushes his lips against mine then pulls back slowly.

"Against every one of my instincts, I treated Parker like a fucking king during his interrogation and then let him go to live his life. He's alive and well and certainly not giving a shit about how you are. He's moved on. Can you?"

"That wasn't nice to say about him not giving a shit about me."

"It's the truth. Accept it."

"I never said we were besties, I just didn't want you to kill him. I don't want you to have to carry such a burden like that on your soul."

"I can deal with my own soul."

"Can you?"

"The part you're not getting is that would have been my business if I had ended his miserable life. It's an ugly part of how things work in my world that I choose to keep away from you for good reason."

"I don't want you making all the choices."

"In my business?"

"In my life!"

"Parker is not a fucking part of your life."

"You made him a part of it when you sent him and Lars to my university to find me. The moment you sent them is the moment they also became a part of my life."

"All I've wanted is your happiness," he exhales harshly. "When will you stop punishing me, Megan?"

"That's not what I'm doing."

"That's what it feels like."

His hand traces the curve of my right breast and I can feel my pussy aching. Everything seems so much more sensitive now that I'm pregnant.

"What are you doing?" I whisper through an exhalation.

"I'm reminding you that a man who would do anything for your sweet, stubborn ass is right here waiting for you to come home where you belong."

One of his fingers rakes against my nipple instantly making it harden through the fabric of my shirt.

"Come home to me, Megan."

It would be so easy to just say *okay*. To ignore all of our trust issues and fall into his arms. I'm carrying his child for God's sake. It's perfectly within my rights to change my mind and go live happily ever after with him.

I love Hunter.

And he loves me.

Particularly when things are on his terms. *Hmm, for a brief moment, I forgot about that part.*

"You'll have to wait a little longer," I say resolutely.

"Why?" His face scrunches into a scowl. "I told you what you wanted to know."

"It's not enough."

His hand falls away from my body.

"Are you adamant about not coming home and having this baby alone?" he asks, his tone acidic.

"I'm just not ready to go back like things are normal when they're not. When you're afraid, Hunter, your default is to go into street fighter mode and street fighters suspect everyone and trust no one. I don't want to live like that."

He straightens his tie and takes several steps back away from me as if I'm poison.

"I understand your point and will give you all the space you require."

His sudden change in demeanor is startling. I don't know what he's thinking. Has he given up on me? Is this what I want?

"You will?"

"Yes, just take care of yourself and the baby. That's all I ask."

That sounds like a final wish.

"And if you need something, call Vaughn and let him know," he continues. "He'll make whatever arrangements are necessary until I find myself a proper assistant."

"Go through Vaughn?" I question softly.

"I don't live in the gray zone, Megan. We're either together or we're not. You've decided that we're not and I'm not in the habit of begging a woman for anything, so yeah, unless it's an emergency go through Vaughn."

"Fine."

"Do you need a ride back home?"

"Am I dismissed?" I ask, put off by the way he's kicking me out of the very club I managed for him a few short weeks ago.

He silently opens the metal door and waits for me to walk through it. I can hear the kitchen staff grow silent, waiting to hear what we're going to say next. They've probably been eavesdropping the entire time, especially Lena.

But Hunter says nothing else, his face an unreadable blank slate.

And it's in that instant the baby moves in my stomach for the very first time.

What have I done?

Chapter 15

Wake The Fuck Up

HUNTER

Work has always been at the center of my consciousness. I live, eat, and breathe it. My need to tame the Los Angeles underworld that once consumed me as a teenager is what motivates me. I never want to be that frightened kid who lost everything and everyone again.

Of course, I've allowed myself room for some vulnerability over the years. My longtime friendships with Vaughn and Christian are proof of that. And then there's Megan.

I've never been in love before. Never. It's not something I ever thought was in the cards for me. It's not that I was even denying myself a relationship. I just never felt that "thing" you're supposed to feel for any woman I've been involved with, at least not until I met her.

When I fuck her, hold her, or simply think about her, I feel exactly like I did after our first explosive meeting. If I had to explain it, I'd say it was more of a warm feeling in my chest that spreads deliciously to my fingertips, my dick, and my toes. A warmth that I never want to let go of. A warmth I would kill for.

That's why I'm so lost right now.

How will I get that feeling back if she doesn't come around? Why won't she listen? Doesn't she understand I have her best interest at heart and that I'll always have the best interest of my child and Megan at the forefront of every decision I make?

"Hunt, wake the fuck up."

Vaughn snaps his finger in front of me, jarring me out of my daze.

"What the hell were you so deep in thought about?" Christian adds from the back of the truck.

"Nothing," I mutter.

The three of us are going to dinner at a restaurant that's over an hour away on Friday night, Los Angeles traffic. Vaughn claims it's one of his favorite spots, which is why we're driving so damn far when Christian and I know this is more of a fact-finding mission. Vaughn's wife is supposedly having an affair with the owner, and we hope to God that she is so that he can finally move on from her toxic ass.

It's our first dinner together since the two of them decided to let Parker go. We've been at odds with each other quite a bit over the last few weeks, and I think we need this time to just eat, drink and talk about shit other than work like we used to.

"How much longer?" I ask.

"About twenty minutes," Vaughn says. "They're holding our reservation."

Out of habit, I check my cell phone. The last text I received was from Vaughn telling me to meet them at the car. The text before that was from Lena. Another was from a work client.

Nothing from Megan.

"So what did you decide about Jack?" Christian asks out of the blue.

Vaughn purses his lips. "I thought we weren't going to talk about work tonight."

"I'm not sure I can eat a lobster tail and pretend that the shit isn't about to hit the fan *again*," Christian says.

"He paid in full and on time, so I will schedule the meeting like I promised," I tell them both.

"Fuck," Vaughn curses. "Things were just settling down."

"It's a meet, nothing more."

"If you think that I believe that you're going to set up a meet between Jack and the man who kidnapped Megan and not a bullet between his eyes, you must think very little of our friendship."

I anxiously tap my feet on the floor mats of the truck, daydreaming about what it would actually feel like to harm the man who terrorized my Megan.

"He deserves a much more violent death than a bullet in the head."

"True," Christian agrees.

"But killing him wouldn't solve the bigger issue going on. His family is making a power move to make some noise out West, and I think they'd do it with or without Fabre. They've been planning this for a long time."

"And that's the bigger issue than him kidnapping Megan?" Vaughn asks, confused by my reaction.

"I know you don't understand it, but yes. Megan is home, and she and the baby are fine. The bigger issue is them coming out here and making things difficult for us. It's taken me years to reach this level. I can't have him and his fucked up family coming out here trying to shake things up."

"We could get some local gangs involved and keep our hands clean."

"I don't want another war on my streets, Christian. The city's only just recovering from the Bloods and Crips thing from twenty years ago."

"True."

"Plus, the whole reason why people come to me is to avoid unnecessary bloodshed. He took Megan to get my attention. He wanted me to know that I wasn't untouchable and that I had stuck my nose in where it didn't belong."

"We didn't know that Naomi was some mafia heiress. Hell, I thought she was from the Bay Area."

"But I knew."

"Not the whole time."

"There's a protocol to this kind of thing. You both know this. When I found out who she was, I should have sent her home or at the very least, called down there and told them where she was."

"Are you justifying that psychopath's actions, Hunt?"

"No, I'm simply saying that I understand them, which is why I'm going to make the meeting happen."

"You're a better man than me," Vaughn mutters under his breath.

"Oh, shut the fuck up," Christian says to him. "We're having dinner a thousand miles from the club, so you can spy on a woman who doesn't give two shits about you. You're not one to talk about how anyone should handle their relationship."

"When we get out of this car, I'm going to body slam you to the ground. Be ready," Vaughn threatens.

"You've gained ten pounds since you ran away from

home. I don't even know if you're capable of body slamming anyone, much less me," Christian jests, and for a moment, I release the biggest belly laugh.

"You two." I laugh some more. "Are so full of shit."

My laughter seems to be contagious as Vaughn begins cackling, and I notice Christian's chest vibrating with chuckles as well.

Things have been so serious these past few months that I'm sure we haven't laughed like this for the longest time.

It feels good.

Like old times.

Then my chest tightens because I can't seem to have a moment of joy without thinking about the one person who has made me the happiest ever in my life.

I used to laugh like this with Megan. Yet lately, all I've seemed to make her do is feel anger or sadness. Now that I think about it, I haven't seen her smile in weeks. The baby isn't even here yet, and already I've proven to be a shitty dad.

"What is it?" Vaughn turns his head, concern etched on his forehead. "What's wrong?"

"I'm an asshole," I say flatly, and they both know exactly what I mean.

"I'm glad you said it," Vaughn agrees.

"Yeah, because if she were mine–" Christian starts.

"But she's not yours," I growl back.

"No, she's not, but if you keep fucking up, you best believe someone will swoop in and take her, new baby and all."

The thought of someone else in Megan's bed or raising my baby makes me sick to my stomach. Never in a million years did I think we'd ever be this far apart from each other, physically or emotionally.

"I don't know how to fix it," I say in a defeated tone that I don't even recognize myself.

"The fuck you don't know how to fix it!" Vaughn exclaims. "Do what you do best. Make your point. Make it over the top. And then you grovel."

"She loves you, Hunt, and I bet she's looking for any excuse to take you back, but you have to give her one," Christian also offers.

Yeah, I ponder to myself.

I have to give her one.

Chapter 16

Ten Percent?

HUNTER

Part of the reason I've become so successful in my business is that I remain neutral in any situation with any criminal.

I'm Switzerland.

I can talk to anyone about anything, and my feelings aren't involved. Why? Because I don't have feelings in these matters, not when it comes to business anyway. I was taught early that business is business, and if you allow emotions to get in the way, it's the kiss of death.

But there's always a first time for everything.

Usually, I set up a meeting between clients at my club because it's a neutral location over which I have complete control. Not this time, though. And I'm incredibly uncomfortable right now.

It doesn't matter that Megan isn't working as the club manager anymore. I'm still not going to let Fabre or anyone related to him, who works for him, or who even breathes the same air as him inside my club. For one, there's the obvious reason. I wouldn't want it to get back to Megan that I've arranged a meeting with the fucker who just kidnapped her. I know that woman of mine and a million different scenarios would run through her head, and none of them are good.

She'd probably be afraid I'd kill him.

Very possible.

Or that she could still save that traitorous Naomi from a future that's been cemented for her since birth.

Not possible.

Lamenting about my reaction toward Fabre, or the idea of still saving Naomi or even Parker, for that matter, is not what I want the future mother of my child to be doing. She should be stuffing her face with delicious food, shopping for the baby, getting foot rubs, and being pampered in all the ways an expectant mother should.

But I still have time to make this right. The second half of her pregnancy will be better than the first half. And it starts with me allowing this meeting to unfold in a very uncomfortable way.

I've got my reasons.

Jack and I got here early. He's clearly nervous as he paces the small balcony off the side of the suite. Lars is sitting quietly in a chair in the corner of the suite, keeping an eye on him. Nervous clients always make Lars uncomfortable. He thinks they're "liable to do any damn thing" when their nerves are involved.

I'm sitting at the large desk in the room, having a cup of coffee with a shot of whiskey...waiting.

Finally, there's a knock at the door.

Lars rises and looks through the peephole, raising three fingers, which means Fabre is there with two other people.

I give a head nod, permitting Lars to open the door, and

it's not until I see the potbelly asshole walk through the threshold that I realize this is a dumb ass idea.

"Middleton," he says with a grin. "I thought we'd meet at your notorious club, but this is nice too."

Fabre sits on one of the sofas as his two men stand close by.

"Hello, Mr. Fabre. My name's Jack Brockington. I used to run with the DiAngelo family."

"But before that, you used to run with Mr. Middleton in the organization, is that right?"

"Yes, I see you did your homework."

"I always do. You must have called in a really big favor to get Mr. Middleton to arrange this meet for you."

Fabre stares at me, and I can sense Lars's body posture shifting in the far corner of the room. He's itching for Fabre to do something stupid, looking for any excuse to put a bullet in his chest.

"Hunter and I do have some history, but this meeting was bound to happen, Mr. Fabre. I know you've taken some interest in things out here on the West Coast, but I'm asking that you leave my business out of it."

"Before we get down to brass tacks, I wanted to introduce my daughter's fiance to you, Middleton. Gabriel's never been to Cali before. I thought I'd show him how the Fabres do business and brought him along."

Naomi's fiance looks indifferent to the introduction and doesn't bother speaking at all. If I had to guess, I'd say he doesn't care much for his new father-in-law, but what else is new? I don't know too many men that say good things about Fabre.

"When is the wedding?" I ask, knowing I shouldn't show any interest at all but remembering part of the conversation I overheard between Naomi, Megan, and Lena before Megan was kidnapped–neither Gabriel nor Naomi wants this.

"My wife is managing the wedding planning. It will be a grand occasion, though, the way we always do it in Louisiana," he says with an extra twang to his voice. "I'd love it if you and Megan could make it."

Every muscle in my body contracts.

He just had to say her name.

"You can't help yourself, can you?" I say through gritted teeth.

"Can we get back to the reason why we're all here, Mr. Fabre?" Jack interrupts, sensing the immediate danger growing in the room. "Can you assure me that you'll leave my business alone as you expand out west?"

"And what do I get out of the arrangement?"

"Ten percent, of course."

"Ten percent?" Fabre scoffs. "You'll pay me ten percent of a business that could be a hundred percent mine if I put a bullet through your head right now?"

Everyone's eyes widen except for mine. If it wasn't clear why he decided to fly across the country for this meeting before, it's crystal clear now. This is it. This is him making his move, daring anyone to stop him. And doing it in front of me is just icing on the cake.

"No one is getting shot inside this suite today," I say steadily. "Not on my watch."

Not today.

"Of course not," Fabre smirks. "I'm just saying that ten percent is a disrespectful offer. I thought your man here would know better. I could simply take all of it from him, and he'd have nothing."

"You're assuming a lot of things. You can't just walk up

in the city of Los Angeles, take a man's livelihood from him, and think there won't be any repercussions."

"Ask around, Middleton. I have a good track record of doing just that."

"Not here, you don't."

We stare off at each other, and I notice a hint of amusement emitting from Gabriel's eyes while the other man with Fabre stands stoically.

"Jack," I say, turning to face him. "You're going to have to do better than ten percent if you want to leave this room with a deal."

"But I already have to give a piece to the organization."

"That's your business," I tell him.

"Rest assured, Jack, when I make my move out here, you won't have to give any of your business to the organization—just the Fabre family."

Another veiled threat.

Jack takes a moment to think carefully about a number. I'm sure he's weighing what he can afford to part with versus giving Fabre a number that doesn't disrespect his power. I'd normally step up and negotiate the price in such instances, but I decide to fall back on this one.

If everything I'm thinking falls into place. This negotiation won't mean shit anyway because Fabre won't be around to collect.

"Then what about twenty percent?" Jack asks.

"What do you think, Gabriel? Cali will be your division to run one day. Are you fine with that arrangement?"

"In my family, we don't settle for anything less than thirty percent," he answers.

"We're your family now," Fabre responds, and it's obvious that Gabriel hates every part of that statement.

"Thirty percent, or we walk," Gabriel cooly tells Jack.

Fabre crosses his fat legs and settles his arms on his stomach. He's pleased with Gabriel's negotiation strategy and, I suppose, with himself as well.

"Then I guess we have a deal," Jack agrees reluctantly. "Thirty percent."

"Do you both enter this agreement of your own free will and, on your honor, will adhere to the terms?" I ask them both, knowing full well that someone like Fabre has no fucking honor, but it's what I have to say. It's why I'm here.

"We do."

I stand up behind the desk, denoting the end of the meeting.

"I'm glad we were able to reach an agreement," I say to the room. "Now, if you excuse me, Jack, I'd like to speak to Mr. Fabre alone for a moment.

Jack shakes my hand, then Fabre's, and Lars shows him out of the suite.

"Alone," I say to Fabre.

"Oh, you want my security to leave?" Fabre grins.

"What I have to say is just between the two of us. You won't need security."

"And what about your man?" he asks, referring to Lars, who I can already tell isn't happy about this request.

"He'll stand outside in the hallway as well."

"Boss," Lars warns.

"Outside," I say in a deeper voice, the one he knows means I don't want to hear shit he has to say.

Fabre stands once the room empties.

"Okay, Middleton, we're alone. What do you have to say that's so important you needed to clear the room?"

I choose my words carefully.

"My fiance will never admit this out loud because she

knows how I feel about the situation, but she wants to know how Naomi is faring."

"Does she?"

"Yes."

"She didn't seem too fond of my *Josephine* when she was traveling with us." He stresses the pronunciation of Naomi's legal first name–Josephine as if I need reminding.

"That's because she was tricked and lied to by your daughter for a long time. She was understandably angry. Deceit must come easy to the Fabre's."

He smirks with amusement. "It does."

Inside, I'm boiling over, but on the outside, I remain a calm and collected adversary. I want the information. While I'm done apologizing for the whole Parker debacle, I think a little intel on Naomi will get me a long way with Megan.

"Well?"

"Josephine is faring quite well. She's living a life of luxury she's accustomed to, eagerly preparing for her wedding day. You can assure Miss Taylor that all is well if she'll even listen to anything you have to say."

What the fuck.

"What are you insinuating?"

"I know that your beloved is back in her old apartment and not living with you. Did you two have a lover's spat? It would be a shame if you're not there to witness the birth of your firstborn child."

I remind myself to text Vaughn just as soon as I step foot outside this hotel and tell him to do a device sweep of the apartment and the club. This psychopath may have bugged one or more of my offices. How is he always a step ahead of me?

"It would be nice if Naomi could assure her of that herself. I'd like them to have a conversation."

"You want them to speak after all that's passed between them?" Fabre walks toward the suite window with his hands clasped behind his back. "You must love your fiance very much to even bother with this."

"You know I fucking do."

He pivots on the ball of one of his shiny Italian-made shoes, turning around with an overconfident swagger I want to crush in the worst way.

Soon.

"Then why haven't you tried to kill me yet?" he asks flippantly.

"Murder is a delicate matter." I stare at him with violent intent. "It needs to be slow-cooked and seasoned properly like a stew, but once ready...it will be utterly delicious."

Fabre knows exactly what I mean.

I'm growing tired of this dance between us. It feels as if I'm only treading water, waiting for the right circumstances to strike. But assuredly, his reckoning is coming...I'm just not sure if the egomaniac believes in his own mortality or not.

"I'll have Josephine call her tomorrow at six pm your time. Just make sure your little artist picks up."

The way this fat fuck pushes my buttons.

Little artist?

I just have to remember this is all for a greater purpose. I need Megan to be happy, and I need her back in my bed where she belongs. She needs to see that I'm doing the work. No matter how excruciating it is.

"Agreed."

Chapter 17

I Am An Artist Dammit

MEGAN

For the first time in weeks, I'm focused on my art, which feels incredible. Growing up, I was made to feel like an outcast in my incredibly toxic family, so I always sought refuge within my art. Sketching and painting have always been the perfect escape, but never in a million years did I think I could forge a real future showing and selling my art. Now that I am, it almost feels surreal.

I am an artist.

I am an artist.

I am an artist.

Perhaps if I say it a hundred more times, I'll actually believe it.

"I love this one, Megan. Have you named it yet?"

I'm having lunch with Miss Linda John, the assistant curator of the Los Angeles Starlight Art Foundation. She seems really interested in a new piece I've been working on for a while now.

"No, I don't name my pieces until they're finished. A lot

can change with just a few strokes, and I like to give them time to morph into what they will become before I title them."

"Ah, that makes sense. Could you perhaps at least tell me the inspiration behind the piece? You're such an upbeat person with a baby coming soon," she points to my growing stomach. "Congratulations, by the way."

"Thank you."

"I'm asking about your inspiration because the shadows of this one skew a bit dark to me."

"But you like it?"

"Yes, there's a weight to it I find particularly interesting."

"I firmly believe that most people have both dark and light parts of themselves. I guess I've just been tapping into the darker areas lately," I smile uncomfortably, not particularly enjoying where this conversation is headed.

Hell yeah, my work has been dark lately. I was kidnapped by a middle-aged gangster and broke up with the overprotective father of my baby all in the same damn month. I paint the darkness to safely escape it, not chat about it over lunch.

"Well, it's fabulous, and I'm confident that the foundation will be very interested in curating this piece for our exhibit next year. The show will feature all local artists, and this piece fits the theme of the show: In The Shade and The Shadows. Oh, and did I mention that it's a year-long installation?"

"A year?"

For new artists like me, art show exhibits typically last about a week. A year-long run is rare.

"Yes."

"I'm thrilled that the foundation is even considering

me." I swallow a bite of my chicken piccata. "But I need to ask." *The one question I've been dreading to ask.* "How did you discover my work?"

I pay close attention to the focus of her gaze when I ask Miss John the question because if I think she's holding something back, like if this is somehow due to Hunter–the underworld patron saint of the arts, I'm out.

She stares me straight in the eyes when she answers, and I wonder if maybe she's trying a little too hard to be convincing. That's one of the problems with being in a relationship with someone like Hunter: you start to suspect everyone and everything.

"Our organization follows the careers of many young people in local university art programs. It's part of our ethos to amplify the voices of new artists."

Duh, Megan.

Get a grip. You know that.

"Right, I just wondered if a particular professor recommended my work or something?"

Or a dangerous millionaire I know.

"You remember there was a write-up about you in the Times after your last show, right?" She gives me a pacifying look. "Many people in the local art community know about your work from that."

"Yes, of course." I nod, embarrassed by my skepticism.

With everything going on in my life, I forgot about the article. Shame on me. Now that she brings it up, I recall how it was a well-written piece about several emerging artists from the Los Angeles area, including myself.

"After reading the article, I searched for a way to contact you online but noticed that you hadn't set up a portfolio website yet, so I contacted your school. They gave me your cell phone number. I hope that was okay?"

"Yes, at some point, I'm sure I checked a box that said it was okay to share my contact information, and I'm so glad I did, or I wouldn't be sitting here with you."

She smiles comfortably.

"Just so I'm clear, these exhibits take a while to plan, and we won't be able to decide on your inclusion until we've seen your final piece."

"Understood."

"Which may possibly fall around the time of your delivery. What are you five or six months along, Megan?"

"Almost six, but I have recently left my job and have nothing but time to work on the piece. It should be finished well before I deliver the baby."

My cell phone rings and I'm startled by the name on the screen.

LYING BITCH

Naomi.

"Do you need to take that?" Miss Lord asks, reading the surprised look on my face.

"Um, if you don't mind?"

"Please, go right ahead. Take your time. I'll be here enjoying my lunch."

I'm not even sure why I decided to take the call. I haven't seen or spoken to Naomi since I snuck out of the motel. Not once did she call to see if I was alive or dead. I mean, what am I supposed to do with that type of betrayal? Nevertheless, I rise and head outside to the front of the restaurant to answer her call. I guess I'm more curious about what she has to say than angry.

"Hello?"

"Megan."

Her voice is not at all Naomi-like. It's small and sad, and it breaks my heart.

"Are you in trouble?" I ask her, concerned that things may have gotten dangerous for her.

"I've been in trouble since the moment I was born."

"Where are you?"

"New Orleans."

"Why are you calling me, Naomi?"

She pauses for a moment before she answers. "I'm sorry, Megan. I've been a horrible friend to you."

I hear a soft, muffled cry. It's a strange sound because now that I think about it, I've never heard Naomi cry before.

"You're right. You have been," I tell her, not mincing any words. Her tears do not absolve her.

"I realize it's selfish of me to bother you with this, and after all that has happened, I should be grateful that you've bothered to pick up the phone, but I can't do this, Megan. I have to get out of here–"

I stop her.

"Naomi, I'm pregnant and in a meeting right now. I don't have the bandwidth for whatever is happening with you and your daddy. I just don't."

Her soft cries escalate into full-blown sobs. "I cannot marry Gabriel."

"Then don't."

"I have to."

"Then marry him!" I say, exasperated with the nerve of this phone call. "What's the worst that can happen?"

"There are so many worse things, Megan. You have no idea."

"I think I have some idea," I answer snidely. "Kidnapping a pregnant woman from in front of her home is a pretty shitty thing to do. Your father is a piece of work, and his henchman is no saint either. I think that dude truly wanted to hurt me."

"Imagine being around him your whole life?"

I don't feel sorry for her. I had my own sociopaths at home.

"Listen, I have to go. There's someone waiting for me."

"Maybe we can talk later?"

"I'm not sure there's much to talk about, Naomi."

"So you have zero interest in talking to me? Ever?"

"At this moment in time, my answer is no. I'm still angry at all the lies you've told and how you didn't have my back at all when your father took me."

"My relationship with my father is complicated, Megan. I am a different person when I'm around him."

"That's obvious."

She sighs heavily. "Can you at least let Hunter know that I called you."

"What does this have to do with Hunter?"

"My father was in Los Angeles, and when he was there, they had a meeting. I don't know what they discussed. All I know is that my father came home and gave me permission to call you, which is another way of giving an order."

"Your father was here?" I ask softly. "In Los Angeles?"

"Did Hunter not even bother to mention it?"

"So you called me because you were ordered to," I state plainly.

"I didn't think I had the right to call you after all that I kept from you."

"And so you were never going to call and explain yourself?"

"That's what I'm doing a piss poor job of right now."

"You haven't explained anything, Naomi. You haven't once explained why you thought it was a smart idea to take on a whole new identity and never tell your best friend about it."

"Telling you about my life in New Orleans would have only put you in danger."

"Yet here we are."

"I realize now that there's no escaping danger when it comes to my family, and I'm also finally realizing that your fiance may be the one person who can help me break free from them."

"If you think Hunter is going to help you with anything, you're delusional. He'll never forgive you for your part in this, Naomi. He just won't, and I'm not sure I can either."

"Funny how he's still communicating with my father, though. I'm not even fucking Gabriel, but I know if someone kidnapped me, he would have already put them six feet under."

"Is that what you want?" I ask, horrified. "You want Hunter to kill your father so you don't have to?"

I'm feeling slightly nauseous now. It's pretty evident that the baby doesn't like it when I argue with people. Not to mention that I've been on this call way longer than I intended. Miss John is probably ten seconds away from ditching this lunch meeting.

"Don't answer that," I tell Naomi. "You've followed your father's orders and called me. I need to go."

"Megan, I'm all messed up in the head. I need another chance to explain myself."

"There's nothing to explain. Not anymore. I sincerely wish you luck, Naomi. I hope you figure out a way to get out of this ridiculous marriage arrangement. But you're not who I thought you were. I don't know who you are, and I'm not sure I ever will. There's just no room in my life for that type of doubt when I'm about to bring a new life into the world."

I inadvertently rub my rounded abdomen. "My baby is all that matters now."

And before I give her any more room to protest, I press the red button on my phone screen to end the call. But as I go back to my meeting, I can't help but ruminate over what Hunter could be up to meeting with Naomi's father.

My stomach swirls again.

Whatever the reason for their meeting, it can't be good.

Chapter 18

Pissed In General

MEGAN

"Are those tears on your face?" Lena asks, her disbelief palpable, as I lounge on the sofa, attempting to hide my emotions by eating my way through a bag of buttered popcorn.

"Nope," I lie, wiping my cheeks with the back of my hand.

"I can see them, Megan. What's wrong?"

I point to the bloody scene on the screen.

"Him."

"Why are you watching the red wedding episode again? You know that it ends badly for them."

"If Robb Stark had just listened to his mother, they'd all still be alive!" I protest. "And what did that poor Beowolf have to do with anything? Why'd they kill him, too?" I cry.

"Megan, I don't know if rewatching every episode of *The Game Of Thrones* is healthy for the baby."

Lena grabs the remote control and clicks the guide button to see what else is on television.

"If that's what kids grow up to do, completely defy their parent's better judgment, then I don't want any."

"I think it's a little too late for that," she snickers.

Growing another human being inside of my body is no joke.

I'm exhausted.

I'm bloated.

And I'm moody as hell.

I guess the pregnancy hormones are responsible for all of the mood swings and the weird dreams I've been having, every dream crazier than the last.

"Why don't we watch Ugly Betty? I always wanted to binge-watch that show but never got the chance. It looks funny."

"What's funny about some ugly girl working in the magazine industry? All they're going to do is bully her for most of the show, and then miraculously, everything will work out for her by the last season?"

"Damn, Megan, you're in a mood today."

"I'm just–"

A sharp pain suddenly takes my breath away.

"Fuck."

I ball up in a fetal position, grabbing my abdomen.

"Megan!" Lena cries out, rushing to my side. "Are you all right?"

I can see that I've frightened her, and rightly so...I'm scared myself. God, I wish Hunter was here. Suddenly, everything we are at odds with each other about doesn't mean half as much as it did yesterday.

But no.

I can't cry for him every time I'm afraid. I'm becoming much too dependent on him. It wasn't that long ago that I was able to escape my family, get a job, and enroll in art school all by myself.

"I'm fine," I blink my wet lashes rapidly. "I think the baby was just mad about what I said earlier."

"What do you mean? Like the baby kicked you?"

"I guess so," I say, sitting myself up on the sofa.

"I'm not sure if you're far enough along in your pregnancy to feel that kind of kicking. Should we call your doctor and maybe get things checked out?"

"How would you know what I'm supposed to feel at this point in the pregnancy?"

"I read a lot."

I grab a tissue from a box on the coffee table and dab the sweat from my temples.

"I'm going to stand under the shower. I think that will fix everything."

"Can I help you?" Lena asks as she assists me off the sofa and to the master bathroom.

"Thanks, Lena. After I shower, maybe we watch a little of your show together."

"Great idea," she smiles. "And while you're in there, I'm going to cook you a real dinner. Popcorn is not dinner."

"Thanks, Lena."

"No thank you needed, roomie. You and my niece or nephew go enjoy your shower."

The warm water feels heavenly as it beats along the backside of my body. I'm aware of each breath I take as I lay my hands on my tiny baby bump and try my best to send the baby good energy. I feel wrong about what I said when I was in the middle of my hormonal tirade.

Of course, I want you, I say to myself. *No matter how frustrated I am with your father, I want you. I already love you.*

A sharp pain ripples through my lower abdomen, very similar to the last one, and I crouch on the shower floor and pray that nothing is wrong with my baby.

Between the oppressive hot steam filling the bathroom and the intensity of the pain, my head begins to feel loopy, and everything becomes increasingly dark...until I see nothing at all.

I'm confused once I awaken.

I'm lying nude in a bed of the softest sheets I've ever felt. I blink several times in an attempt to get my bearings. There's a dark ceiling fixture adorned with crystals on the ceiling that I don't recognize.

Where am I?

"She's awake," a relieved voice from the distance says.

"Lena?"

"Hi, there." She moves closer to the side of the bed, holding a food tray. "I brought your dinner."

"This isn't my room, though," I say. Things are still a little fuzzy, but not fuzzy enough that I don't know I'm not home.

" I know." Her eyes shoot down to the floor. "I called my brother."

Of course.

I look around as things start to make more sense. He's changed a few things around and bought some new sheets, but this is the room where I slept many nights with him. Where I fell into his arms when I was dead tired. Hell, this is the room where the baby was conceived.

"Lena," I say with disappointment.

"I had to call him," she offers defensively. "You passed out in the shower, and I couldn't lift you. You're freaking pregnant, Megan. You're lucky I didn't take you to the emergency room."

"You should have just called the ambulance," I admonish her.

"That can still be arranged," a deep voice that wraps around my heart and travels down my spine says from the doorway.

Hunter.

My eyes widen once they focus on his shadow from across the room. And fuck, he looks magnificent. The answer to how I've found myself in this pregnant predicament is staring me right in the face: all six feet, four brooding inches of him.

"I feel fine," I finally say.

"But you're not fine," he says in a gravelly voice.

"I think I read about this. These pains are normal. The baby is growing and stretching me out."

"Have you earned a medical degree while we've had this time apart?"

I shift uncomfortably. His sarcasm weighs heavier on me than this overpriced, down-feather comforter.

"If you were so concerned, maybe you should have taken me to the hospital."

"As if you would have accepted that."

"I wouldn't have known, now would I?"

"Good thing for you; I know a few people."

"What's that supposed to mean?"

Lena ignores our salty banter and mixes the Mexican tortilla soup she's brought in for me to eat. It smells incredible, but I'm not quite in the mood for soup and a sandwich.

"I've brought one of the best OBGYNs in the city to give you an exam. She's in the other room waiting for you to wake up."

"She?"

I don't know what made me question the sex of the

physician. It was a knee-jerk response. The more time we spend apart, the more I worry he'll move on. I'm not an idiot. I know that there are women just waiting for me to fuck this up. Smart, beautiful, accomplished women. But I'm no dummy. I also know that I need to start the way I want to finish. I can't just let him walk all over me now in the name of "protection" because if I do — that's how it will always be.

Hunter moves closer inside the room, an obvious smirk on his face. He knows I'm jealous, and he loves it.

"Yes, *she*."

I'm dying to ask all the questions a jealous lover would ask. *How do you know her? How long have you known her? In what capacity do you know her?*

But I won't give him the satisfaction.

"Since the baby is my number one priority, let her in."

I notice a slight look of surprise cross his face, but he nods in approval and leaves the room to get her.

"Now, maybe you take a few sips of this soup before she starts the exam?" Lena fusses over me.

"Lena."

"Are you still pissed with me?"

"No, I'm just pissed in general."

"Understood. I'll just leave this all here and you can dig in once the exam is over."

"Where are you going?" I ask, slightly panicked, that she will leave me alone with Hunter.

"Back downstairs."

"Why?"

"Because you don't need me here."

"The hell I don't!"

Lena sits on the edge of the bed and clasps one of my

hands. She's not a touchy-feely kind of person, so I figure whatever she's going to say matters a lot to her.

"I'm going to tell you this whether or not you want to hear it, Megan. I may be new in my brother's life, and yours for that matter, and while he may be many things, I know that he is in love with you in a way that some women can only dream of. If you keep this wall up you've built–"

"What, he may leave me?" I interrupt contemptuously.

"Yes, and is that what you want, Megan?"

My eyes water at the thought of not having Hunter in my life or our child's life.

"I think you have your answer."

Lena walks out as the doctor walks inside, leaving me with much to consider after her poignant words.

"Hi, Megan. I'm Dr. Brentwood. I heard you've been having some pain."

"Debilitating pain," Hunter adds. His voice was laced with concern. "And she fainted."

"You have a regular physician at LA Mercy, right?"

"Yes, Dr. Lawson."

"Oh, yes, I've heard of him. Would you like me to give him a call after your exam and keep him in the loop?"

Ugh, why does she have to be so nice?

"Yes, that would be helpful."

"I've brought a portable sonogram machine with me. I want to have a look and make sure Baby Middleton isn't in any distress."

Baby Middleton?

Humph.

Hunter gives me a smug look after the doctor presumes my baby's last name, which I do my best to ignore.

Dr. Brentwood takes her time listening to the baby's heartbeat, then giving me a cautious vaginal examination.

She's slow, gentle, and perhaps slightly nervous because Hunter hasn't moved an inch during the exam.

She pulls off her latex gloves and starts to pack up her things when Hunter abruptly asks, "So, what's going on with my baby?"

"Nothing."

"Really?" I say, part relieved, part surprised.

"In my professional opinion, you've been dealing with some Braxton Hicks contractions."

"But I read that those were mild. These hurt like hell."

"Every woman is different, but I assure you that the baby is not in any distress, and it's just the way your body is preparing for childbirth."

"She fainted," Hunter adds.

"She was in a hot shower," the doctor retorts, facing him head-on. "These things happen."

The doctor turns her head back to face me. "To be on the safe side, be sure to stay hydrated and limit any strenuous activity for a while or at least until your next visit with your regular OBGYN."

"What kind of strenuous activity?"

"No standing on your feet all day. No sports. And be careful with sex."

"No sex?!" Hunter cuts in, and the doctor chuckles in response.

Wait a ding-dong minute.

Dr. Brentwood emits the kind of laugh you make around someone familiar.

"Do you two know each other?" I ask them both, my eyes slightly slanted with curiosity...or perhaps jealousy.

"Same neighborhood growing up," she says.

I look directly at him. "Is that right?"

"We've both come a long way since the old days," she

reflects. "Did you know your fiance helped me pay my way through medical school?"

"No, I sure didn't."

He acts as if he's suddenly embarrassed.

Puh-lease.

"Thank you for coming, Tara," he tells her. "Please be sure to send your bill to my office."

"You know I'm not going to do that," she says in a matter-of-fact tone as she packs up her things. "Please call me any time, day or night, if you have another episode. It was a pleasure meeting you, Megan."

"Same."

When Hunter returns after seeing Dr. Brentwood out, he catches me looking for my sneakers. They've got to be in here somewhere.

"What are you doing?"

"Going home."

"This is your home."

"No, downstairs is my home, and I thought you bought me another home in the Hollywood Hills somewhere? Why aren't you there?"

"I canceled the sale."

My eyes pop up to meet his.

"You did?"

"If and when you want to move, I have a realtor on standby waiting for your instruction."

That's huge for a control freak like Hunter.

"And what about security?"

"I just wanted you to be safe and thought moving to a better neighborhood would exponentially improve those odds, but I may have jumped the gun a little. I can wait."

Wow, that's progress.

"Naomi called me," I tell him to gauge his reaction.

"What did she want?" he asks flatly as if he had nothing to do with it.

"She called because you made her call."

"I suggested it would be a nice gesture after all the hell she's put you through."

"But you asked her father to make her call me."

"Damn, did she tell you everything?"

"Why did you do that, Hunter?"

"Because even after all the fucked up shit that girl did, I knew speaking to her would make you happy."

"I'm not exactly sure how it made me feel. But what I do know is that I don't want you communicating with that man anymore."

"Now, who's being bossy?"

"I'm serious."

"Don't leave, Megan."

He slides a hand along the side of my face, cradling it like I'm the most precious figurine in the world.

"Hunter–"

"I love you, and there's nothing more important to me than you and our baby. It kills me that you've spent any part of this pregnancy alone. This little person is *our* creation." He places a hand on my baby bump. "And you both belong here with me."

"You know my history, Hunter. I don't want to go back to a situation of being controlled."

"I would never hurt you the way your father did." He looks offended, and I realize my words may have come off the wrong way.

"I didn't mean it like that. I know you would never intentionally hurt me. I just mean that I have a voice, you know? And I need you to hear it."

"I do."

His lips suddenly find the side of my neck, and he kisses a pulse point at the base of my neck.

"I hear you loud and clear, baby," he speaks into my skin.

My eyes close in rapture as I run my hand into the base of his scalp.

God, I've missed this man.

He raises his lips to meet mine, and we share a sensual kiss. It's a kiss that echoes all the feelings that we both have been suppressing. One that borders on possession but dwells in love.

It's laughable that I ever thought I could live without Hunter Middleton, I think to myself as his hand dominantly wraps around my throat and his mouth devours mine.

Or that he'd ever let me.

Chapter 19

This Shit Is Spiritual

MEGAN

I spent a huge part of my childhood immersed in fictionalized worlds of books and television. I understand now that it was a coping mechanism, an escape, a place where I could go and not have to deal with the real people in my life.

In many of those romance books or drama series, couples would often talk about "making love" as if it were some spiritual experience. First of all, I was too young to read or watch adults making love, so I didn't get it then. And then, when I started having sex, I didn't understand it then either.

Sex was great.

Orgasms were very enjoyable.

But a spiritual experience? *Eh.*

But as Hunter spoons me from the back, our legs delicately entangled in a sensual dance as he enters me from behind over and over...I'm starting to get this whole spiritual thing.

Maybe it's because I'm knocked up, and the hormones are raging inside of me, or perhaps it's because I've missed this man something fierce. Still, my eyes practically roll up inside of my head as he alternates between pinching the nipple of my right breast and massaging my clit in between, taking deep strokes inside of my pussy.

Yeah, this shit is definitely spiritual.

"Are you okay, baby?" he whispers, which is another telltale sign that we're making love because when has Hunter ever worried about me being *okay* while we're fucking?

"Mmm, very okay," I moan, reaching my arm behind my head to touch the side of his face. "More than okay."

"That's good, Megan because we have a lot of missed time to make up for," he growls into the skin of my neck. "We're in for a long night now that you're back where you belong."

I spend the morning pattering barefoot around the penthouse on a high from the night Hunter and I spent together. I spear a chunk of mango on a fork and am nibbling on it when I walk back into the bedroom to check on him. He's been asleep for an unusually long amount of time. In fact, he's still sleeping when I sit on the edge of the bed and watch his chest peacefully rise and fall.

I've spent so much time battling him lately; it's been a long time since I've appreciated the view. Hunter is a beautiful man. He has a set of long, black eyelashes that most women would envy, a nose that is slightly crooked but in the most perfect way, and a chiseled jaw that would put the fictitious Thor to shame.

He shifts in his sleep, and I stare in appreciation of every dip and valley of muscle in his chest and arms. Incredibly, my desire for him surfaces again, and I gently touch the center of his chest with a light touch of my pointer finger.

"You're such a greedy girl," he says with his eyes still shut but smirking. "Didn't I give you enough last night?"

"I'm starting to see what women say about pregnancy hormones. I didn't believe them at first, but now I do. I want you to fuck me in the worst way."

His eyes open slowly.

That woke him right up.

"Megan."

"Yes?" I grin.

"You just had a scare yesterday. You were in a lot of pain, and you heard what the doctor said."

"What your doctor said."

"What's that supposed to mean? She's not my doctor; she's *a* doctor. A very well respected one."

"Did you ever have a romantic relationship with her?" I ask, dying to know the truth.

"I felt her up once when I was sixteen years old. We've been friends ever since."

"Eww."

He chuckles as he sits up and plants a kiss on my lips, lifting my legs up on the bed so that I'm entirely in his embrace.

"You taste like mango."

"And you taste like me."

"I should taste like you; I ate you half the night."

I smile. "So you don't want more of me this morning?"

He stares hungrily at my breasts, which sit heavily under my sleep tank top, but then he glances at my baby bump.

"How are you feeling this morning?" he asks hesitantly.

"Better than I have in a really long time, Hunter."

I wrap my arms around his neck and wiggle my ass on his lap.

"Still—"

"Still what?" I interrupt him.

"There's nothing more I'd like to do than make love to you repeatedly, but we've established that we're very good at the physical thing. I think we need to focus more on our non-physical communication."

"You want to focus on our *non-physical* communication?" I ask in disbelief.

"Your engagement ring is sitting in that box on the dresser over there." He points to a medium-sized, intricately carved wooden box I've never seen before.

"You've been shopping," I say.

"It's a recreation of a box my mother used to have in her bedroom. It was one of her favorite possessions. I've been thinking about her more lately. I'm trying to remember all the little things I can about her so that I can tell Lena."

I nod my head in understanding. "She'll like that."

"Back to us, as I was saying, your ring is in that box, and I don't want to put it back on your finger until you're sure that you won't take it off again because once you put it back on, you're mine, Megan. I'm not going stand for any more wishy-washy bullshit just because we argue once or twice."

A part of me feels guilty for my past behavior. If it were me advising anyone else, like a girl from the nightclub, I'd tell her she was crazy. I'd tell her that she'd probably never do any better than a man like Hunter and to act accordingly. Seriously. What are the chances of someone like me falling in love with one of the wealthiest, most respected, and most feared men in Los Angeles?

Slim.

But this isn't about the odds of this love story.

This is about real life and how I want to live it.

"You're right. Just because we're bringing a baby into this world doesn't mean that we should jump into marriage."

His left eye twitches at that comment. "I didn't say exactly that."

"No, but I know what you meant. So where do you think we should start with this whole working on our non-physical communication?"

"Honesty."

"Honesty?"

"Brutal honesty. It goes against everything I've ever learned in the streets about keeping myself alive and staying one step ahead, but if I'm going to trust one person completely in this world, I'd like it to be you and vice-versa. The only way that's going to happen is if we try being honest with each other no matter how much we think it may hurt the other person's feelings."

It sounds like everything I've ever wanted from Hunter, but now that he's said the words out loud, the whole concept seems a bit daunting.

Do I actually want brutal honesty?

Does anyone?

"What do you want me to be honest about?" I ask him.

"Do you want to marry me, Megan?"

Well, shit, he's not pulling any punches.

"I think so."

He gives me a light peck on the lips.

"I appreciate your honesty, but that answer is not what a man wants to hear when he proposes to the woman he loves, so we put marriage off for now. Agreed?"

I swallow thickly, and it feels like a lump of clay is becoming stuck in my lower esophagus. Put our marriage off? Just like that? Well, damn, brutal honesty hurts.

"Agreed," I say softly.

"How about one more question? Then we will go fix you and my baby a proper breakfast."

"Okay," I reply, afraid of what he will ask next.

"No, I mean you ask me one this time."

"Oh."

I think carefully about my question, not wanting to ruin the intimacy of the moment or our recent reconciliation.

"Is my family alive?"

Hunter's face goes blank. He wasn't expecting me to ask about them ever again, but I'm not sure that was a realistic expectation. I need closure about those psychopaths either way, plus a part of me wants to know who I'm genuinely sleeping with.

"Yes."

Knowing what I know about Hunter and everything I've seen, I ask him the next logical question.

"Why?"

"Because a part of you is still emotionally tied to them, or you wouldn't have asked the question. I knew that already. There are many ways to keep them permanently out of your life without putting them in the ground. Killing them would have weighed heavily on your conscience."

"And not yours?"

"Are you worried that you are having a baby with the devil?"

"No, I'm just worried that I'm sleeping with a devil I don't know."

He cradles my face with his hands and kisses my forehead. "You know this devil better than anyone on this earth, but you need to get to a place where you believe that. We'll get there, but for now, let's eat."

He lifts me, and I naturally wrap my legs around his waist as he walks us into the kitchen. He places me on the granite counter and kisses the inside of my left palm before he walks away.

"You start the bacon while I go pee."

"And after breakfast?" I ask as he heads to the bathroom.

"We move your pretty ass back into this apartment where you belong, and then...we fuck."

Chapter 20

Another Round For Table 21

HUNTER

"We're celebrating!" Vaughn exclaims, placing down a glass of amber-hued liquor at the table where the three of us are sitting. "Let's hang out tonight."

He loosens the silk tie around his neck and then pulls it free from his collar.

"We're already hanging out," Christian responds.

"Eating appetizers and drinking whiskey at the club is what we do every other normal night of the week. I'm proposing we go out and get wasted out of our minds like we did back in the day."

Vaughn is excited about something. What it is, I don't know, and I only halfway care. I've got a difficult business negotiation on my mind that I need to tie up, as well as a beautiful woman at home who is growing very impatient with her pregnancy. Her recent texts only confirm that.

> Megan: How much longer are you going to be at the club?

> Me: Maybe an hour or so.

> Megan: What are you doing there that you can't do here?

> Me: The staff need to see me in the building, Megan.

> Megan: That's why you have a manager.

> Me: I also run my other business from here.

> Megan: At eight o'clock at night?

> Me: Really, babe?

She knows all this already.

> Megan: Fine, but don't you dare think you can walk in here after midnight, and I'll just spread my legs for you. I'm tired.

She's the one wearing me out every night, but I play along.

> Me: No expectations at all.

> Megan: You suck.

I chuckle as I place my phone back on the table. Megan is so restless at times that it took me over thirty minutes tonight to convince her that stopping by the club was a bad idea at this point in her pregnancy. She took it way too personally and accused me of pregnancy bigotry (whatever the hell that is). All I told her was that nobody wants to party at a nightclub next to a pregnant woman.

She was livid, although I understand her frustration. The weight of the pregnancy makes her feel uncomfortable at times, and she's often bored at home. While she loves to paint, which keeps her busy up to a certain point, I think she misses human interaction with someone other than me and her security detail. Once I wrap up this negotiation I'm working on, I think I'll take her to Paradise Cove for a week-long beach getaway. She'll like that, and we both need the escape.

"What the hell are we celebrating anyway?" Christian asks Vaughn, breaking my train of thought.

"My divorce."

"I didn't get any finalized paperwork," Christian replies in a confused tone.

"I handled it myself."

"Get the fuck out of here!" Christian jests.

"Yep, sure did."

"What did you do?" I ask, worried about how exactly Vaughn handled his scandalous ex.

"I told her I was sick of paying lawyers and that we were both grown people who could handle the end of our relationship in a civil manner."

"Sick of paying lawyers? You haven't paid me one red cent," Christian scoffs.

I laugh because Christian's just fucking with Vaughn. We're friends, so it's assumed that Christian is helping Vaughn with his divorce because of their longstanding friendship, not for money. Christian doesn't need the money, and divorce law isn't even his specialty.

"I still have to pay *her* legal fees."

"You pay them only if she wins, idiot, and I'd never let

that happen," Christian blusters. "I hope you didn't give her all your damn money because that's all she wants."

"I didn't."

"But you gave her more than what you should have, didn't you?"

I don't want to hear the answer to that, so I raise a quiet hand to get a server's attention. I notice that another new girl is working in the main room of the club tonight, and I wonder what's going on. Why is there such a staff turnover? I thought Gage had a handle on things.

"May I help you?" the server approaches. Like most of the women who work at the club, she's relatively young and attractive, but something about her reminds me of when Megan first started, almost like she's like a fish out of water.

I can tell by the way she directs her greeting to Vaughn that she doesn't know who I am. It's how I've always preferred it, though. I like to watch new hires from a distance and make sure that they fit in here. This is not the easiest place to work. One night, there may be a table of haughty investment bankers, and another night, a party of rowdy motorcycle gang members—a true reflection of how wide my reach is in the city. Servers who work here need to know how to navigate the personalities of all sorts of people.

Vaughn grins, taking pleasure in the fact that the new server is flirting with him—something she should have been told not to do the minute she was hired.

"We'd like everything on the sampler appetizer menu and another round of drinks for the table, beautiful."

She blushes at Vaughn's lame flirting attempt. "May I ask what you all are drinking?"

"The bartender will already know," I interrupt. "Just tell him another round for Table 21."

"Okay." Her face drops, probably a reaction to my

abruptness. When she starts to walk away, Vaughn calls after her.

"And don't forget our appetizers, beautiful."

She turns her head to smile and almost bumps into a customer by mistake. "Right away, sir."

"I think my dick just got hard," Vaughn chuckles.

"It's been so long that you don't know the difference?" Christian quips.

"I thought you wanted to go out to celebrate," I say to Vaughn, annoyed that he's just flustered one of the new hires.

"I do, but I would rather eat here first. With Lena in the kitchen, at least I know the food will taste good. Then we can go and drink somewhere else."

"You and Christian should go hang out, but my mind is on other things. Happy for you, though, friend. Now you can move on."

"Just say what you want to say, dammit."

"Hmm, let me think," I quip. "Maybe that your impulsive marriage was a mistake from the beginning."

"Or how about you can't turn a whore into a housewife," Christian laughs.

"You two are the worst friends a man could ask for," Vaughn sucks his teeth and takes a swig of his drink.

"We tried to warn you," I say, shrugging my shoulders.

"And you never listened," Christian scoffs.

"But now that you're free, just make sure you don't celebrate with one of my employees," I warn him as I watch the new girl get an earful from Gage.

"You mean with your hot new server over there? Did you see the ass on her? Is that thing real? You know how the ladies are getting butt implants nowadays."

"Good thing you'll never find out," I say.

"Why? She could be just the woman to convince me that not all of them are bad like–"

"Don't say her name!" Christian abruptly interrupts with a laugh. "It's like saying Valdemort's name out loud. Bad things will happen."

"Just don't do it," I tell Vaughn with a grin, knowing that he's just talking crap about messing with the new employee, or at least he better be. I've got enough on my plate without having to worry about his extracurricular activities.

"You don't play by a fair set of rules, Hunt. Why are you the only one who gets to pursue a hot employee, whisk her off to Paris, move her into your building, get her pregnant, and live happily ever after."

"Watch yourself."

"I'm just saying."

"The key part of that story is that she was *my* employee, and they're *my* rules. I can play by them any damn way I want."

Christian and Vaughn chuckle at my prickly response but immediately quiet down when a recognizable group of men enter the club. It's Dante DiAngelo and two of his right-hand men. It's highly unusual that DiAngelo would visit the club without calling me first as a courtesy, which puts the three of us on high alert.

"Did he call?" Vaughn asks the question.

"No, he didn't," I say as all three of us continue to stare them down as they approach.

"Where's Lars?" Christian asks in a low tone.

"He's at the apartment."

"Why?"

"I wanted my best men on Megan. Stop worrying. Dante DiAngelo is a friend."

When it's convenient for him.

"DiAngelo," I greet him tersely.

"My apologies for just dropping by, Hunter, but a matter has been brought to my attention that I need to discuss with you."

"Have a seat," I offer.

He looks at Christian and Vaughn cautiously. "This needs to be in private."

I take a sip of my whiskey and assess Dante's intent through his body language. He's trying hard to remain emotionless, as if whatever he has to say isn't that important, but the tension in his hands tells me otherwise. He keeps twisting that signet ring of his that he never takes off.

"Let's go to my office," I offer as I stand. "Tell the server to send up some food and drinks," I tell Vaughn and Christian.

"Will do," Vaughn agrees reluctantly.

Dante's men stay downstairs with Vaughn and Christian, which feels like a gesture to make me feel more comfortable.

It doesn't.

"How can I help you?" I start the conversation once I close the door to my office.

"We've known each other a long time, Middleton."

"Yes, we have."

"I've helped you when you needed it." He's referring to Megan's family and perhaps a handful of other favors.

"And I've done the same," I say, reminding him of the time I saved his fucking life from his own grandfather, who wanted him dead.

"True; I think it's fair to say that our lives are the sum of our choices."

"Meaning?"

"I was approached three days ago by a man named Fabre out of New Orleans."

My heart slows.

"And?"

"You know him?"

"I do."

My Glock is in a locked drawer on the left-hand side of my desk. I'll never get to it in time.

"I'm not going to bullshit you, Middleton." He pulls back his suit jacket and flashes a .38 seated in his waistband. "If I eliminate you, I was promised a seat at the table."

That fat fucker.

This is what I get for thinking Fabre could be reasoned with.

"So you're going to kill me in my own club and think you're going to walk out of here alive?"

"Oh, I'll definitely walk out of here."

He pulls the gun out of his waistband but holds it down by the side of his thigh. DiAngelo and I have a long history, and he's hesitant, probably still weighing his options. If he kills me, will Fabre deliver on his promise? Or if he doesn't, will I reward him with something more?

"Are you waiting for something?" I ask cooly. Pissed that this douchebag has the balls to kill me in my own damn club. Fabre probably requested that be part of the arrangement in order to make my whole operation look weak.

The funny thing is—he was right.

I see the very moment in Dante's eyes when he realizes this, too, and makes his final decision.

I could try to run for it and call downstairs for help, or I could leap for my drawer and try to force it open to grab my gun, but I know that neither of these choices will get me my desired result.

There's just not enough time.

Once DiAngelo raises his arm, the only image that flashes through my mind as the shot rings out is of the woman I love.

Megan.

Who will protect her now?

Chapter 21

What A Mind Fuck

MEGAN

I've had an uncomfortable feeling gnawing at my subconscious for a while, but like most people, I tried to ignore it. At first, I thought it was because of my pregnancy and the natural fear of bringing a new life into this world...this dangerous fucked up world. Now, I know my uneasiness was based on something more horrible than I could have imagined.

I'm not sure how we got here, but Naomi's father put a hit on Hunter, and now he's lying in a hospital bed, helpless, with various tubes running in and out of his body.

What a mind fuck.

As the life slowly drains from Hunter's body, I can feel another life growing inside of me.

"Megan," Lars reservedly addresses me, standing in the doorway of the hospital room—my mind so clouded with despair that I didn't even feel his presence.

The two of us haven't exchanged more than a few words since Hunter was savagely shot at the club. He's been avoiding me mostly and I understand why. Lars takes Hunter's attack personally, but he shouldn't. Hunter assigned him to my security detail that night. There is nothing he could have done to help Hunter, but it doesn't matter; he still blames himself. I don't have the time or the temperament to soothe his feelings of guilt right now. All I care about is the man I love lying helpless in this bed.

"What are you doing here, Lars?" I ask cooly.

"Do you want me to leave?"

"I'm asking you what you're doing here?"

"I just wanted to check...to see how the boss is."

"He's the same as yesterday and the day before that."

"What have the doctors said about his condition?" Lars shifts uncomfortably between both feet and then bows his head. "It's been three days. When will he wake up?"

I remind myself that Lars has known Hunter much longer than I have and is truly concerned about his welfare. I'm being a bitch for no reason, or, as Hunter would probably say, "not being helpful."

"They don't know, Lars, but I can tell there's growing concern for every additional day he spends on the ventilator."

I gently stroke Hunter's forearm as our child moves inside of me. The small fluttery movements remind me that I haven't eaten much today except for a few saltine crackers a nurse was kind enough to bring me.

Lars steps inside the room.

"We need to talk, Megan."

I rub my fingertips against the back of Hunter's thick knuckles, hoping he can sense my presence.

"About what?"

"Maybe we can step outside first?"

"For privacy?" I scoff.

"Well–"

"Hunter is in a coma, and I'm not getting out of this chair. Just say whatever you have to say right here."

Lars sighs. "The Boss was very organized and always had contingency plans in place for most situations, except he didn't account for feelings."

"Feelings?" I reply impatiently. "What are you talking about, Lars?"

"In case of an emergency, I think it was always his plan or intention that Vaughn and Christian would handle the business, but they are not in the right headspace to do so. The shooting happened right under their noses while they drank with DiAngelo's security. They feel incredibly responsible for what happened, so all they're thinking about is—retribution."

"What's your point, Lars?" I'm getting annoyed by this conversation. I don't care what those two are thinking about. It's of no consequence to me. Hell, the shooting did happen right under their noses. Maybe they should feel guilty.

"You need to return to the Blue Whiskey and run it."

"Gage can run it. It's his actual job to manage it, remember?"

"Gage has Hunter's back, that's true, but I'm not really sure about his management style. Even the boss was wondering about it lately. People listened when you were in charge, Megan. I think they respected that you used to do their job."

Funny, that's not how I remember it.

"Lars, I'm not leaving this hospital. What part of that do you not understand? I'm pregnant, Hunter is in a coma, and it's my job to advocate for him because he can't advocate for himself. Between you, Gage, Vaughn, and Christian, somebody should be able to run the damn business."

Lars takes a few more tentative steps towards me.

"All I'm suggesting is that you have a conversation with them because what I do know is that The Boss is not going to want to wake up and hear that his business is in shambles. He'll never forgive any of us for that."

While I'm irked that Lars is bothering me with this save-the-business conversation, a part of me understands what he means. Hunter has had to fight for everything he has in this world, and it would crush him if he woke up and most of it was gone. While his health should be the primary focus, I must also consider other things. I hate to admit it, but maybe Lars is right.

"I just don't want to leave him. What if he wakes up alone? He may be frightened not knowing where he is."

Or I could simply be projecting my own fears onto him.

"I'll stay with him while you're at the club, and when you're here, I'll be at the club. We can work together, Megan. I failed him once, but I won't fail him again."

I stare up silently at Lars and study the look on his face. It's a pained one. Maybe I must consider that other people feel just as emotional about Hunter as I do.

"You'll call me if there's any sudden change in his condition?"

"Immediately."

"I'll let the nurse the nursing staff know you'll be here in my place."

He nods. "I've got him."

I stand and bend over close to Hunter's ear and whisper, "I need you to wake up, Hunter. I need you to fight. The baby and I love you."

I wait for some sort of sign that he can hear me. A finger tap. An eyelid flutter. But there's nothing. I guess miracles like that only happen in the movies.

When I arrive at Blue Whiskey, it's ninety minutes before opening, yet there's barely any staff. The only person I see on the floor is Gage.

"Megan," he greets me in a surprised tone. "How's Hunter doing?"

"There hasn't been any change," I answer somewhat dismissively. "Where are the servers, Gage?"

"They called out."

"Why?"

He raises an eyebrow as if my question is an odd one. "Because the owner was shot in the head here three days ago, Megan. They don't feel safe."

"Bad things can happen anywhere at any time. It shouldn't stop people from coming to work."

"Megan–"

"We can't run a nightclub if there's nobody in here to serve customers."

The bartop is already spotless but Gage wipes it down as we talk, a habit I'm learning is common for him when he deeply considers what he will say next.

"Are we sure it's even a good idea to keep the club open right now?" he asks.

"You want to close the club?"

I hear heavy footsteps walking towards the two of us. Vaughn and Christian are descending the staircase with scowls on both of their faces. Each of them gives me a tight bear hug and has a seat at the bar.

"Closing the bar is not an option," Vaughn says to both of us. "I was lax with security because I underestimated just how many enemies we have, but I won't make the same mistake again."

I haven't said it out loud because I haven't had the time or opportunity to, but when I look down at my swelling belly (and feet), I finally find the nerve to say what I've been thinking since this happened.

"You won't make the same mistake? I'd hope not because Hunter won't survive another shot to the head."

Vaughn's expression tightens but I continue with my rant.

"Security is what you do for a living. You're supposed to be an expert. What do you mean you were lax about it? Why? There have been nothing but life-threatening situations at this club and at the apartment since I met Hunter. Were you lax those times, too? How many more lucky chances do you think Hunter has?"

Vaughn's eyes drop to the floor. I don't mean to hurt him like this, but it's time for everybody to get a reality check including Hunter's friends.

"That's not fair, Megan," Christian retorts, sitting on the other side of me

"What's not fair is that Hunter is on a ventilator, and we're all sitting here discussing the future of his business," I say.

"Well, since you seem to be in the mood for difficult conversations, the reality is that Hunter's priorities have changed since you entered his life," Christian counters.

"Are you saying I'm the problem?" I reply in disbelief.

"I'm just saying that things are different. He doesn't always take Vaughn's security recommendations or my legal recommendations because now there's a new variable in his life: you."

"So you guys suck at your jobs now because I'm around?"

"Megan, I know you're upset, and I know you're scared, and I get that you blame me for Hunter getting shot, but no more than I blame myself."

Vaughn's eyes grow glassy.

Shit, I'm sure this isn't what Lars had in mind when he suggested I have a talk with them.

"I'm sorry," I quickly backpedal. "I know you both love him, and I'm not here to blame anyone. I'm here because I just want to ensure that everything is fine when he wakes up."

I stand up and pace the floor, explaining what needs to happen as the thoughts come to me.

"Gage, the club is not going to close. In fact, I want it packed in here. I want our DJ, servers, and a full kitchen staff because I want the club busy and making money so that Fabre doesn't get any satisfaction from what he's done. I don't care what you need to do to make that happen. Just make it happen. That's why Hunter hired you; he was confident you could do whatever needs to be done."

Gage offers me an impressed look. "Okay, I'll start making some calls."

My eyes settle on Christian.

"Christian, I know you're privy to all the details of Hunter's business in a way that I'm not. He wants me to live a soft life, make my art, and have his babies, but it looks like fate has other plans for me. If you have knowledge of any ongoing negotiations he was having, you need to figure out how to either continue them or put them on hold until he recovers. I can't tell you how to do that. I just know that it needs to be done."

Then, my eyes turned to Vaughn.

"Vaughn, I know that your priority is probably finding DiAngelo."

"It is."

"What are you gonna do when you find him?"

"You know what I'm gonna do. The same thing Hunter would do if the roles were reversed."

I pace the floor, rubbing the base of my spine, which has been starting to ache lately.

"That's a lot of energy you're expending on the messenger when maybe you should use that energy to deal with the person who made the call. I don't know much, but I grew up in this city, and I know enough to know that Fabre is the problem. He's making a serious move by trying to get Hunter out of the way. I don't think any of this was personal. So, I need you and Christian to figure out who or what Hunter was in the way of."

"Damn, Megan," Vaughn comments. "I don't know that I've ever seen this side of you."

"I'm more than just Hunter's fiance or an art student who paints pretty things on a canvas. I'm carrying the reason why Hunter will wake up and come back to us. I may not know everything, but I know what's important to him."

Actually, I don't know shit. I'm simply flying by the seat of my pants, but I've got to do something to light a fire under these guys. I can feel it all falling apart if I don't.

"Let's all agree to do the work needed to keep the business running and leave the vengeance to him."

"But, Megan, we can't just let this go unchecked, or every criminal in the city will come after us."

"Hunter had a plan for Fabre. A long game. I don't know what it was, and maybe he'll have to readjust that plan when he wakes up, but it's his plan, not ours."

"Everything you're saying makes a lot of sense, but what about you?" Christian speaks. "I hate that you feel you have to take all of this on."

"That's the cool thing. For once in my life, I'm not alone. You all will help me."

The three of them offer me a smile and agree in unison, "We will."

And finally, I exhale the breath I'd been holding since I walked into the building.

I can't force Hunter to wake up yet, but I can fix this.

Chapter 22

Where The Fuck Is She?

HUNTER

My head feels like a balloon packed with wet sand as I slowly open my eyes to a harshly lit room. Immediately, I cough, choking on what I soon realize is a tube down my throat. I blink and try to gain my bearings. I'm not even sure if what I'm experiencing is reality or a dream, but if this is a dream, why isn't Megan in it?

Where is she?

A serious-looking man wearing thin, silver-rimmed glasses and a white lab coat is standing over me, examining what I assume is an important machine behind my bed. For some strange reason, the man reminds me of my high school chemistry teacher. A class I cut more times than I can count.

Why the hell am I thinking about that guy? He was an asshole.

It takes a while for me to comprehend where I'm at, but soon, it's obvious that I'm in a hospital, although I'm not sure which one or why. Everything's fuzzy in my head, but not in a good way, like when I've had a few too many glasses of whiskey.

"Welcome back, Mr. Middleton," the man says in a perfunctory tone. "It's been almost five days."

Five days?

"Don't try to speak because it will hurt like hell," he advises. "I'm Dr. Wickoff and I performed your surgery a few days ago."

My surgery?

"All the bullet fragments were removed, but you'll probably continue to feel some discomfort. And we'll need to keep the tubing down your throat for now."

Bullets.

The doctor walks around to the other side of the bed, inspecting some other piece of machinery keeping me alive. "We've started slowly weaning you off the sedation medication, but we'll need to keep you on oxygen support until you can breathe on your own."

It infuriates me that I can't respond to this man with words—this apparent surgeon with a bedside manner that needs a lot of work. Instead, I'm resigned to following him around the room with my eyes, hoping I will remember everything he is saying to me.

Eventually, a nurse enters the room and scribbles a few things on the whiteboard across from my bed. She and the surgeon exchange a few words I can't hear.

"I'll come back tomorrow to check on your progress," he says to me, leaving the room.

The nurse turns and offers me what I believe is a genuine smile. "Glad to see you're awake, Mr. Middleton. Your friend has been outside patiently waiting for days. Should I let him in?"

I try nodding so that she understands, but it's difficult. My entire body feels weighted, and everything seems like a difficult task. I'm relieved to see a familiar face when Lars enters the room although it's His under-eyes are hollow, as if he hasn't had any sleep.

"Good to see you're still in one piece," he says, standing several feet from the bed, almost as if he's afraid to approach any closer.

I offer him a slight smile to try and ease his clear discomfort with the situation, but what's most important to me is to try communicating what I want to know from him with my eyes.

Where the fuck is Megan?

I want to make sure she isn't in the state I'm in or worse.

"We haven't found DiAngelo," Lars offers. "I'm not even sure how that slippery fucker walked out of the club. Fabre must have him in a safe house somewhere."

So DiAngelo shot me, and Fabre is behind it? What in the actual fuck. Why can't I remember any of this?

I want to rip every hose and tube out of my body. This, not being able to talk shit, is torture. I have a million questions for Lars, and he's spoon-feeding me information like I'm a newborn baby.

"Calm down, boss," Lars says, noticing I'm becoming anxious—the heart rate monitor a dead giveaway. "You just woke up."

He wants me to calm down? Has he just met me yesterday?

I manage to eke out one word, although it's painful to do so.

"Megan."

"I'm going to call her now. She'll be excited to know you're finally awake."

Relief settles slowly in my bones. If she's taking Lars's calls, that means Megan must be okay.

"It may take her a minute to drive over from the club. Traffic is pretty bad right now."

Why is she at the club? The safest place for her to be is in this hospital room with me.

I can't say anything else because of the pain, but I tap one of my fingers on the bed and hope that Lars will understand that I want more information from him.

He takes a seat in a chair next to my bed. "After the shooting, we were all over the place about what to do. Emotions were running high, especially once we learned that DiAngelo turned out to be Fabre's gun for hire."

Fucking Fabre.

Yes, some of that night is coming back to me.

"It was Megan who reeled us all in."

My eyes widen in surprise. My Megan?

"If I ever doubted her ability to fit into our world, or rather your world, my opinion has now changed. She told us that we'd have to wait on revenge because you'd probably have a plan for DiAngelo of your own. Then she explained that the mission is to keep the business running as if it hasn't missed a step, nothing more. She was adamant about that."

I close my eyes in despair, saddened that Megan's been put in a position where she not only has to worry about me but also about the future of my entire business. This isn't the life I wanted for her. I wanted to give her a soft life. She's already come from hard.

When I get out of this hospital bed, I'm going to kick everybody's ass. Why would they allow my very pregnant fiancee to take on this role?

Lars continues, "Vaughn and Christian are handling meetings. Gage is managing the staff. Megan and I alternate our time between the hospital and the club. And before you get pissed, that's how Megan wants it. She wouldn't take no for an answer."

I slowly shake my head in protest.

How could they let this happen?

"We all recognize and accept that she is a permanent part of your life, Hunter. She is your partner. The soon-to-be mother of your child. It was either walk all over the woman you love or allow her to make decisions for you that she thought were best. Which would have rather happened?"

Sometimes, I hate it when Lars makes complete sense. I offer him a slight nod of understanding and smile to myself. I think my little kitten has grown into a lioness. I can see her bossing everyone around right now. Hand on her hip. Pouty mouth. I'm just sorry I missed it.

"I'm glad you understand because you may be in this bed for a while, and I don't want you to worry. I'm not going to let her fail, boss. I promise you."

If I were the emotional type, I'd give Lars a hug. Beyond Christian and Vaughn, this is the one man who I know can't be bought or sold. He is a true friend. Like the older brother I never had. And I'm so fortunate that he's looking out for me and the woman I adore.

Lars takes a glance at his phone and snickers. "Your woman must have superpowers. I'm not sure how she's only ten minutes away in thirty minutes worth of LA traffic."

Yeah, my lioness can fly.

Chapter 23

Stop Talking

MEGAN

I didn't think my body could still tremble like this.

Not after everything.

Not after watching Hunter's chest rise and fall so slowly, so helplessly, through the haze of medical machines. But here I am, staring at my phone screen, fingers shaking, barely able to keep my thoughts straight as Lars' recorded words echo in my head.

Hunter's awake.

The moment I heard those words, it felt like the world around me shifted. The hospital room, the muted beeps, and the sterile smells all faded into the background, leaving just one undeniable fact: Hunter is alive. Awake. And somewhere beyond these walls, he is waiting for me.

I press my palm against my belly, feeling the light flutter of the baby moving inside me, reminding me that despite everything, I'm not alone. But the thought of facing Hunter again... I don't know how I'm supposed to feel.

He's alive—that should be enough, right?

But what if it's not the same? No matter how strong he may be, will a man who wakes up from a traumatic brain injury be the same? What if...?

"Stop it," I whisper, my voice trembling. "You have to be strong, Megan."

As soon as I returned Lars's call, I shared the good news with Lena, Vaughn, and Christian, but we all agreed that I should be the one to visit Hunter first.

I force myself to stand, each movement feeling like an uphill battle. Every step toward his room feels like stepping closer to an unknown I'm not sure I'm ready to face.

Hunter has always been my rock, the one person who can ground me in the midst of all the chaos that surrounds us. Seeing him in a coma this past week has shattered something inside me. I felt so powerless, so lost as if a piece of myself was missing. And now, knowing he's awake, I should feel whole again.

But I don't. Not yet.

I make my way down the hospital corridor, the cold tiles beneath my feet doing nothing to soothe the storm raging inside me. Lars is waiting for me just outside the nurses' station. His normally stoic expression is softer today, relieved.

"Hey," he says, his voice low, almost hesitant. "You okay?"

I nod, though I'm not sure if it's true. "Does he... remember everything?" The question slips out before I can stop it. It's the only thing I can think about. What if he doesn't remember me? Us?

Lars rubs the back of his neck, his gaze flicking toward the door down the hall. "He's still piecing things together, but he remembers you, Megan. He's been asking for you."

Something in my chest loosens, and for the first time

since I got Lars' call, I take a breath. He remembers me. That should be enough to calm the torrent of emotions swirling inside me. But the anxiety gnaws at me still.

I try to smile, but it feels more like a grimace. "I guess I should go in then."

"Take your time," Lars says, his accented tone understanding. He knows this is bigger than just a reunion. Hunter waking up changes everything, but we still have a long road ahead. "They just took the breathing tube out, but he's still a little worse for wear."

I bite my bottom lip anxiously.

"I promise it looks worse than it is. He's not going anywhere."

I nod again, but my feet feel like they're stuck in quicksand. Finally, after what feels like an eternity, I manage to force myself to walk toward his room. The door looms ahead of me, and my hand hovers over the handle, my heart pounding in my ears. What if he's different? What if *we're* different?

The door swings open with a soft creak, and the first thing I notice is the quiet. There aren't as many beeping machines and no more hushed voices of stoic doctors. Just the soft sound of Hunter breathing. And there he is, sitting up in bed, looking both familiar and entirely different at the same time.

His eyes meet mine, and for a moment, everything else fades away.

"Megan," he attempts to greet me. His voice is rough and raspy from disuse, but it's Hunter. My Hunter. My knees almost give out, and I have to grip the edge of the doorframe to steady myself.

I swallow the lump in my throat, forcing myself to walk toward him. "You're awake."

He gives me a tired smile, a ghost of the one that used to make my heart race.

I don't know what to say. I should be overjoyed, but there's this strange sense of distance between us, like an invisible barrier that I don't know how to break through. The last time I saw him, he was a broken man—battered, unconscious, and on life support. The love of my life was slipping away from me while I sat helplessly by his bedside, praying for a miracle.

And now he's back. But the wounds run deeper than I can see.

"Come," Hunter says, his hand reaching out toward me. His fingers tremble slightly, but the familiar command in his strained is undeniable.

"Don't talk," I tell him.

Then I take his hand, feeling the warmth of his pale skin against mine, and all the tension I've been holding onto melts away. Without thinking, I sit on the edge of the bed, my other hand still cradling my belly. His gaze drops for a moment, and I can see the questions swirling in his eyes.

"The baby's fine. We're both fine."

Relief floods his expression, but it's quickly replaced by something else—guilt?

"I don't want you worrying about my business," he mutters, his grip tightening on my hand. "You should be—"

"Stop." I cut him off, shaking my head. "Don't do that. You've spent your life building that business. It's our son or daughter's legacy," I remind him, patting my stomach.

His jaw clenches, the tension in his body palpable. "I didn't protect you," he coughs. "You were left alone to deal with all of this. I—"

"Stop fucking talking I said."

I place a finger over his lips, silencing him. "You

survived. That's all that matters." My voice cracks, and I hate how vulnerable I sound, but it's the truth. As long as Hunter is drawing breath, we'll always be okay. I know this just as sure as I know the sun will set tonight.

Hunter's eyes soften, but I can see the war going on inside him. "Megan, I—"

Before he can finish, I move closer, resting my head against his chest, just listening to the steady rhythm of his heartbeat. It's the only sound I need right now. His hand moves to the back of my head, fingers tangling in my hair as he holds me close.

"I missed you," I whisper, my voice muffled against his hospital gown. "I missed you so much."

"I'm here now," he murmurs into my hair. "And I'm not going anywhere."

For a long time, we sit like that, wrapped in each other's presence, not saying anything. There's nothing left to say. We've both been through hell and now we have to find a way back to each other. I feel the weight of his arm as it drapes over my shoulders, holding me close as if he's afraid I'll disappear.

But the truth is, we're both scared. Scared of what comes next. Scared of what we've lost and what we might never get back. But at this moment, with Hunter's heartbeat beneath my cheek, I realize something.

We're still here.

Together.

And that's more than enough.

After what feels like hours, I pull back slightly, just enough to look into his eyes.

"We have a lot to talk about."

Hunter nods, his expression serious. "I know."

"I don't even know where to start," I admit, biting my lip. "Everything's changed."

It will be a long time before Hunter is going to be well enough to be who he was in his world. And until he gets back on his feet, I'm going to have to keep everything afloat. I won't fail.

He reaches up, brushing a strand of hair from my face. "I'll figure it out. I always do."

His words are meant to be reassuring, but there's an uncertainty in his eyes that wasn't there before. We both know things won't be the same, not after everything he's been through. Fabre has to be dealt with, and there will be fallout, but I suppose we'll have to take it one step at a time. It's our only choice now.

"We'll figure it out," I correct him. "Together."

"I love you," he adds, his hand resting gently on my belly.

There was a moment when I thought I'd never hear Hunter say those words again, and I want to cry. Like, I really want to have a good old ugly cry. But that would only worry him. So, instead, I place my hand over his, feeling the warmth of his touch seep into me.

I slowly rise from the position I'm in on the bed and kiss Hunter on his cracked lips.

"You better," I whisper into his mouth.

And for the first time since all of this began, I'm actually believing that there is a *real* happily-ever-after in our future.

Except it's my turn to be Prince Charming.

Chapter 24

Can Anyone Hear You?

MEGAN
Eight Weeks Later

I'm sitting in the familiar shadows of the club, the hum of the deep bass vibrating under my feet. The crowd is light tonight—thank God. I'm not sure my swollen ankles could handle the usual rush. At this late stage of my pregnancy, I feel like a balloon that could pop at any moment, but I wouldn't trade this feeling for the world. I run my hand over my belly, smiling at the kick I feel in return. *Damn, that one was a little hard.*

As if on cue to distract me from the rather swift kick my baby just gave me, I receive a call from the little soccer player's father, who has been a terrible patient at his rehabilitation facility lately.

"Hello, beautiful."

"Is everything okay?"

"Everything's fine."

"Then why aren't you sleeping?"

"You're micro-managing my sleep schedule as well as everything else, I see."

"The doctor was clear. Rest is an integral part of your recovery. Eating, sleeping, and physical therapy is all you should be doing."

"And you're eight months pregnant with my child. You shouldn't be sitting in a smoke-filled club."

"Sitting here is literally part of the job."

Knowing that I'm right, he lets out an annoyed growl. Hunter still hasn't gotten comfortable with the fact that I call the shots until he's back on his feet. While there's nothing wrong with his beautiful brain, he still has quite a few physical challenges that would make him look weak in front of clients and, more importantly, his enemies.

"It's not healthy for the baby."

"Most people vape now. I don't even smell the smoke," I quip.

"Not helping, Megan."

"Seriously, get some sleep, Hunter. I'm going to head home in a little while. The guys can handle the rest of the night."

"Lars is driving you, correct?"

"Like he does every single night," I sigh.

"And you'd tell me if you felt like something was off?"

"Everything's fine, Hunter. You've got to try and relax. It's quiet as a church in here tonight."

"I'm going fucking stir crazy in this place. Everyone is old enough to be my grandfather."

"If you keep doing everything your therapy team tells you to do, then you'll be home before you know it."

"Is my sister there?"

"In the kitchen as usual."

"And Christian?"

I know why he's asking about those two in particular, but I feign ignorance. I'm not going to get involved in any of that drama. Who am I to judge if Lena likes older men?

"He's at Table 21."

"Vaughn, too?"

"Yes, he's here as well. Like I said, they're here every night. I feel very safe."

"You know that Vaugn can take over if you're not feeling up to this anymore? He was always the most logical choice to do it."

"Except he wasn't, was he? I was the one with the rational head when the shit hit the fan. Don't forget that, my love."

"It appears as if you're never going to let me forget it."

I grin hard to myself.

"You're absolutely right."

"I wish you were in this bed with me." His voice drops.

"There's not enough room for the three of us," I chuckle, reminding him that I'm carrying another human being.

"I'd make room."

"What are you doing, Hunter?" I ask suspiciously, fully understanding what it means when his voice thickens like that.

"I'm thinking about how sweet you taste."

"Do you even remember?" I tease.

"Oh, I remember everything about that sweet pussy of yours. It smells like ripe berries and tastes even sweeter."

I scan my surroundings, taking note that no one is within earshot of me, so I indulge him.

"Can you smell me from there because my pussy is soaking wet?"

"Fuck, Megan," he grunts.

"It's a shame visiting hours are over. Who's going to take care of that hard dick of yours?"

"Megan," he growls.

"God, I love that fat dick when it's inside me. In my mouth. In my pussy. Hell, it doesn't matter."

"Megan! Can anyone hear you?"

"I don't give a shit who can hear," I say in the best sex kitten voice I can muster. "Do you remember how wet I get for you, Hunter? I'm sitting in your club, drenched, in need of a good fuck. What are you going to do about it?"

"Shit–" I hear him violently grunt, then there's a moment of heavy breathing and then complete silence.

I wait for a moment and then speak, "Hunter, you okay?"

"I expect you to come by here tomorrow before you go to the club, Megan."

"To finish this up?" I chuckle.

"Good night, Megan," he says before ending the call. I love it when I leave him hot and bothered. It's fine. Tomorrow, I'll lock the door to his private room and give him a quickie blow job.

Gage, the manager, moves behind the bar with practiced ease, filling drink orders without a second glance at me. He's grown used to me sitting back here, keeping an eye on things.

"You doing okay, Megan?" he asks, glancing over his shoulder as he polishes a glass.

"Yeah, I just said goodnight to Hunter, and now I'm enjoying the quiet," I answer, stretching my back. It's been a long day already, but quiet nights like this make it easier. Less chaos means fewer problems to deal with, and that's what I need right now. A little peace.

But I've learned the hard way—peace doesn't last long around here.

My phone buzzes on the table. I glance down at the screen, seeing an unknown number flash. My stomach twists. Calls from unknown numbers rarely bring good news.

I hesitate for a moment before answering, keeping my voice steady. "Hello?"

There's a pause on the other end, then a woman's voice, shaking and laced with panic. "Is... is this the number? The one I was given? The one I'm supposed to call if... if something went wrong?"

I straighten up, tension rolling down my spine. I was told a call like this may happen, but it doesn't make hearing the fear in her voice any easier. "Yes, this is the right number. What's the problem?"

There is another pause, and then she speaks again, her voice barely above a whisper. "I was told a man would answer. The one who fixes things. The one who makes problems go away."

Her confusion is palpable, and I understand it. She's expecting Hunter—someone tough, intimidating, the guy who steps in when things get messy.

Not me.

But unfortunately, tonight, I'm all she's got.

"Well, I'm the one handling things tonight," I say firmly, leaving no room for doubt. Then I try remembering the script I was given to use if one of these calls ever occurred. Hunter made me practice it a million times, although I don't think he ever believed I'd need it.

"Who gave you this number?" I ask her.

"He told me to say a friend from the bottom."

That's the correct answer, so I move on.

"Tell me what happened."

She's quiet for a second, and I can hear her breathing shakily on the other end, clearly debating whether to hang up. But then she lets out a long, unsteady breath.

"There's a body," she whispers, her voice cracking. "He's dead, and I... I didn't mean for this to happen. I just..."

Fuck me.

A dead body?

Seriously?

Chapter 25

Did You Tell Hunter?

MEGAN

"Where are you?" I ask, cutting through the panic in the woman's voice. She's falling apart, and if I'm going to pull this off, I know I need to keep her calm.

"The Shaded Lamp," she says, almost in a daze. "In the back room. I don't know what to do. They told me this number would—"

"I'll handle it," I say, my voice firm but calm. I quickly remember the next question I'm supposed to ask.

"Is there anyone else with you?"

"No."

"Has anyone seen you or...the body?"

"No."

"Good, just stay where you are. I'll be there in fifteen minutes. Don't touch anything."

She starts to say something, but I hang up before she can continue. I don't need to hear any more right now—I've got enough to go on.

I grab my coat, the weight of the baby making every movement slower than I'd like. As I stand, I wince as another sharp kick lands against my ribs. "Easy, baby Middleton," I mutter, rubbing my belly. "We've got work to do."

Gage notices me standing and frowns. "Something up?"

"A call came in," I say, pulling on my coat. "Just need to handle it."

"Did you tell Hunter?"

"And why would I do that? You know he's recovering."

"Okay, well, are you sure you don't want Vaughn or Christian to go with you?" His eyes flicker to my belly, concern etched on his face.

"I'm sure," I say firmly, not bothering to defend my decision. I've learned that most people still don't understand how deep I am in Hunter's world now.

I can handle this.

Christian and Vaughn immediately spot me waddling to the exit door and follow after me.

"And where do you think you're headed in such a hurry?" Vaughn asks.

"I got a call."

Both of their faces contort in a look that screams, "Oh my fucking god."

"What kind of a call?"

"A clean up."

Hunter explained to me a few weeks ago that at this point in his career, albeit begrudgingly, he mainly handles negotiations between underworld figures in disputes and charges them a shit ton of money to do so. He doesn't do cleanups much anymore, but if a call comes in from a trusted source, he won't ignore it.

"A cleanup?" Christian echoes.

"Yes."

"The streets are already questioning if Hunter is out of commission," Vaughn tells me.

"And?"

"And a sudden clean-up call feels like a setup."

"I have Hunter's emergency cell phone in my possession. We can't ignore the fact that she called the number and sounded scared as shit on the call," I tell them.

"Some random woman called Hunter for a cleanup?" Christian asks. "That's definitely a setup. You're not going."

"I'm going."

"This makes no fucking sense, Megan. You're about to drop a baby any minute," Vaughn counters, pointing toward my stomach for effect. "You're putting yourself in danger. Hunter couldn't have possibly agreed to this."

He's right.

Hunter would kill me if he knew what I was up to. He made it clear that if, by some small chance, I actually received a call on that bat phone of his, I should tell Vaughn and Christian right away and let them handle it.

At least I kept half my word.

"Listen, I know that none of us expected an actual call to come in, but it has. What do you want me to do? We're supposed to be running things as if it's business as usual. And I'm not dropping this baby in any minute. I've got a whole month."

"The jig will be up when whoever called sees a pregnant college student come to the rescue. What the hell can you do?"

"I have a brain, if you recall, and if there's any heavy lifting, Lars will take care of it. You all can't keep this side of the business from me forever, especially when I've already been on the receiving end of some of your mistakes," I say, reminding them both of when I was abducted and almost shot.

"I'm coming then," Christian says.

"No, Lars is coming. You don't send a whole team to a clean-up."

"You've been talking to Hunter."

"Obviously!" I say, flustered. "He has more faith in me than you two do."

"And if I call him to check that he's on board with this?" Vaughn asks me.

"Then you and I are going to have problems. I told everyone that he's to be left alone until he's released."

"Well, I'm definitely putting a team on you," Vaughn says through a growl. He's never been on board with me in charge, but it doesn't come from a spiteful place. I know he truly cares about my safety and thinks it would be best if I stayed home and painted landscapes until the baby comes.

Hell, he's probably right.

"There's been a security team on me for weeks, so let's not pretend otherwise," I say with a hand on my hip.

"You know?"

"Of course I do."

"Do I need to fire somebody?"

"No, Vaughn," I chuckle. "Hunter told me weeks ago."

"That henpecked motherfucker. You weren't supposed to know."

"I'll call you with an update," I tell them both, ending the conversation. "I promise."

I step outside into the cool night air, the chill instantly making my skin tingle. Lars is waiting by the car, leaning against the hood with his arms crossed. He knows something's up as soon as he sees me. This is not the usual time I leave the club.

"What's going on?" he asks, his voice low and steady, but I can tell by the way he's watching me that he's already in problem-solving mode.

I walk over to him, feeling the weight of the situation settle on my shoulders. "I got a call from a woman at The Shaded Lamp. There's a body in the back room."

Lars straightens immediately, his eyes narrowing. "You're not going there alone."

"I wasn't planning on it," I reply, giving him a pointed look. I know better than to walk into a situation like this without backup. Plus, Lars still feels guilty about Naomi's father abducting me, so this is an opportunity for him to redeem himself, although I've never assigned any blame to him for that.

He nods, his expression hard. "Let's go, then."

We climb into the car, and the ride is quiet as we drive through the city. The streets blur past, but my mind is focused on what's coming next. I've run the scenario script through my head a thousand times, but this is real life. There is always the risk of something going wrong. Always the chance that one mistake could unravel everything.

I want to call Hunter and hear his voice, for a pep talk, for some guidance, but that would be a terrible idea. All I want is for him to focus on his recovery and to be a hundred percent healthy when the baby comes. But I know that man; if I told him what I was about to do, he'd check out of the rehab and come after me in a flash.

The Shaded Lamp comes into view, its neon sign flickering weakly in the night. It's a dive bar—one that caters to a rough crowd—and the thought of dealing with whatever's waiting inside makes my stomach churn.

Maybe this was a dumb idea?

But I push the feeling down. I have to stay focused.

As we pull up, I spot a woman pacing nervously near the entrance. She looks out of place here—like she doesn't belong, but she's trying to blend in anyway. Her hands are shaking, and she's chewing on her bottom lip like she might chew it clean off.

Lars and I step out of the car, and as soon as she sees me, her face falls.

"You're the one I talked to?" she asks, her eyes wide with disbelief. "You're... you're pregnant."

The disappointment in her voice is clear, and I don't blame her. She was expecting a legendary fixer—my Hunter. Instead, she gets me, a pregnant woman who paints portraits.

"I am," I say, standing taller. "But that doesn't matter. I'm here to help you with your problem. Now, take me to the body."

She blinks at me, then at Lars, clearly unsure of what to make of the situation, but eventually, she nods and leads us inside. The bar is dark and dingy, smelling of stale beer and desperation. The few patrons at the front don't even glance our way, too drunk or too tired to care about what's happening around them.

The woman pushes open a door at the back, and my heart tightens as I see the body. It's a man slumped against the wall, his face bruised and bloody, a deep gash on his head. Blood pools around him, staining the cracked floor.

Lars steps forward, his gaze sweeping over the scene. "What happened?"

"He... he was causing trouble," the woman stammers, her hands trembling. "He wouldn't leave, got into a fight with one of my guys. He tripped, hit his head on the bar, and then... then he wasn't moving."

I remember my script.

Hunter is only called for important people and as gross as this bar may be, this woman must be connected to someone who matters.

"Where's your guy?" I ask her.

Her eyes drop to the floor. "He ran."

"Who is he?" I ask about the body.

Her voice quivers as she explains. "I didn't see the tattoo on his wrist until I tried searching him for ID. He's part of the Blood Nation."

While I don't know all the intricacies of every group that Hunter has worked with, I know enough to understand that a dead Blood Nation member on a bar room floor is never a good thing.

I take a deep breath, the weight of the situation settling on my shoulders. "Alright," I say, keeping my voice calm. "We're going to handle this. You got it?" I ask Lars.

Lars nods, already with his phone out, texting whoever Hunter usually calls to handle scenarios like this. Meanwhile, I turn back to the woman. She's on the verge of tears, her hands shaking as she wrings them together.

"You need to keep calm," I tell her, my tone firm but reassuring. "No one can or will know about this. We'll take care of the body, but you need to make sure no one in the bar talks, especially your guy on the run. It would be best if you found him. Understood?"

She nods quickly, swallowing hard. "I understand. I'll make sure no one says anything."

As Lars finishes making the call, I take one last look at the scene and wonder how young Hunter was when he first had to handle something like this. Was he my age? Was he even younger? It would explain so much.

"How much longer before the bar closes?" I ask her.

"Hours."

"I suggest you go out there, announce last call, then go home and handle finding your person. That's the priority."

"Okay...I'm sorry, what's your name?"

Lars gives me a side-eye warning.

"We don't need to get into names," I tell her. "Let's get to work," I say, my voice steady, even as the baby kicks again—a jab to the ribs that feels even stronger than the last time.

"Oww!" I bend at the waist.

"Are you okay?" the woman asks.

Before I assure her that I'm an incubator for a future soccer star, another intense kick takes my breath away.

"Hey?" Lars approaches, ending his text exchange and placing a hand on my shoulder.

Another kick happens, and the pain seems to travel around the side of my belly and up my spine.

"Fuckkkk!" I bellow.

"She might be in labor," the woman says to Lars.

"No," I interject firmly. "I have another month."

The pain intensifies.

It doesn't feel like just a kick anymore.

Just pain.

And that's when it hits me.

I'm in a dive bar with a dead body, and something is very wrong with my baby.

Hunter's going to lose his shit when he hears about this.

Chapter 26

I'm Not Going To Ask You Twice

HUNTER

I now completely understand why teenage boys play with their dicks so much. I can relate. With this kind of downtime on their hands, what the hell else are they supposed to do? I've been laying in this bed, it seems like, for months, twiddling my thumbs in between half-ass physical therapy sessions.

Physical fucking therapy.

Talk about a hustle.

All they do every day is make me walk around, check my balance, and lift light-ass hand weights. I can't believe they get paid for that shit. I worked out harder back when I was a scrawny thirteen-year-old, hoping to be recruited by the organization. The best therapy for me would be to simply get back to my life, especially my woman.

Megan is all I need.

She's mine.

And while she's always at the center of my thoughts, for some reason, she is taking up a significant amount of my consciousness tonight. Fuck, I miss her luscious ass and infectious smile. Everything in my life is always better when she's around.

It's way too late at night for me to call and check on her, but I have an excuse. She's carrying my child, which makes her more of a target than she's ever been, and regular check-ins help me sleep at night.

So...I text her.

> Me: How's my baby?

While I anxiously await her response, I do random leg stretches in bed. Anything to speed up the process of getting out of this hell hole. After several repetitions, I slowly rise to get up to pee. Everything feels ache, not because I was shot but because all I'm required to do in this place between sessions is lay like broccoli. It's infuriating and frankly counterproductive.

I check the time.

At this point in the evening, Megan should be in the penthouse by now, meticulously lotioning her skin after a long shower. Her cell phone usually sits on a dresser at her side of the bed or is parked on a charging station. I wonder if she's seen my text yet.

She's probably exhausted, but my gut tells me something is not quite right. And I trust my gut. It's gotten me out of more precarious situations than I can count over the years.

I call Lars to make sure he's dropped her off at the apartment building, but his phone goes straight to voicemail. Then I call Vaughn. Same thing. Next, I call Christian. Ditto. Finally, I call Lena. When she answers, the tone of her voice makes my chest tighten.

"Hunter?"

"What's wrong?" I say, skipping the formalities of a greeting. "Why is no one picking up their phones?"

"It's Megan."

"What about her?" I skip a breath, fearing the very worst.

"Something with the baby."

"Where is she?"

I slowly stand and head toward the closet of my room. I need my street clothes so I can get the fuck out of here. I need to get to her now. She's probably petrified.

Hell, so am I.

Ever since Megan told me she was pregnant, I've been flip-flopping between polar opposite emotions. On one hand, I'm elated that the woman I love is giving birth to a human being that the two of us created. But on the other, I worry that all we've done is create another moving target for my enemies. If Johnathan was alive, he'd laugh in my face and tell me how soft I've become.

He'd be right.

"Lena, did you hear me? I asked you where she is."

"LA General."

"Tell me exactly what happened."

She sighs softly over the phone. As I begin to learn all the mannerisms of my little sister, I can sense that she's stalling. She doesn't want to give me details, which means I'm not going to like them.

"Lena, I'm not going to ask you twice."

"I don't know everything."

"Then tell me what you know."

I struggle to pull up one of my socks.

"She got a phone call on the emergency line."

"And?"

"Let me just have Christian explain."

The fuck?

"He's been sitting next to you this entire time?"

"Um, hold on."

"Hey, Hunt."

"Don't answer the phone like it's a casual Monday, motherfucker. Why didn't you pick up the phone when I called?"

"Let's argue later. You want to hear about Megan or not?"

Jackass.

"What happened?"

"We didn't think it would happen, but she got a call. A real one. It was a clean-up job."

"A clean-up? That sounds like–"

"I know, and I thought it was a setup at first, too, but it was legit. The body was at the Shaded Lamp, and it's some-body from Blood Nation."

So, it's truly begun.

Fabre is making moves.

Bodies from Blood Nation don't just show up dead in random bars.

First, he tried to put me out of commission, and now he's hitting the organizations I have relationships with. But that's not my primary concern right now. First, I need to get to Megan and my child.

"So you're telling me my pregnant fiancee was dealing with a dead body across town in that fucking dump, and now she's in the hospital?"

"We tried to stop her."

"You tried to stop her," I parrot back his words flatly. "You didn't try hard enough."

"To be fair, your woman is formidable when she wants to be."

"If she didn't put a Glock to your temple and threaten your sorry ass life, I don't want to hear shit from you."

"That's harsh, man, even for you."

I can hear Lena in the background asking Christian, "What'd he say? What's he saying?"

"Nothing. It's fine," he assures her in a gentle voice that you use with someone you're intimately involved with either emotionally or, God help him...physically.

"Hunt," he returns to our conversation. "Lars got her to the hospital in record time. He's with her right now. Lena and I had to help Gage close the club, but we're on our way. We'll be there in ten minutes. And Vaughn is dealing with the situation at the Shaded Lamp."

"I'll be there in thirty minutes," I tell him as I struggle to gain my balance. Even with all this physical therapy crap I've been doing, things are still quite wobbly.

"I imagine there's no scenario in which you'd stay put until we can send over security to escort you to the hospital?"

"Fuck no."

"Got it," he huffs. "See you when you get there."

"And Christian–"

"Yeah?"

"When we're on the other side of this, we're going to have to talk seriously about my sister."

"Agreed."

"Mr. Middleton, this really won't do. It's not standard protocol to allow patients to check themselves out of the facility in the middle of the night," the no-nonsense, heavy-set nurse says to me.

I read her name tag.

"It's an emergency, Portia."

"A police emergency?"

"It's personal," is my simple response. I don't owe anyone in here an explanation about where I'm going or what I'm doing.

"You're not well, Mr. Middleton."

"What papers do you need me to sign relieving you of any liability because I'm leaving," I say sternly. "You're holding me up."

I'm trying to be polite because this poor woman is only doing her job, but every moment we spend in this exchange is one more second I'm not at Megan's side.

"Give me a minute," she huffs as she prints out several sheets of paper.

As my discharge instructions print, she grabs a wheelchair and points to the seat. "Sit."

I do what I'm told as she hands me a pen and the paperwork. "Sign everywhere it asks for a patient signature as I roll your stubborn butt to the elevator.

"My fiancee was rushed to the hospital. She's pregnant with our first child," I finally explain, relieved I'm almost out of here.

"Oh, my God!" the nurse exclaims. "You should have led with that. Is there a ride waiting for you downstairs?"

"No, I'm going to have to call an Uber."

"Don't worry, I'll have someone at the security desk call you one. I hope everything goes okay, Mr. Middleton. Babies are my favorite thing in the world."

As I sit in the back of the Uber, the driver tapping his fingers on the steering wheel to some mindless pop song, my phone vibrates on my lap. I snatch it up, praying it's Megan, Lars, or anyone with an update from the hospital.

But the message isn't from anyone I expect.

> Unknown Number: If you want to see
> Megan and your baby alive, turn back
> around.

My blood turns cold.

The car slows for a red light, and I glance out the window, scanning the streets for anything—or anyone—watching.

A second message pings immediately after.

> Unknown Number: We're closer than you
> think.

Chapter 27

Not A Small Ask

HUNTER

The back of the driver's head blurs slightly as I stare, the tension wrapping around my chest, squeezing tighter with every heartbeat. For the first time in a long time, I feel uncertain, helpless—like a kid trapped in a game where the stakes are just too high. Every option feels like a dead end. Whatever move I make now could shape the rest of my life, and that of Megan, our child, and too many others.

With a steadying breath, I type a response to the anonymous message, keeping my fingers calm, even though my mind is racing.

Me: Who is this?

The wait for their reply stretches longer than I'd like, each second thick with the hum of the car engine, the faint smell of stale coffee, and my own pulse drumming in my ears. Then finally, the screen lights up.

Unknown Number: Wrong question.

A flicker of anger burns through my frustration. They think they're calling the shots. I grip my phone tightly, the plastic casing creaking under the pressure, and respond like this is just business as usual.

Me: Then I'm done.

It's a bluff. I don't negotiate with cowards hiding behind blocked numbers. If I'm going to protect Megan, I need to act like I have nothing to lose. I sink back into the seat, feeling the car jostle slightly as we drive over a patch of rough road. A few heartbeats later, the next message buzzes in.

Unknown Number: You shouldn't call our bluff.

I clench my jaw, forcing down the instinct to respond with rage. My emotions and logic battle it out, and for once, I'm unsure which side to follow. The stakes are too high, and this isn't a game.

I dial Christian. He picks up on the first ring, his voice sharp with tension.

"Where are you?" he snaps, anxiety pulsing through the line.

"What's going on in there? Can I talk to her?" My words spill out, tighter than I intended.

"Hell no, you can't talk to her!" he shoots back. "She's scared shitless, man."

The driver glances at me in the rearview mirror as I slam my fist on my thigh, ignoring the questioning look he gives me.

"Christian!" I grit out, my patience slipping away.

"Alright, listen—Megan's safe for now. But where are you? How far out?"

"There's someone following me. They've threatened her safety if I get any closer to the hospital."

The phone line goes silent as he processes my words, then comes back with grim determination. "I'll call Vaughn. We can get extra men and more firepower. We're not letting some–"

"No." I interrupt him, each word controlled, deliberate. "I'm not putting Megan and my baby through a damn gunfight outside the hospital doors. That's not what I want for either of them."

Christian lets out a frustrated huff. "You're really going to let a random threat keep you from being there for the birth of your kid?"

"It's not about me," I tell him, swallowing back the urge to lash out. "It's about keeping them safe, whatever it takes."

"Then what are you gonna do, Hunt?" His words are strained, verging on desperate.

Just then, another text flashes across my screen.

> Unknown Number: If you get any closer to the hospital, we're going to assume you aren't taking us seriously.

I close my eyes briefly, the weight of the situation pressing down hard. I need a plan, and I need it now. I lean forward, catching the driver's eye.

"Hey. Change of plans. I need you to take me somewhere else."

He frowns at me in the mirror, eyebrows raised. "You have to update the address in the app, man. I can't just–"

"Just pull over for a second," I snap, tapping through my

phone to update the destination, trying to quiet the dread curling in my gut.

"Hunter?" Christian's voice drags me back. "What should I tell Megan? She's going to know something's off if you're not here soon."

"Tell her... tell her I'm coming," I lie, the words sticking in my throat. "Tell her whatever she needs to hear to keep calm."

Christian's silence hangs thick for a moment. "And Lena? You want me to lie to her, too?"

"Of course," I say, exasperated.

"She'll know something's off, too."

"What the fuck are you talking about, Christian? Neither of you know each other well enough to understand each other's tells. Whatever you have to tell my sister or Megan, just do it and make sure they both feel safe."

Christian mutters a string of curses under his breath. "This isn't exactly a small ask, Hunt."

"There's a reason why I called you," I add, my voice low and urgent. "And only you."

Christian sighs, resignation laced in every word. "Fine. But Megan isn't stupid. She's going to know something's off."

"You're a lawyer, aren't you? Then lie. Be convincing. It's your job to ensure she doesn't think anything is off. Do I need to remind you of what's at stake?"

There's a pause, and he huffs, "Fine."

The driver looks back, clearly growing impatient. "You still back there changing the address?"

"Yes, almost done," I say, glancing back at my phone. The screen stays blank, but the tension in my gut tells me they're still watching, waiting.

"Hunt?" Christian's voice drops, laced with worry. "Where exactly are you going? I should know."

"It's better if I don't tell you," I mutter, looking out the window at the blurred lights. "But if I'm not there by tomorrow night, send Lars to look for me."

"And tell him what, exactly?"

"Tell him the truth if it comes to that. But not now—I want him with Megan. She's the priority."

Another long pause. Then, with a resigned sigh, Christian mutters, "You better show up, man. She needs you. We all do."

I end the call and turn to the driver, my phone raised with a crisp hundred-dollar bill folded underneath it.

"Forget the app," I say, my tone low and demanding. "Take me to this address in East LA, and the cash is yours."

He eyes the money, weighing the offer with a shrewd look before nodding.

"Alright," he murmurs, the unspoken agreement hanging between us.

He changes course, the car veering off onto a darkened street as I settle back, gripping my phone with white-knuckled determination.

And as we plunge into the night, the only thought in my head is a cold, steely resolve.

I'm coming, Megan.

Hold on, baby.

Chapter 28

Is This Your First?

MEGAN

The chaotic hum of the emergency room swirls around me as I press my hand against my stomach, the pain pulsing in waves. Every nerve in my body is raw, fraying with each jolt, each sensation that crashes through me. I try to tune out the nonsense Lena and Christian are mumbling.

"What kind of language is Lars speaking?" Lena's voice pierces through the discomfort.

"Hell, if I know," Christian mutters, his eyes flicking toward Lars, who's barking something that sounds distinctly Nordic and unrestrained. "I've never heard him use it before."

"I wonder if Hunter knows he speaks it?"

"If he does, he's never mentioned it. Kind of wild, right?"

I clench my fists and grind my teeth, the dull ache in my lower back throbbing with the rhythm of each heartbeat. "Could you two be quiet!" I bark, shooting them a glare through the haze of pain. "Lars is the only one trying to get me and my baby some help."

"Aww, Megan, that's not true," Lena says softly, her hand rubbing circles on my lower back, trying to soothe me. Her touch is warm and comforting, but the pain is relentless, digging its claws deeper by the second.

Christian steps away to take a call, leaving Lena and me to watch Lars work his magic—or his frustration—on the nursing staff.

"Is that Hunter?" I shout after him, hoping for a sliver of reassurance, but Christian just shakes his head, and disappointment hits me in a fresh wave of irritation.

Where is he? I need him here, not only to talk me through this but to bulldoze our way past this waiting room full of people. He'd know what to do, know how to get us the attention we need. Lars is already causing a scene, his low, aggravated voice slipping in and out of Danish. I've never seen him this upset before, and from the looks of it, neither has anyone else.

The nurse, looking overwhelmed and exhausted, finally raises her head and meets my gaze. We exchange a look—a silent understanding that we're both at our limits. She grabs an empty wheelchair, her sigh almost inaudible under the fluorescent hum of the hospital lighting. "Can you sit?"

I nod, carefully lowering myself into the seat, feeling every movement jolt through my body like an electric current.

"How far along are you?" she asks, a tired kindness in her voice.

"Eight months," I say, trying to keep my voice steady.

"Has this pain been constant?"

"It's been building up all day," I admit, a shiver of worry

slipping through me. "But now it's…it feels like more than that. Could I be in labor? It's too early, isn't it?"

The nurse's expression is neutral, reassuring, but firm. "It could be labor. At eight months, you're in a relatively safe range. We see plenty of babies born around now who are perfectly healthy."

That should calm me, but her words hang in the air, the uncertainty prickling my already frayed nerves.

I force a weak smile and nod, but the worry gnaws at me. "It just doesn't feel right."

The nurse's gaze softens, a hint of sympathy slipping through. "Is this your first?"

"Yes," I whisper, almost embarrassed by how lost I feel.

"It's normal to feel overwhelmed," she assures me. "A lot of first-time mothers are shocked by how intense the pain can be. I'll do my best to get you a bed soon, but right now, we're packed."

A ripple of irritation passes through Lena. "So what, she should have the baby on the waiting room floor?" she snaps, surprising even me. Lena's normally the calm, collected one, but seeing me like this must be setting her off.

The nurse raises a brow but keeps her composure. "We'll get her seen," she says, holding up a calming hand. "If you can, try to call your OBGYN's emergency line. We're overextended tonight."

"Damn," Lena mutters under her breath, rolling her eyes. "Might as well deliver this baby in the parking lot."

I blink at her in surprise. Twice now, Lena has let her sass slip—something I rarely see. But the fierce determination on her face makes me feel…protected, somehow.

Lars maneuvers the wheelchair to a quieter corner of the waiting room, near a woman sprawled across three chairs. She's middle-aged, with silver-streaked braids, a black leather jacket embroidered with pink flowers, and heavy combat boots propped up on the seat across from her. She looks up with a start as Lars approaches, his large frame casting a shadow over her.

"Lars," I say in a warning tone, sensing his irritation, but he silences me with a hard look that tells me to stay quiet. He leans down and taps her shoulder.

"We need the seats," he says, his voice gruff.

She blinks at him, momentarily startled, before breaking into a grin. "Sure thing, handsome."

If I weren't in so much pain, I'd giggle. I've never seen someone flirt with Lars like this.

Her eyes soften when she notices me, her gaze dropping to my stomach. "In labor, huh?"

"I think so," I say, gritting my teeth as another wave of pain surges through me. She gives me a sympathetic smile.

"Delivered three of my own," she says with a wink. "It gets easier each time, I promise."

Lars clears his throat, sending her a look that makes it clear the conversation is over. I think about telling him to lighten up, but at this moment, I just don't have the energy. He's still on high alert from the Parker fiasco, and any new person—especially one like her—is just another potential disappointment in his eyes.

I let my head fall back against the seat, feeling Lena's hand steady on my shoulder as she watches Christian, who's just come back around the corner, talking low on his phone. Her eyes narrow, picking up on something I hadn't noticed.

"Did Hunter call back?" she asks.

"No," Christian says a little too quickly, his gaze avoiding hers. "That was work."

My stomach twists, and not just from the pain. I glance at him, my instincts flaring. Is he lying?

"Then where is he?" I demand, my voice tight. "Do you all know something I don't? Why isn't he here yet?" I look from Christian to Lena, then to Lars, who remains silent, his eyes like steel.

"Give me my phone, Lars," I snap, holding out my hand. Lars hesitates but finally hands it over, his face a mask of conflicted loyalty.

Just as I'm about to unlock it, the nurse approaches us again, a spark of relief in her eyes. "I found a bed. Did you manage to reach your doctor?"

"No, I'm doing it right now," I say, fumbling to dial with trembling hands.

"I'll call for you," Lena says, reaching for the phone with a steadying hand.

For the first time all night, I feel a flicker of relief, but it's fleeting. Because as soon as I'm rolled into the examination room, I feel a wetness grow slowly between my legs.

I'm officially petrified.

Chapter 29

Calling In A Favor

HUNTER

"This is unexpected," Psycho greets me, his voice carrying the slightest edge of amusement as I step into the dimly lit house. The air inside is thick with the scent of tobacco, sweat, and something metallic that lingers just beneath the surface—blood, perhaps, though I don't care to confirm.

The headquarters of Blood Nation in East Los Angeles is unassuming from the outside, but inside, it hums with quiet menace. A low murmur of voices filters through the walls, punctuated by laughter and the occasional sharp bark of command. It's the kind of place where secrets live and die in the same breath, where loyalty is earned with blood, and betrayal is met with it.

"I'm calling in a favor," I reply, my voice steady as I meet Psycho's sharp, dark eyes. He's aptly nicknamed—there's something unhinged in the way he tilts his head, like he's already imagining how he'd take me apart if given the chance.

"El Jefe wasn't expecting you, Middleton."

"I realize that. Nevertheless, I need to speak to him."

"And you came alone?" His smirk widens, a predator catching the scent of a challenge.

"I did."

"Armed?"

"You're seriously asking?"

His body shakes with a low chuckle, an unsettling sound that seems to vibrate in the walls around us.

"Frisk him," he orders two men who step forward from the shadows. They're big, broad, and silent, the kind of men whose names you never need to know because they only serve one purpose.

"No need," I say, keeping my movements deliberate as I pull my piece from its holster. The weight of the gun in my hand is both reassuring and regretful—I'd never walk into a place like this unarmed under normal circumstances. But tonight isn't normal. I set it carefully on a maple wood accent table to my right. Its polished surface gleams under the dim overhead light, a sharp contrast to the peeling wall-paper and scuffed floorboards.

Psycho stares me down, his grin unwavering. I hold his gaze, unflinching. Finally, he snorts.

"I'll go see if El Jefe has time for you."

I exhale slowly as he disappears down a hallway. This needs to go smoothly, but nothing is ever easy when you're dealing with men who've spent their entire lives learning to trust no one.

When Mateo finally enters, he does so with the force of a storm. Short but solidly built, his presence fills the room like a thunderclap. His heavy boots thud against the floor, each step deliberate, each movement speaking of power barely restrained. He looks like a man born to fight, his body a map of scars and muscle that tells a story of battles won and lost.

"Middleton," he says, his voice low and gravelly.

"Mateo," I return evenly.

"We didn't have a meeting on the books, and this isn't your local stomping grounds. What brings you here? Must be serious as fuck."

"I'm calling in my favor," I say, getting right to the point.

Mateo raises an eyebrow, his expression unreadable. In this business, favors are worth more than gold—currency that can buy you anything from loyalty to a second chance at life. A flicker of understanding passes over his face.

"What is it?"

I lean forward slightly, lowering my voice. "I received several anonymous texts. Someone's watching me. Threatening me to stay away from my fiancée."

Mateo leans back against the wall, crossing his thick arms over his chest. His brow furrows, but his eyes remain sharp and calculating.

"Okay," he says slowly. "What's that got to do with Blood Nation? We don't threaten people over the phone."

"I know it isn't you," I say. "But I know who it is."

"Fabre." His lip curls in distaste, the name landing like a curse between us.

"Exactly. He's making a move in L.A., Mateo. Think about it. If I'm out of the way, he can pull all the strings he wants unchecked, turning this city into his playground. By the end of the year, he'll have everyone at each other's throats, which is exactly what he wants—chaos."

Mateo's jaw tightens, his expression hardening. He doesn't like where this is going. "This sounds like a *you* problem, vato."

"Then why did I just clean up a dead member of your organization tonight?"

Mateo stiffens, his dark eyes narrowing. "What the fuck did you just say?"

"A Blood Nation member," I repeat, my tone measured. "Dead. At The Shaded Lamp."

His eyes dart to the side, his mind racing. "Who?"

"I don't know his name, but my team saw his ink. He's definitely one of yours."

He mutters something in Spanish, his words sharp and clipped. "Who the hell would be all the way over at The Shaded Lamp?" He looks at me again, suspicion and anger flickering across his face. "Why didn't you call me right away?"

"You weren't my client, Mateo. The client who hired me wanted the body gone, and that's the service we provided. I'm only telling you now because it's odd—a Blood Nation member, dead in East Rider territory, and no one saw anything. This has Fabre's fingerprints written all over it."

Mateo rubs his jaw, his movements tense. "What do you want from me, Middleton?"

"Fabre's fucking with me tonight," I say bluntly. "And yes, my fiancée is involved."

"He knows she's your weakness."

"Yes, it's no secret I'd burn down this entire city for her. I'm just trying my damndest not to have to."

Mateo studies me for a long moment, his eyes unreadable. Then he nods. "We all have our Achilles heels, vato."

"And it usually involves family, doesn't it?" I remind him of why he owes me a favor in the first place, my voice steady.

"Verdadero," he mutters what I think is the word truth in Spanish. "What's the favor?"

I meet his gaze, unflinching. "Fabre thinks he's untouchable. I suggest we use your manpower and my resources to prove him wrong. We put him down like the dog he is."

I glance at my Rolex. Time is slipping away. "Your job starts immediately. I need to get to the hospital to see my child born. You need to make sure I get there in one piece."

Mateo smirks, but there's steel behind it. "With your luck, that sounds like a tall order."

"I don't believe in luck," I reply. "And neither should you."

Mateo puts me in the back seat of a black SUV flanked by two of his "most trusted" soldiers. Their trustworthiness doesn't inspire much confidence—they're stoic and silent, their eyes sharp as they scan the streets, hands never far from their concealed weapons. Every pothole we hit rattles my nerves, and I grip my phone like a lifeline. Vulnerability isn't something I wear well, and tonight it feels like a second skin I can't peel off.

As we drive through the darkened streets of East L.A., I tap out a quick text to Christian.

> Me: On my way. Keep your head on a
> swivel.

The last thing I need is for him to be caught off guard. My screen lights up with texts from Lena, rapid-fire messages asking where I am. At least I know Christian hasn't told her much yet, though that won't last long. I reply to her as well, keeping it brief.

> Me: Almost there.

The hospital looms ahead, its fluorescent lights glaring against the night sky. The soldiers don't say a word as they pull up to the emergency room entrance, but I feel their eyes on me as I step out. I glance back once—they give me a curt nod, then drive off into the shadows. Mateo keeps his promises, at least for now.

The moment I walk inside, the sterile smell of antiseptic mixed with the faint aroma of stale coffee hits me. The hum of the ER surrounds me—phones ringing, nurses calling out patient names, the shuffle of hurried feet against linoleum floors. But I don't see any of it because Lena spots me, and her scream cuts through the chaos.

"Hunter!"

She launches herself at me like a bullet train, crashing into my chest with enough force to knock the wind out of me. Her arms wrap around my waist, clutching me like I'm a lifeline, and I hold her just as tightly. For a moment, the world narrows to this embrace, a shared assurance that, despite everything, we're here, and we're okay.

"Is she all right?" I ask, my voice hoarse.

Christian appears beside us, his hand landing on my shoulder—a rare gesture that catches me off guard. His usual stoic expression cracks ever so slightly, betraying the stress he's been under.

"Lars is with her," he says. "I'll tell the nurses that you're here."

My blood turns to ice at his words. Something about his tone, about the fact that *Lars* is with Megan, sends a shiver down my spine.

"Is she dead?" I blurt, the one question I've been dreading to ask since I got that first frantic text.

"Dead?" Lena repeats, her face pale with shock. "No, of course not. Go see her!"

I don't wait for more. My legs carry me down the hallway on autopilot, my heart pounding louder with every step. I push open the door to her room, bracing myself for the worst.

Megan lies on her back, her legs propped up at a ninety-degree angle with pillows. She looks exhausted, her rich skin tone sallow but alive, her hands clasped tightly with Lars's. His head droops like he's seconds away from passing out himself.

Our eyes meet the moment she sees me, and relief floods through me like a tidal wave. She's here. She's alive. She's safe.

"Hunter," she whispers, her voice fragile but filled with more emotion than I've ever heard from her before.

"I'm sorry I'm late," I say, crossing the room in three strides.

Lars lifts his head, his expression softening with a look of palpable relief.

"Thank you, Lars," I say earnestly.

He stands, stretching his arms. "I'll be right outside."

The look I give him is sharp, a silent warning I've given him a dozen times before. *Don't let your guard down.* He nods and steps out without another word. I know he'll stay by the door like a sentry, ready to act if anything—or anyone —threatens her.

Before I can say anything else, my lips cover Megan's in a possessive kiss I'm not sure which one of us needs more.

Afterward, I lay my hand on Megan's swollen belly. Her warmth grounds me, but the sight of her hooked up to a monitor twists something deep in my gut.

"Are you okay?"

"I am now." She smiles.

"No, but really."

"They've given me an epidural," she explains, her voice steady but tired. "For the pain. They're keeping an eye on me because I was bleeding earlier."

"Bleeding?" My voice rises, my chest tightening.

"It was frightening," she admits, "but the doctor said it wasn't dangerous."

"And the baby?"

"Your future little badass wants to join us tonight," she says with a small smile. "But I'm not dilated enough to start pushing yet."

"So I didn't miss anything?"

Her smile softens into something more intimate, more profound. "No. You're right on time."

The tenderness of her words barely has time to sink in before her face contorts with discomfort. I'm at her side in an instant, leaning over her, searching for a way to help. I desperately want to take her pain away, but in this circumstance, I detest how helpless I am.

"I thought you were on pain meds," I say, brushing a strand of damp hair from her forehead. Her curls have been styled into two long braids with a middle part, making her appear even younger than she is.

"It's not pain exactly," she says through gritted teeth. "More like pressure."

"I'll get the doctor."

Her hand shoots out, grabbing mine. "No, don't leave!"

"I won't." I press a kiss to her forehead, guilt gnawing at me for not being here sooner. "Where's the nurse's button?"

She presses it herself, grimacing as another contraction takes hold. Minutes later, a nurse enters, her dark blue scrubs wrinkled but her demeanor calm and professional.

"You're coming along nicely," she says after a quick check.

"And the earlier bleeding?" I demand, my voice sharper than intended.

The nurse hesitates, glancing at Megan for what feels like permission to speak to me.

"He's my fiancé," Megan assures her.

"It was just a bloody show, which is perfectly normal," the nurse explains. "Her body is preparing for delivery."

The words ease some of the tension coiled in my chest, but not all. After she leaves, I pull up a chair and sit as close to Megan as possible.

"Turn on your side if you can," I tell her. "I'll massage your back."

"Get under the gown," she orders, a spark of humor lighting her tired eyes.

"Are you trying to seduce me in the middle of labor?" I tease, earning a weak chuckle.

But her laughter fades as another contraction grips her, and I hold her hand tightly, helpless but determined to be here for her.

A text lights up my phone.

Mateo: Assholes watching you at the hospital have been eliminated. Enjoy the night, vato.

Relief floods through me, though I quickly pocket the phone before Megan notices.

"Hunter?" Her voice pulls me back.

"Yeah, babe?"

"Can you get Mary? I think my water just broke."

Chapter 30

The Wrong One

HUNTER

A brief flash of artificial light cuts through the dim hospital room, casting fleeting shadows across the walls. I glance down, making sure the glow from my phone doesn't disturb the two most important people in my life. Megan lies on the hospital bed, her breathing slow and steady as she sleeps, her body still recovering from the ordeal of childbirth. Cradled in the crook of her arm, our son is swaddled in a soft blue and white blanket, his tiny chest rising and falling in perfect rhythm with hers.

My chest tightens as I watch them, the weight of gratitude nearly overwhelming. They're here. Safe. Mine.

I pick up my phone, silencing the screen quickly. Megan stirs slightly but doesn't wake. She deserves this rest—God knows she's earned it.

We chose not to find out the baby's sex, wanting to be surprised when he arrived. The look on Megan's face when the doctor announced, *"It's a boy!"* was something I'll never forget. It was as if she thought giving me a son was the greatest gift she could ever offer as if that mattered more than the fact that she and the baby were alive and healthy.

Now, don't get me wrong—I'm over the moon to have a son. A *son*. The word feels strange on my tongue, like something precious I'm afraid to mishandle. And he's beautiful, with a head full of lush dark hair, a button nose, and long legs that seem to promise he'll outgrow me one day. His skin is the perfect creamy blend of Megan's gorgeous brown complexion and my fairer tone.

When the nurse placed him in my arms after Megan held him first, I felt something powerful explode in my chest, shooting straight to my eyes and blurring my vision.

The memory still hits me like a freight train. I've never felt anything like it.

The phone buzzes in my hand, pulling me from my thoughts.

"What?" I whisper, assuming it's Christian or Vaughn checking in.

"Congratulations," comes a raspy voice on the other end, thick with a sneer. My stomach drops, ice shooting through my veins. I know that voice.

Fabre.

I stand immediately, careful not to make a sound as I slip out of the room. The hospital hallway is quiet except for the occasional beep of a monitor and the low murmur of voices from the nurses' station. Lars isn't at his usual post outside the door—he mentioned grabbing food from the cafeteria. Christian, Vaughn, and Lena are all at home, resting. I've shut down the Blue Whiskey for the first time since opening it, just to carve out a few days to bask in this fleeting love bubble with Megan and our son.

But of course, the bubble never lasts.

"This is starting to get creepy," I say, my tone dripping with sarcasm as I press the phone to my ear.

"Creepy?" Fabre's laugh is like nails on a chalkboard.

"I'm starting to think you're obsessed with me. Unfortunately, I'm already spoken for."

"You think you're untouchable, don't you, Middleton?" he snarls.

"I think you're definitely dying to touch me," I reply coolly, though every muscle in my body is coiled with tension.

The smugness in his voice vanishes, replaced by venom. "I'm coming for your city."

"It's not mine to take."

"You're in my way," he continues with his warnings. "But not for long."

"Is that a threat?"

"You've seen a bit of what I can do," he snarls. "How far my reach stretches. I'm going to take your city, your fiancée, and your goddamn life."

My jaw tightens, and my voice drops, the calm tone masking the storm raging beneath. "Listen to me carefully, Fabre. I get threatened every day by half-ass gangsters like you. And I get why you want L.A.—it's a business move. But what you *will not do* is threaten my woman. Megan is mine. Mine to love. Mine to protect. Mine to kill for and mine to die for. For some ridiculous reason that only you understand, you've decided to make this personal, and if there's one thing you should know about me, it's that I handle personal shit better than anyone."

Inside, I'm seething. My entire world is just a few feet away, blissfully unaware of the chaos that threatens to spill into their lives. And they should remain unaware—because it's *my job* to make sure they never have to carry the weight of my world.

Megan should only have to worry about simple things such as breastfeeding our son or painting her next masterpiece. My son should grow up in warmth and love, never knowing a damn thing about this petty gangster shit.

Fabre's laugh cuts through the silence, grating and mocking. "Tough words for a man I could've taken out a million times today. I've had eyes on you and everyone you care about all week."

His words twist in my gut, but I don't falter. "And who's watching Naomi?" I ask darkly.

The silence on the other end is immediate and suffocating.

"Leave Naomi out of this," he finally says, his tone faltering.

"That's not how this works," I snap, my voice hardening. "You threaten what's mine, I threaten what's yours."

"You know I could've hurt Megan a dozen times already," he says, trying to regain control.

"And yet you did hurt her," I growl. "You kidnapped her."

"She's back with you safe and sound," he replies dismissively.

"She's home now, not because of you—but because she got away. Did you really think I'd let that slide? That I'd forget? I'm going to fucking destroy you, Fabre. You, and every single person in that backwater town you call home. You fucked with the wrong one."

I end the call without waiting for his reply, my hand trembling with rage. But beneath the fury, there's relief. The lines have been drawn. No more games, no more passive threats.

This is war.

I glance back at the hospital room door. Inside, my family sleeps peacefully, unaware of the storm brewing just outside their sanctuary. I take a deep breath, forcing the tension to drain from my shoulders. For them, I'll be the shield that never breaks.

Because no one touches what's mine.

In fact, no one should even consider it.

Chapter 31

I Can't Wait

MEGAN

There are countless advantages to being engaged to one of the wealthiest men I've ever met, and at the top of the list right now are these *damn sheets*. Soft as clouds, cool against my skin, they're a luxury I never knew I needed. Wrapped in their embrace, it feels like the world outside doesn't exist—just me, Hunter, and the gentle quiet of the early morning.

If it weren't for our precious baby boy, I'm not sure we'd ever leave this bed. But life has changed in the best way possible. Every few hours, I'm up to feed him, change him, and, of course, perform the obligatory millionth check to make sure he's still breathing. Motherhood has turned me into someone I barely recognize, but I can't say I mind.

"Don't move," Hunter murmurs from his side of the bed, his voice low and commanding as his strong arm snakes across my waist, pulling me close. His touch is firm yet tender, sending a shiver down my spine.

"Wait," I giggle, though the sound is breathless. "I have to check on the baby first."

"Wait?" His voice drops another octave, gravelly and full of desire. "I've been waiting for weeks." He nuzzles into the crook of my neck, his stubble grazing my skin, leaving goosebumps in its wake.

"And you can wait at least another hour," I tease, though I'm already melting under his touch.

"I can't wait another *fucking second*," he growls, his lips brushing against the sensitive spot just below my ear.

"You're impossible," I laugh, squirming slightly.

"There's a monitor in every room of this house," he argues, his tone a mix of logic and lust. "I can see him from here, and so can you. Hunter Middleton, the second, is fast asleep, dreaming about whatever it is angels dream."

I glance at the monitor on the dresser, the tiny screen showing Deuce's peaceful form, his chest rising and falling in a perfect rhythm. He's fine—more than fine, really. He's perfect.

It's been six weeks since I gave birth, and while my love for our son is a tidal wave of emotions I never knew I was capable of, there's another kind of love I've been missing. The fiery, consuming connection Hunter and I share has been simmering on the back burner, waiting for this moment. And God, do I want him.

But he knows me too well. As his hand slides beneath my oversized sleep shirt, his fingers trailing gently along my skin, I remember that this is love, too—urgent, raw, and powerful.

"Mmmm, that feels good," I whisper, my voice betraying how much I've missed his touch.

"You're still in your head," he says, his tone firm and knowing.

"I'm not," I lie, though I can't help but think about the possibility of breast milk ruining the moment. Not exactly sexy.

"Get out of your head and focus on this," he orders, his words laced with authority that sends a thrill straight to my core.

I huff playfully, but he's right. Hunter's been lost in his own thoughts for weeks, pacing the apartment with Deuce in his arms, murmuring words I can never quite hear. I know he's worried—about us, about the city, about the future. But right now, he's fully present, and I want to be, too.

"I'm here," I say softly, trailing my hand down the center of his broad chest, my fingers grazing the hard lines of muscle beneath.

His body is a masterpiece, but it's not just his strength that captivates me—it's the vulnerability he reserves only for me. And as my hand ventures lower, finding him hard and ready, I realize how much I've been craving this connection.

"I need you," I admit, my voice thick with longing.

"And I need you," he replies, his words like a promise.

When his hand finds me, stroking with expert precision, I feel a fire ignite deep within me. His lips capture mine, part passion, part reverence, and I lose myself in the moment.

"I think you're wetter than you've ever been for me," he murmurs against my lips, his voice tinged with wonder.

"I told you," I gasp. "I need you more than I ever have."

For a fleeting second, I worry about the moment he'll finally be inside me—will it hurt after so much time? But the worry vanishes the instant he enters me. I feel full, deliciously full, and my body remembers him like no time has passed.

"Fuck, you feel good," he groans, his hips meeting mine with a rhythm that feels like coming home.

"Let me ride," I say, my voice trembling with desire.

He grins, his smile wicked and full of hunger. "Ride me, baby."

It takes a moment to lower myself completely, but once I do, it's like I've unlocked something primal. I move with abandon, hard and fast, letting weeks of pent-up longing pour into every motion.

"Shit," he grunts, gripping my hips tightly. "Slow down, baby. I'm going to come."

I lean down, pressing a kiss to his lips, my grin teasing. "Slower for the old man?"

His laugh is dark and full of promise. "Careful, Miss Taylor. That kind of talk will get you a sore pussy *and* ass."

"Promises, promises," I retort, turning into a reverse cowgirl position. The angle gives me control, and I revel in it, grinding low and slow as I chase my release.

"*Yess*," he hisses, his hands finding the curve of my back, pressing me forward to deepen the connection. "That feels so fucking good."

The tension coils tighter with every movement, and when he grabs my hips and thrusts up into me, I lose myself entirely.

"Did you miss this dick?" he growls, his voice raw.

"Yes," I cry out as the waves of my orgasm crash over me. "Yes!"

As his own release follows, I collapse onto his chest, both of us slick with sweat and grinning like fools.

"I love you, baby," he murmurs, pressing a kiss to my hair.

"I love you more," I reply, my heart full and my body sated. "Now that was worth the wait, wasn't it, Mr. Middleton?"

"I'm not sure," he teases.

"Wait, what?"

"I think I need more convincing." He playfully slaps one of my ass cheeks.

I glance at the monitor. Deuce is still sound asleep. And honestly, even if he wasn't, I don't think I could deny this man.

Climbing back on top of him, this time face to face, I meet his smoldering grey eyes with a playful smile. "Let me try again. I can be very convincing."

Hunter's rare, infectious smile spreads across his face. It's a look he rarely gives anyone, and I feel special that he often shares it with me.

"Good answer."

Chapter 32

New Blood In The Club

HUNTER

"Have a seat," I offer.

It's been several months since the attempt on my life and the birth of my son, and all has been quiet with Fabre and his obvious attempt to make a power move in Los Angeles. While this moment of tranquility has my team a little on edge, I'm not fazed. This thing with Fabre is not a game of checkers but of chess. He comes off as this brash, overweight, uncouth slob, but really, the fucker is incredibly smart and deliberately patient. All this means is that I have more time to plan my offense instead of always playing defense against him. In the meantime, though, I have other little fires to put out in my life, starting with my sister.

"When your voice gets deep like that, I know I'm in a world of trouble," Lena says with a giggle. I love that little laugh of hers and how our relationship has grown from a strained to a genuine sibling connection. It feels good to be the big brother—the role I was robbed of for much of Lena's life.

"You're not in any trouble."

"Problem with the food then?"

"From what I hear, the food is good as always."

"I mean, it's pretty hard to mess up a buffalo chicken wing." She rolls her eyes in aggravation.

"I know you want to try serving something a little more sophisticated, Lena, but we cater to a certain crowd here. Plus, the real money is at the bar, and that's where I want our focus."

"I get it." She shrugs her shoulders. "But not all of your patrons want hot wings and truffle fries. Hell, you don't even eat the food we serve."

"That's because I've got to watch my figure," I jest. "I can't let some young boy swoop in and take my wife away."

"As if that would ever happen," Lena snorts, and I smile at how easily my plan is falling into place. I lean back in my chair and act as if I'm contemplating her thoughts on the Blue Whiskey's menu.

"Now that you mention it, it does seem kind of silly that we don't serve some alternative dishes, maybe for a less salty palate."

Her face illuminates with hope. "Right, that's exactly what I mean. I've been playing around with a few dishes at home that I think would be a perfect fit. A tomato-based shrimp dish, a garlicky pasta dish, and a more sophisticated kind of beef slider made with short ribs."

"Garlic pasta?"

"Yeah, what about it?"

"Garlic breath at a club?"

"A few glasses of wine from the bar is the best solution for counteracting garlic breath. You'll sell more drinks, especially from the women. It's actually a brilliant idea if I do say so myself."

"A varied menu would mean more work, though. The kitchen is already understaffed."

"That's because anyone half-decent is probably too afraid to work here. Someone is always getting stabbed, or shot at, or tossed through a glass table." She turns the side of her mouth up.

"Hmmm." I pretend to scroll through the contacts on my phone. "I may have someone who could help us out."

"Gage already offered, but–"

"No, Gage needs to stay exactly where he is. I like him at the front of the club keeping an eye on things."

"Then who?"

"His name is Oliver, and I've known him for a few years. I'm not sure why I didn't think of him when Megan wanted to hire some more people for the kitchen before, but he actually might be a good fit."

Lena studies me suspiciously for a moment, and I'm afraid that she's getting to know me a little too well and will see right through my deception.

"You just happen to have a friend in your rolodex who has experience?" she questions.

"The use of the term friend might be a stretch, but yes, he ran a kitchen for a few years in Chinatown."

"Chinatown? He sounds overqualified." Her arms crossed. Yeah, she definitely suspects this isn't exactly what I'm saying it is, but the great thing about being the big brother is that she's probably not going to challenge me on it —at least, that's what I'm hoping.

"I think he may be interested in a less hectic situation. We might be just what he needs."

"If he runs the kitchen, then what am I going to do?"

"He wouldn't take your place, Lena. You're my sister, and you'll always run the kitchen of the Blue Whiskey if that's your choice. I'd just hire him to help you put more systems in place so that you can offer the old and new menu items."

"So I could work on the new dishes while he handles other stuff?"

Damn, I'm good.

"Exactly."

Lena takes a spin in the chair she's sitting in, reminding me of her youth and also that I'm doing the right thing.

"I'll think about it," she tells me, knowing full well that the decision has already been made.

"How about this? He'll come by tomorrow, you feel him out, and then you tell me what you think."

"I can make the final call?"

Lena raises an eyebrow.

"Of course."

"Fine."

I failed to mention to Lena that I invited Oliver and some of his friends to the club as my special guests at Table 21 *tonight*. That would have made my agenda of distracting her attention from Christian too obvious. It's rare that I give anyone with who I don't have direct business ties carte blanche in my club, but this is just as important as any negotiation I've ever conducted. Plus, Christian has other plans tonight and won't be coming by the club.

But Megan is here, dammit.

Climbing up the steps toward my office.

And she looks fucking gorgeous.

She's wearing one of my favorite red dresses that tastefully skims her body, ends right above her knees, and flatters her rich skin tone. She looks even better in the dress than she used to because her body has several more lush curves than it did due to carrying our son, and those curves are in all the right places.

Fuck me.

Since the doctor has given us the all-clear, she's been very determined to seduce the hell out of me at every turn, and I can see that tonight she's on a mission. I'm a lucky motherfucker, but tonight is just bad timing.

"Hey, beautiful."

"Hey, yourself, Mr. Middleton."

"Where's Deuce?"

"Home with the baby nurse." She cocks her head to the side. "Obviously."

"Right, that was silly of me to ask."

She ignores my blunder and spins around on one of her heels, showcasing how good she looks.

"You like?"

"I love."

A staff member walks by my open office door, taking a peep inside, admiring Megan's silhouette. Prettier than any picture she's ever drawn.

"Close the door," I tell her. "Then bring your pretty ass over here."

She smirks. "Yes, sir."

Megan walks seductively over to the door, carefully locking it as my dick hardens beneath my zipper. Her ass has a special jiggle that speaks to my soul as if it's only talking to me.

Baiting me.

Driving me to a delicious madness.

Does she not have any underwear on?

I covertly check the time and am expecting Oliver to arrive in about ten minutes. Shit. I had plans to show him around personally, then accidentally bump into Lena (on purpose), but all that's just been shot to hell when Megan straddles my lap, and I discover, just as I'd hoped, she's pantiless, wet and ready for me to give her the fuck of her life.

Chapter 33

The One In Blue

LENA

"Ouch!" The sharp sting of hot oil on my skin snaps me out of my thoughts as I burn the side of my palm on the fryer. I mutter a curse under my breath, quickly moving to the sink to run cold water over the tender spot. The stream feels like tiny needles against the burn, but I welcome the sensation—anything to keep me grounded.

My mind's been buzzing ever since my conversation with Hunter. The idea of revamping the menu at Blue Whiskey is exhilarating, a chance to prove myself and bring something fresh to the table. This place is no Zagat-rated steakhouse, sure, but I know I can do better than wings and fries.

"You alright?" Gage's voice cuts through my thoughts.

"Yeah," I say, waving him off as I inspect my reddened palm. "Just not paying attention. What's up?"

"Some dude at Table 21 has questions about the food."

"Questions?" My tone drips with irritation as I dry my hand.

"I know," he says, holding up his hands defensively. "But it's Table 21."

I frown. "So? This isn't The Four Seasons. I don't personally answer questions about wings."

"You're becoming a real snob, you know that?"

"Whatever," I mutter, turning back to the fryer. "Isn't dealing with customers your job? Especially since Megan's on extended maternity leave?"

"Do you want to be the one to tell your brother you couldn't be bothered with customer service in his club?"

I glare at him, but Gage stands firm, his smirk almost daring me to argue.

"Fine," I huff, untying my apron. "But you owe me."

"Sure thing, chef," he says with a wink.

As I step into the main room, the steady hum of conversation and clinking glasses fills the air. The dim, moody lighting casts a warm glow over the sleek tables and dark wood accents, a far cry from the chaos of the kitchen. Gage gestures toward Table 21, where two men sit surrounded by plates of food and imported beer.

"The one in blue," he says, pointing subtly.

I let out a slow breath, still cradling my burned hand in a tea towel. If I'm going to turn Blue Whiskey into something better, I have to learn to deal with situations like this. Plastering on a professional smile, I approach the table.

"Hello, I'm Lena, the chef here," I say, my voice polite but firm.

The man in the ink-blue jacket turns his head, and my breath catches. He's... striking. Dark hair, almond-shaped eyes, and creamy tan skin that suggests a mixed heritage—maybe Asian and Latino, or Black? His broad shoulders and sharp jawline only add to the effect, and for a moment, I'm speechless.

"Lena," he repeats, his voice rich and smooth.

I clear my throat, trying to regain my composure. "Yes. You had a question about the food?"

"Not a question," he says, his tone casual but edged with arrogance. "A comment."

The man beside him snickers, clearly anticipating what's coming next.

"Oh?"

"Our meal tastes like we're paying you for a heart attack."

My smile falters. "Excuse me?"

"It's ridiculously salty."

His words land like a slap, and suddenly, he's not striking—he's infuriating.

"You brought me out here to tell me that parmesan wings and truffle fries from a nightclub are salty?"

"I thought you should know."

"Order something else."

"I would," he says with a smirk, "but I'm afraid for my life."

His friend snorts, barely containing his laughter.

"Sorry to hear you don't like the cuisine," I say, my tone icy. "Why don't you and your friend go somewhere else?"

"Is that how you talk to your customers?"

"Just the rude ones."

"You don't take criticism well, do you?" he asks, a dimple appearing as his smirk deepens.

I resist the urge to slap him. "I'll tell the manager to comp your check."

Turning on my heel, I make a beeline for the kitchen, my heart pounding. Criticism has always been my weak spot, and his smug delivery hits a nerve. But as I walk away, Hunter steps into my path.

"Lena," he says, gesturing toward the table. "I see you've met Oliver."

I whip around, my eyes narrowing. "What do you mean, *met Oliver?* How do you know these jerks?"

"Hey," the second guy protests, raising his hands. "I'm innocent. He's the jerk."

"This is Oliver," Hunter says, his tone patient. "The guy I was telling you about."

My stomach drops. *"You're* Oliver?"

Oliver stands, and my brain short-circuits. He's tall—ridiculously tall—and his tailored jacket only emphasizes his lean, muscular frame. He looks like he stepped out of a high-end fashion ad, rugged and polished all at once.

"I am," he says, his voice dropping an octave.

Focus, Lena.

He's a dick.

"You insult my food and think you're going to help me run my kitchen?" I snap.

"It wasn't an insult," he says, his cool arrogance unshaken. "Just an observation."

I turn to Hunter, lowering my voice. "You said it's up to me."

"It is," he says gently. "But you've known Oliver for five minutes. You can't make a decision yet. Let him come back tomorrow, show him around the kitchen, and then decide."

"This is *not* what I agreed to," I hiss.

"He's got the experience we talked about."

"How? He can't be that much older than me."

Oliver steps closer, his presence commanding. "I have a baby face," he says with a faint smirk. "But I know my way around a kitchen. It's the family business."

"Then why don't you go back and work for your family?"

"Lena," Hunter warns, his tone sharp.

Oliver raises his hands in mock surrender. "Listen, I think we got off on the wrong foot. I'm a straight shooter, and sometimes that comes off as... overbearing."

"You think?"

"Let's try again tomorrow," he says, extending a hand. "If you still hate me, I'll move on. No hard feelings."

Before I can respond, my smartwatch vibrates with a call from Christian. It's the perfect escape.

"I'll give you an hour tomorrow," I say, ignoring Hunter's disapproving look as I answer the call.

"Hey, Christian..."

Chapter 34

Did You Say Usurp?

MEGAN

"So then what happened?" I ask, cradling Deuce on the floor of the living room as I watch his tiny hands reach for my hair. His smile lights up my whole world, making it hard to focus entirely on Lena's complaints, but I do my best.

Lena exhales dramatically from the couch, the picture of exasperation. "I showed him around the kitchen and then the club, like Hunter made me."

"And?"

"And what?" she snaps, her tone defensive—too defensive.

"And why are you so angry about it?"

"I told you. He's forcing this guy into *my* space."

"To help you at the club," I counter, holding back a smile. "So you can be more creative with the menu. Isn't that what you wanted?"

"Oh, so you're in on it, too?"

Deuce gurgles happily, his bright eyes locking on mine

as I lean down to pepper kisses across his chubby cheeks. The softness of his skin, the pure innocence of his laughter —it's impossible to feel anything but joy when he's in my arms.

"I'm not in on anything, Lena," I say, laughing softly as I nuzzle my son. "I just know your brother. All he ever wants to do is make the people he loves happy. And like it or not, that includes you."

"What he's doing," she says, crossing her arms like a petulant teenager, "is making me sorry I even brought up extending the menu in the first place."

"Lena..."

"What?"

"What is it about this guy that's got you so... *bothered?*" My voice is gentle, teasing even, but her reaction is telling. She bristles, her lips pressing into a thin line, as if I've hit a nerve.

Hunter would never admit it to me, but I'd bet good money he's hired this Oliver guy not just for the club but as a distraction to keep Lena away from Christian. And knowing my husband, the guy is probably hot as hell. If he's going to do something, he's not going to half-ass it.

"You should understand what I'm dealing with. I've just finally started to gain some respect from the staff," Lena says, her frustration spilling out in a rush. "And now Hunter brings in some 'master chef' to waltz in and usurp my power."

"*Usurp your power?*" I chuckle. "Have you been reading that fantasy romance book of yours again?"

"Whatever, Megan."

"What's this guy's name again?"

"As if you don't know."

"Seriously, Lena, Hunter hasn't mentioned anything about him to me."

She huffs. "His name is Oliver. And he's... well, he seems very sure of himself. I think someone in his family owns a restaurant in Chinatown. So yeah, he's got experience running a busy kitchen."

"That's a good thing, right? He could be helpful."

"Running the Blue Whiskey kitchen is *my* job. I may not have gotten the position the old-fashioned way, but I've worked my ass off since to prove myself. I just don't want this Oliver guy overstepping."

I pick up Deuce, pressing his tiny body to my chest as I rub his back. The little burp he lets out makes me grin. "Listen, Lena. Neither of us are brain surgeons, but we're both more than qualified to do our jobs. And you know as well as I do that Hunter would never let anyone overstep *you* at the club."

She leans back against the couch, her irritation softening slightly. "I just feel blindsided, you know? One minute I mention wanting to change the menu, and the next thing I know, Hunter's already lined up some guy like he's been planning this for weeks."

I could tell her what I suspect about Hunter's motives, but that would only make her feel manipulated. And besides, I have a hunch there's more to her feelings than she's letting on.

"So, you really don't like this Oliver dude?"

"I wouldn't say that," she admits, her voice softer now. "It's just... a feeling I have about him."

"A feeling?"

"Yeah, a feeling. Now give me the baby."

"Aren't you cooking us dinner?"

"It's in the oven already. Now hand him over."

I pass Deuce to her, watching as she makes silly zerbert noises on his belly. His giggles fill the room, light and infectious.

"Tell me more about him," I prod.

"I don't know anything more than what I told you," she says, though her tone suggests otherwise.

"What does he look like?"

"Why does that matter?"

"I'm just curious. Trying to put a face to the name."

She rolls her eyes but humors me. "Tall. Sort of muscular. Black hair, almond-shaped dark eyes, tan skin. And, um, he has a dimple, too."

"That's... very specific," I smirk. "I could probably pick him out of a lineup with that description."

"You *asked* what he looked like!"

"And you definitely told me," I chuckle.

"What are you trying to say, Megan?"

She hands Deuce back to me, her mood shifting from defensive to annoyed. But I've danced around this long enough—it's time to address the elephant in the room.

"I just think you might be protesting more than the occasion calls for because... maybe you're attracted to him?"

"I'm *not* attracted to that smug asshole. And even if I was, why would that bother me?"

She's going to make me say it.

"Because," I say, standing with Deuce and pacing the room to calm his fussing, "you feel like it would betray the feelings you're already having for someone else."

"Feelings?" she repeats, her voice rising slightly.

"Can you grab a bottle from the fridge and warm it for me?" I ask, ignoring her question as I focus on Deuce. "I think he's hungry."

She does as I ask, but the look on her face tells me she's

still waiting for an answer. "What are you talking about, Megan?"

"Lena..."

"What?"

I take a deep breath, rocking Deuce gently in my arms. "Can we stop pretending? You have feelings for Christian. Maybe that's why you feel guilty that someone else caught your attention."

"What? No! Christian is my brother's friend."

"I know who he is, Lena."

"It's not like that," she says, her voice unsteady. "He's just... someone who's been there for me. While you and Hunter were dealing with all your... drama."

Her words hit me like a slap, and I pause mid-step. Have Hunter and I been so wrapped up in our own chaos that we missed what Lena's been going through? Has Christian become her lifeline in our absence?

"No, you're right," I say softly. "There's been a lot of drama, and too much scary shit has happened. Hunter sent Christian to watch over you because he trusts him. It makes sense that you'd start to develop feelings for someone who's been your rock. He's attractive, single, and you've spent a lot of time together."

She grabs the bottle from the warmer, handing it to me with a look of disbelief.

"Christian would never look at me like that," she says, her voice barely above a whisper.

"Why not?"

"He's older. He has an actual career. And, more importantly, he's my brother's best friend. There's no way he'd ever cross that line."

"Are you sure about that?" I ask, raising an eyebrow.

"Yes!"

"Well," I say, smirking as Deuce calms down in my arms, "if Christian *is* interested, it sounds like he might have some competition now. Oliver sounds pretty hot."

Lena stares at me, her cheeks flushing as she struggles to find a retort.

I settle into the chaise, feeding Deuce as his tiny hand rests on mine. The room falls quiet, save for the soft sound of him drinking, but the unspoken words between Lena and me linger in the air. She's not ready to admit the truth, but I see it in her eyes: her heart is more conflicted than she'll ever let on.

Maybe Hunter's plan is falling exactly into place, but only time will tell. Something tells me that Christian hasn't heard about Oliver yet.

Chapter 35

Fifteen Minutes

MEGAN

After putting Deuce down for his nap, I step out of the nursery, stretching my sore shoulders as I make my way to the living room. The apartment is quiet, save for the muffled hum of the city beyond the glass windows. I expect to find Lars doing what he always does—standing watch like an immovable sentry. Instead, something in his expression stops me cold. His face, usually a blank mask of stoic disinterest, is drawn tight with something close to concern.

I know that look. I don't like it.

"What's wrong?" I ask, scanning his face.

Lars hesitates, as if debating whether to tell me the truth. That alone makes my stomach knot. I cross my arms, my stance firm. "Tell me," I demand.

He exhales through his nose. "There's someone downstairs to see you."

My heart stutters. For the briefest, most naive moment, I allow myself to hope—*maybe it's Naomi.*

"Your sister," Lars clarifies.

My chest tightens. So Hunter didn't kill my family like I once feared.

My voice is careful when I ask, "Did you tell Hunter?"

"Not yet."

"Don't."

"Megan—"

"I'm not the same person I was the last time I saw her, Lars. I can handle whatever she came here to say."

He eyes me warily, but there's something knowing in his gaze. "I bet she's a different person now, too," he says, a quiet warning in his voice.

I already know what he means. Hunter is a man of vengeance, and my sister's past actions—her betrayal—haven't been forgotten. If she's had a rough time of it, it's because she earned it.

Still, she's my sister.

I weigh my options. There's no way in hell I want Rachel near Deuce. She doesn't even need to know he exists. Which means the only choice is to go downstairs alone. The baby nurse isn't due for another hour, so Lars will have to stay up here with my son.

"You'll have to stay with the baby. I'll go see what she wants."

His frown deepens. "Not a good idea."

"It's not the *best* idea," I concede. "But I'm not an idiot. Hunter has eyes everywhere. I know there's a car stationed outside, probably someone lurking in the damn bushes for all I know. I won't leave the lobby. I'll stay in plain sight."

"I don't like this," Lars mutters, jaw clenched. "My job is to protect you. And that includes reporting anything suspicious to Hunter."

"But she's here," I press. "And I need to see her." My voice softens, just a little. "She's still my sister, Lars."

He scoffs. "Blood isn't everything. It just means you didn't get a choice in the matter growing up. Now you do. I'd choose *not*."

I meet his gaze and say firmly, "This isn't a negotiation. I know you work for Hunter, but I'm marrying him—which means you work for me, too."

The words leave my mouth before I even process them, but I don't regret them. I respect Lars. He's older, wiser, and damn good at his job. But this is my life. My decision.

His expression hardens, but after a long beat, he relents. "Fifteen minutes," he growls. "Then I'm calling my *other* boss."

Ooh, he's pissed.

But I don't care.

I need this closure.

"Deal."

I slip into my room, change into a clean shirt, and make my way to the elevator. As I descend, my pulse pounds in my ears. The moment the doors slide open, a new guy at the front desk gives me a nod and subtly gestures to the far left corner of the lobby.

Rachel stands with her back to me, staring out the floor-to-ceiling windows at the city beyond.

At first glance, she looks... unfamiliar. Like any other young woman lost in thought. But when she turns around, my breath catches.

She's unrecognizable.

Gaunt. Sallow-skinned. Her once-lustrous hair hangs in limp strands around her sunken face. Her clothes are loose, hanging off her body like she's been starving. And for the briefest moment, I mourn for the selfish, reckless girl she used to be—because the person standing before me now is *broken*.

Her eyes flick over me, assessing. "Megan."

"What are you doing here, Rachel?" My voice is sharper than I intend, but I can't help it. I fight the urge to ask when she last had a meal. "What do you want?"

Her lip trembles. "I haven't seen you in a year, and *that's* what you ask me?"

"Rachel, I have a lot on my plate. Your showing up here was unexpected. And frankly, *unwanted*." I level my gaze. "What. Do. You. Want."

Tears slip down her face, but I don't trust them. She's always known how to cry on command.

"I was kidnapped," she whispers. "I don't know where our parents are. And you want me to leave?" Her voice rises, raw and pleading. "I have *nowhere* else to go."

I knew Hunter had something to do with this. But the fact that she doesn't know that? That's a miracle.

"You were kidnapped," I repeat.

"Yes!"

"And you *escaped*?"

"Yes!"

"Well," I say slowly, shifting uncomfortably. "Then you're safe now."

"Megan!"

"What?"

"I need help! I'm your *freakin' sister*!"

I cross my arms. "You've never been a sister to me, Rachel. *Not ever*."

Her eyes flash with something unreadable. "What do you mean? Is this about what happened with your ex?"

I scoff, barely able to believe my ears. "It's *every-*

thing, Rachel. I'm not saying it's all your fault, but you're missing something inside you."

A brain.

A heart.

A soul.

"Something I don't think you can just *learn*."

Her face crumples. "Are you saying I'm a monster?"

I shrug. "You *come* from monsters."

"And so do you!"

I tilt my head. "I remember my mother. She wasn't a monster."

"And *mine* is?"

"The fact that you have to ask that is the problem."

Her shoulders shake as silent sobs wrack her body. For the first time, the tears seem real. Her pain? *Real.*

She swallows hard. "Megan..." Her voice cracks. "I'm sorry."

I slide my hands into my sweatpants pocket, fingers brushing over the cash I grabbed on my way down.

This apology is enough for closure. But not enough for anything more.

I pull out the cash—one hundred and twelve dollars—and press it into her palm. "Use this to get something to eat."

She stares at the bills, then up at me. "Can I stay here for the night?"

"No," I say simply. "But I can give you the name of a shelter."

I scribble down the address of the one Lena told me about—the one that actually helps women get back on their feet.

"A shelter?" Rachel whispers, looking defeated.

"Yes," I say.

She looks at the paper, her fingers trembling. "So this is goodbye, isn't it?"

"Yes." I hold her gaze. "And Rachel—"

She lifts her chin. "Huh?"

"Don't come here again. If Hunter had been home, this would have ended *very* differently. Do you understand what I'm saying?"

She gives me a bitter smile. "You're in love with a psychopath."

I smile back. "No. I'm in love with a *protector*."

Saying the words out loud settles something inside me.

Hunter isn't a monster.

He's what a *man* should be.

Protective.

Loyal.

Loving.

And undeniably, *all mine.*

"Good luck, Rachel."

Then I turn and walk away without looking back with a smile on my face and, more importantly—one in my heart.

Chapter 36

Always Prepared With A Plan B

HUNTER

A year ago, I wouldn't have imagined that I'd be on a date with my fiance and our brand-new baby.

Me, in a committed relationship?

Me, a father?

Neither of those things were ever in the cards for me. But here I am...loving every single minute of it. And truthfully, it feels good not to worry about being shot or shanked at any given moment. Even if this period of peace is just a moment in time, life has taught me that I need to savor every second of it as if it's my last.

"What kind of place is this?" Megan asks, staring around the room with a bright look on her face.

The San Vista House is an upscale, members-only club with modern architecture and moody lighting. Membership is exclusive and expensive. I've been a member for over five years but rarely come. It's the kind of place you come to when you're trying to impress a client or a woman, something I never do. Well, until now.

"You like it?"

"You've never mentioned this place? Is it okay for us to be here with Deuce?"

"I'm a member. It's fine."

"I don't see any other babies around."

"If you come on your own one day on a random Tuesday morning, you'll see quite a few babies, some with their mothers or with their nannies."

"Ah, okay."

"This doesn't really seem to be your style. I bet there's not a lot of Blue Whiskey clientele in here."

"There aren't," I smirk. "Which is exactly why we're here."

"Welcome back, Mr. Middleton," a man in a black suit with a slender white tie greets us.

"Thank you, Daniel, right?"

"You remembered," he smiles. "Yes."

"This is my fiance, Megan, and our son, Deuce."

Daniel peeps into the carriage to take a look, giving a nod of approval, not that either of us needs it. We already know we have the most handsome boy on the planet, thanks to his mama's good looks.

"Pleased to meet you both. I have your private room ready for you all. Please let me know when you're ready for lunch and if you need anything else."

"Thank you, Daniel."

"A room?" Megan asks as we walk toward the elevators.

"We can have lunch up in the suite or down here in the main dining room, your choice." I lean over and give her a kiss on the lips. "Either way, we'll have some private space if we need to change Deuce or put him down for a nap."

"So, is this some sort of hotel for private members?"

"It's a members-only club that has rooms reserved for

long stays upon request." She admires the oversized, ornate chandelier hanging above us. "Do you like it?" I ask, hoping that she does.

"It's definitely nice. So nice that maybe we should've gotten a babysitter?"

"Already on it." I grin, thankful we're both on the same page. I already scheduled the baby nurse to come and allow us some time alone. "Ruby is coming in ninety minutes."

"Hunter." The look of joy on her face as she places a gentle hand on my chest assures me that I did a good thing.

"I know—I'm amazing."

"And modest," she chuckles.

Megan shifts in her seat, her bare shoulder catching the low, golden light of the club's dining room. I don't know what it is about this woman, but even after months of loving her—of touching her, tasting her—she still manages to make me want her like I've never wanted anyone or anything before.

Deuce is upstairs, sound asleep under the watchful eye of Ruby. And for the first time in what feels like forever, Megan and I are alone.

With no threats.

No chaos.

Just us.

"You really went all out, didn't you?" she muses, trailing her fingertips along the rim of her wine glass. "A private suite and"—she gestures to the floor-to-ceiling windows—"a perfect view of the city skyline. If I didn't know better, I'd think you were trying to seduce me. Just like in Paris."

I smirk, leaning back in my chair. "Who says I'm not?"

She raises a playful brow. "You don't have to try so hard, you know."

"That so?"

Megan shifts forward, propping her chin on her palm as she studies me with a mischievous gleam in her eye. "I hate to break it to you, but you had me the moment we walked through the doors of this place. And the fact that you scheduled Ruby to give us time alone tonight only seals the deal. I'm what you call a sure bet, Mr. Middleton."

I reach across the table and hook my fingers around her wrist, tugging her hand into mine. "I love a sure bet."

She laughs, the sound filling the quiet space between us. "I know you do."

The waiter arrives with our entrées—perfectly seared filet mignon for me, a delicate truffle risotto for her. Megan takes one bite and lets out a small, satisfied moan.

I grip my fork a little tighter.

I want inside of her in the worst way.

"Okay," she sighs, eyes fluttering shut for a moment. "You were right, as usual. This place is amazing."

I grin. "Being right wasn't the goal, but I'll take it."

She tilts her head. "Then what was the goal?"

I study her, the way the candlelight catches in her brown eyes, the way her heart-shaped, full lips curve in amusement, the way every little thing about her makes me feel...whole.

"To give you a night where you don't have to think about anything else but us."

Her teasing expression softens, and for a brief moment, she doesn't say anything. Then, she exhales, shaking her head as if I've knocked the wind out of her.

"Damn it, Hunter," she murmurs, setting her fork down

and leaning closer. "You're making it very hard for me to pretend like I'm not completely in love with you."

I smirk. "Then stop pretending."

Her gaze flickers to my mouth, and just like that, the air thickens. We've been here before—this dance of push and pull, teasing and taking. But something about tonight feels different. Maybe it's the privacy. Maybe it's the fact that, for the first time in a long time, we're allowed to just be.

Megan shifts in her seat, her hand tightening around mine. "Are you gonna kiss me or just sit there looking smug?"

I stand, walking around the table to pull her up and against me. "I was thinking of doing a lot more than just kissing you."

She smiles against my lips. "You better be, but how? Our private room is a little occupied right now."

"The great thing about being me is that I always have a Plan B."

"Is that right?" she says seductively.

"Always," I whisper.

I kiss her, slow and deep, my hands slipping around her waist, fingers splaying over her lower back. When I finally pull away, she's breathless, her lips still parted like she wants more.

Hell, I definitely want more.

I brush a strand of hair from her cheek, my voice low. "Marry me."

"Hunter–" Her eyes dance with amusement. "We're already engaged."

"That's not an answer."

She lets out a soft laugh. "What other answer could there be? I've already said yes." She flashes her ring for me to see. "The ring is proof."

"The ring is a promise, but I want you to marry me now," I demand.

"You're impossible."

"I'm determined to make an honest woman out of my baby's mama." I trace slow circles on her lower back, keeping her close. "So, what's stopping you from picking a date?"

Megan pulls back slightly, rolling her eyes. "Oh, I don't know. Maybe the fact that we just had a baby? That I'm exhausted? That I still don't know if you'll survive a day without someone trying to kill you or kidnap me?"

"Survive a day?" I arch a brow. "Trust me, no one's ever going to take you from me again and give me some credit—I haven't been shot, stabbed, or kidnapped in months. That's got to count for something."

She shakes her head, smiling despite herself. "The wild part about that statement is just how true it is."

"So, we're in agreement. Let's set a date."

Megan exhales, clearly trying to play it cool, but I see the hesitation in her eyes. "Hunter, I just—"

I cup her face, my thumb stroking over her cheek. "Do you love me?"

She blinks, caught off guard. "You know I do."

"Then what are we waiting for?" My voice drops, softer now. "I want this, Megan. I want you. I don't want our son growing up the way either of us did. I want him to grow up knowing his parents are in love and we're in this for the long haul. No doubts. No hesitations."

Her throat bobs with a swallow. "We're already in this for the long haul."

"Stop stalling, beautiful." I press a lingering kiss to the corner of her mouth with no concern about the other people in the dining room. "Marry me next month."

Megan chuckles, resting her forehead against mine. "Next month? Who can plan a wedding in a month?"

"Justice of the Peace is fine by me."

She's quiet for a long moment, and for a second, I think she's about to find another excuse. But then, she tilts her head, studying me with something unreadable in her expression. "Three months," she finally says.

I lean back, my smirk widening. "That sounds like a yes."

"As long as there's no drama–"

"Like your sister showing up at our house?" I quip back, knowing that she thinks she was able to keep that little visit under wraps.

"Lars is such a snitch," she laments.

"Who works for me." I remind her.

"And will also work for me when we get married in three months. He'll have to reevaluate his loyalties then."

I kiss her again, long and slow, until I feel her melt against me. "If you marry me in three months, I'll make sure Lars only takes orders from you moving forward."

"You'd give up your most loyal employee just to marry me?"

"Do you really need me to answer that?" I growl. Her head tilts up, and her lips meet mine.

"Nope."

And just like that, the deal is sealed.

We're getting married.

Chapter 37

What's The Catch?

MEGAN

When I got the call, I was stunned.

Linda John, assistant curator of the Los Angeles Starlight Art Foundation, wanted to have lunch. Just when I was sure she had completely given up on me. Honestly, I wouldn't have blamed her.

The last time we spoke, she had tentatively offered me a spot in an upcoming art exhibit, In The Shade and The Shadows. But it wasn't a guaranteed spot—I had to submit my final piece for approval before she could make it official.

A piece I never finished.

So, basically... I flaked.

At the time, I hadn't realized just how much pregnancy —and the chaos at the club—would drain my motivation to paint. My life had become a never-ending cycle of fires to put out, and my art, which once felt as natural as breathing, suddenly felt like an afterthought.

And now?

Now, I'm a mother. My entire world has begun to

revolve around Deuce, every hour of my day measured in feeding schedules, diaper changes, and the occasional nap where I can steal a moment of peace.

And to top it all off, Hunter wants to add another distraction: a wedding.

First world problems, I tell myself wryly.

A year ago, I was scraping by in a shitty apartment, dodging advances from my creep of a landlord, and doing everything I could to avoid my toxic family. Now, I'm engaged to the most incredible man I've ever met and raising our perfect son. Most women would kill to be in my position.

And yet... I feel like I'm losing pieces of myself in the whirlwind.

The restaurant is all sleek wood and floor-to-ceiling windows, the kind of place where artists and collectors sit across from each other discussing the next big thing in the contemporary art world.

The moment I step inside, I spot Linda John immediately.

She's the epitome of effortless cool—her chunky silver sweater glimmers in the light, her dark-wash jeans hugging her long legs, her black leather high-heeled boots screaming money and power. She radiates that unbothered confidence that only people who have never had to worry about money seem to possess.

I, on the other hand, am wearing a tan cotton mini dress that suddenly feels too casual, too wrinkled. I smooth my palms down the fabric, silently regretting my choice.

The only impressive thing about my outfit today? My engagement ring.

She stands, offering me a warm smile.

"Hi, Megan."

"Hi, Miss John."

She waves a dismissive hand. "Linda, please."

I nod, correcting myself. "Hi, Linda."

"I took the liberty of ordering us some iced teas with lemon. I hope that's okay—I wasn't sure if you were still breastfeeding."

"Oh, that's perfectly fine," I assure her. Deuce is at home with Ruby, probably drinking the milk I pumped two days ago.

Linda studies me for a beat, then leans forward slightly. "So, how's motherhood?"

I hesitate. How do you summarize something so monumental in a few words?

"It's... really good."

She nods. "I imagine you've been tremendously busy. I was raised by a young mother too, so I get it."

Something about the way she says young mother makes me stiffen.

I arch a brow. "I'm busy like any mother would be, but I have an amazing support system, so..."

Linda picks up on my defensive tone immediately. "I meant no offense," she says quickly. "I just wanted to check in—see if you've had time to create. You have such a special gift."

I glance down at my glass, watching the condensation bead down the side, pooling on the table.

"Thank you," I say, my voice careful. "But the truth is, I haven't been able to make art a priority. Not just because of the baby, but... everything else, too."

She nods, taking a sip of her tea. "Are you still attending State Arts?"

I shake my head. "I took some time off."

"Do you plan on finishing your degree?"

"Absolutely." I straighten slightly. "I never had formal art training before college, so those classes are really important to me. I feel like there's still so much to learn."

Linda's eyes soften. "That's good to hear, Megan, because I strongly advocated for your piece to be included in the Shade and Shadows exhibit, even though we haven't seen the final submission yet."

My heart stops. "You did?"

She nods. "That's how much I believe in your talent. I just hope you believe in it as much as I do."

A lump forms in my throat. Shit.

I swallow a gulp of my iced tea, trying to figure out what to say next. I'm grateful—so fucking grateful—but also terrified.

My piece isn't anywhere close to done. And now, the pressure is on to finish it—and not just finish it, but make it a damn masterpiece.

Still, I force a smile. "Thank you, Linda. I do believe in it."

She reaches into her nylon black messenger bag and pulls out a manila envelope with the Starlight Foundation branding on the front.

"Here's the official contract."

My fingers tremble as I take it from her.

"There's an expectation sheet, a timeline, and a contract for you to review, initial, and sign. You have five business days to go over it with your lawyer. As long as your piece is done by next month, we're good to go."

I nod, the weight of the moment settling over me.

One of my paintings—on display at a Starlight exhibit.

This is the kind of exposure most new artists dream about.

But as usual, I can't help but question my good fortune.

Why me? There are so many better artists.

Is there a catch?

Did Hunter pull some strings behind the scenes to make this happen?

I don't know why it's so hard for me to just accept good things without assuming there's an ulterior motive but it is.

"Thank you, Linda," I say. "I'll review this with my husband and our lawyer and get back to you."

She pauses, tilting her head. "Did you get married recently?"

"That was a slip of the tongue." I shake my head, blushing slightly. "We're getting married in a few months."

Her lips curve. "Nice. If you're planning on changing your name, let me know when you submit your final piece. We'll need to have it listed correct on all the promotional materials."

Change my last name?

I hadn't even thought about that.

Megan Middleton.

It does have a nice ring to it.

"I'll let you know."

Linda stands, grabbing her bag. "I have another meeting across town, but stay and have lunch on me. Then, go home and get to work. I want to be able to tell people that I discovered our next great homegrown artist."

I grin. "Thank you, Linda. I appreciate you not giving up on me."

She winks. "Oh, I'm not a quitter, Megan. And I'd bet the farm that you aren't either."

Later that night...

Hunter sits on the chaise lounge in our living room, reading over the contract for the third time while Deuce sleeps soundly on his chest.

I glance over from the kitchen. "It's too good to be true, right?"

"No," he answers plainly.

"Then why are you reading it over and over?"

He smirks. "Because that's what you do with a contract before you sign it."

I roll my eyes. "Don't be a smartass, Middleton."

His gaze lifts, amusement flickering in his steel-gray eyes. "Maybe you need to learn not to be so suspicious of everything and everybody."

I scoff. "I get it from you!"

He grins. "Don't you dare project your paranoia onto me."

I lower my knife, laughing. "Hunter, you have a security team on me that rivals the damn Secret Service."

"Which we have plenty of real world evidence to prove that it's a necessary evil. This is something entirely different. Your talent is obvious and special, and I shouldn't be the only one to benefit from seeing it."

Suddenly, I grin. "Are you trying to get some tonight with those flowery words?"

"That's not what I would say if I were trying to make you spread those thighs for me tonight."

"Is that right?" I smile. "And what would you say?"

Hunter silently slides my contract carefully back in the envelope and places it on the side table. Next, he lifts a sleeping Deuce in his arms, kisses his belly, and then walks him into the nursery, placing him in his bassinet.

"No snappy comeback?" I chuckle as I get back to chopping the ingredients for my salad.

When Hunter returns, he's actively rolling up the sleeves of his shirt. "Do you need help with dinner?" he asks.

"No, I'm almost done."

"Then I'll watch," he says in his signature deep baritone voice, and I immediately realize...I didn't win that one. The flirtation game isn't over.

When I'm finished chopping my last piece of chicken, I feel the heat of Hunter's breath behind me the moment I place the knife down on the cutting board.

"As I was saying before, I'm a pretty simple man. I say what I mean, and mean what I say. Therefore, I wouldn't have to say anything extra or flowery, as you put it, to get you to spread your legs for me."

My panties dampen as his lips grow closer to the back of the neck.

"All I'd have to say is spread them, shoulder-width apart, wouldn't you?"

His hand trails down the side of my neck and travels to my right breast. He gently squeezes my right nipple and whispers against my skin, "spread 'em".

Obediently, I spread my legs and my hands grip the edge of the counter.

"Wider," his voice commands with an edge I haven't heard in a long time.

I'm wearing a pair of loose workout shorts, which he slowly lowers down my legs, revealing a pair of powder-blue panties with lace trim. He loves this color on me.

"Did you wear these for me?" he growls.

"Maybe," I flirt.

"It's good to know that I'm always on the mind of my wife."

"Future wife," I tease.

"Wife," he growls defiantly as he moves my hair to one side and peppers my neck with kisses, then moves one of his hands between my legs.

"Okay, okay," I moan, loving his caress of my pussy. "What's two months and a marriage license mean—wife it is."

He chuckles sinisterly. "That's the right answer, Mrs. Middleton."

"Oh, about that," I say as his fingers slide between my folds.

"About what, baby?"

"I'm not sure if I'm going to take your last name."

His fingers stop their glorious work, and I curse myself. *Why the hell would I bring this up now?* God, I hate when I get diarrhea of the mouth.

"Why the fuck not?"

Welp, I put it out there now. I might as well follow through. "It seems a little outdated, don't you think?"

"No, Megan, I don't think it is, but what I know is I'm going to spend the rest of the night convincing you why you *should* take it. Dinner can wait."

Chapter 38

Who Said I'm Angry?

MEGAN

Lena pepper kisses across Deuce's chubby belly, gently lifting him into the air with the ease of someone who has done this a million times before. His bright-eyed giggles fill the room, his tiny hands grasping at the air, reaching for her. My heart melts at the sight.

"Who's your favorite auntie?" she coos, her voice dripping with exaggerated affection.

Deuce lets out another delighted squeal, utterly enchanted by Lena, which is no surprise. She has a natural way with him, her energy always playful yet protective.

"You're his only auntie," I remind her with a knowing smirk.

"Which is why I'm his *favorite*," she quips, flashing me a smug grin before blowing a raspberry against Deuce's stomach.

I watch them for a moment, soaking in the easy warmth between them before she abruptly levels me with a pointed look.

"Now, remind me why you're still here?"

Hunter had practically vibrated with excitement when I told him about my meeting with Linda John. Within a matter of hours, he had gone full alpha-mode, securing a private studio space for me so I could finish my piece without distractions. And he wasn't wrong—if I stayed here, I'd spend every spare second hovering over Deuce instead of painting.

I sigh dramatically. "Stop rushing me."

"Your painting isn't going to paint itself," Lena scolds. "Now skedaddle. Deuce and I will be fine."

"Skedaddle?" I arch an eyebrow. "Has anyone ever told you that you use sayings like a seventy-year-old woman?"

"I worked with a lot of seventy-year-olds at the shelter," she fires back. "They were amazing people, so thank you for the compliment."

I roll my eyes. "Whatever."

I lean down, pressing a lingering kiss against Deuce's soft little lips. His sleepy baby scent—powder, milk, and something uniquely him—fills my senses.

I could stay here all day.

But Lena is right.

If I want to see my painting hanging in the Starlight exhibit, I have to get to work.

When I step into the lobby, I spot Lars sitting in one of the sleek leather chairs, his broad frame hunched slightly as he focuses on his phone. His usually impassive face is uncharacteristically soft, his brows furrowed in concentration.

Then, something startling happens.

He smiles.

I freeze in my tracks. I have rarely seen Lars smile. It's almost like spotting a unicorn in the wild.

It's not big, but it's there—a small, quiet thing that tugs at the corner of his mouth. He's on a video call, and his deep voice is lower, softer than usual. It's so human, so intimate, that I feel like I've accidentally walked in on something private.

Then he notices me.

His expression snaps back into place, his posture going rigid as he ends the call with a quick word.

I approach with my bags, curiosity buzzing inside me like an electrical current.

He stands, effortlessly taking my bags from my hands. "Let me get those."

We settle into the car, and I try to push down the urge to ask what I just walked in on. But the longer we drive, the more my curiosity burns.

Finally, I can't help myself. "Who were you talking to, Lars?"

His gray-blue eyes flick to mine in the rearview mirror, unreadable as ever. "Hmm?"

"On the video call," I press. "Who was that?"

He hesitates.

For a split second, I swear I see a flicker of uncertainty in his usually impenetrable gaze.

Then he exhales.

"My daughter."

I blink. My brain short-circuits.

"Wait—your *what*?" I nearly gasp.

I've known Lars for a long damn time. He's Hunter's right-hand man, a shadow in the background of my life— always watching, protecting, never revealing anything personal.

And now, he's casually telling me he has a daughter?

"You've never mentioned that you have children."

His expression remains stoic, but there's something guarded in his tone. "Are you surprised?" His accent—usually faint—becomes more pronounced, his Nordic roots suddenly peeking through.

"Well, *yeah*, Lars." I stare at him, still processing. "Does Hunter know?"

He nods once. "Yes."

And that pisses me off a little.

Hunter knew.

Of course, he did.

And he didn't tell me.

I cross my arms, fuming in the backseat. "Don't be angry."

I scoff. "Who said I'm angry?"

Lars gives me a knowing look in the mirror.

"I'm not angry!" I insist, even though my tone is a little too sharp to be convincing.

A beat of silence passes.

Then, his voice is lower, more measured. "My past is complicated, Megan."

I exhale, trying to temper my annoyance.

"There's no need to explain," I say, even though I *do* want an explanation.

"Then why are you angry?"

"Oh my God, Lars." I throw my hands up. "I said I'm *not* angry!"

A long pause.

Then, finally—his voice drops into something quieter.

"My Elsa is twenty-four years old."

That stuns me into silence.

"Twenty-four?" I echo.

Lars nods. "Her mother moved her to London when she was small." He exhales, his fingers tightening slightly around the steering wheel. "Today was the first time I've spoken to her in three years."

My stomach twists.

Shit.

"And I interrupted that?" I whisper.

"It's fine." He shrugs. "The call was basically over."

I frown. "You haven't spoken to your daughter in three years, and the call was *over?*"

His jaw tightens. "I'm done talking now."

And just like that, the wall is back up.

I stare at him, my chest aching with something I can't quite name.

I've spent my life yearning for the kind of father that Lars could have been. A father who protected, cared, loved.

I bet his daughter doesn't even know how lucky she is.

***

The moment I step into my new studio, my breath catches.

It's beautiful.

The space is expansive and sunlit, with exposed brick walls and floor-to-ceiling windows that flood the room with golden afternoon light.

Everything is set up perfectly.

A freshly assembled easel stands in the center. Jars of clean paintbrushes rest on the work table. A cold lunch waits on the counter—because, of course, Hunter thought of everything.

I should be thrilled.

But instead, I stand there, phone in hand, glaring at the unsent text I've rewritten five times.

I want to tell Hunter that I hate how easily he keeps secrets from me.

That I can't believe he never told me about Lars's daughter.

That it bothers me more than I care to admit.

Just as I perfect my wording, my phone rings.

For a second, I assume it's Hunter—maybe his ears are burning.

But then I see the name flashing across my screen.

Not Hunter.

Not even close.

It's the number saved under "Lying Ass Bitch."

Naomi.

What the hell does she want?

Chapter 39

Before She Betrayed Me

MEGAN

"You've got to be kidding me," I say flatly as I answer the phone, my grip tightening around the device. Naomi's name flashing across my screen is like a ghost from the past, a reminder of all the ways she's failed me.

"What do you want?"

A soft chuckle floats through the receiver, casual, almost amused, as if we're still old friends catching up over coffee instead of former roommates estranged by betrayal.

"Wow," Naomi muses, completely unfazed by my hostility. "You were never this mean when we lived together."

I scoff. Is she serious right now?

"That was before I realized you had a habit of standing by while your father *kidnapped me and tried to kill the man I love.*"

There's a pause. A beat of silence.

"I deserved that," she finally says, her voice quieter.

"But no, I'm not calling because of my father. And I don't know anything about him trying to hurt Hunter."

I let out a cold laugh. Typical Naomi.

"You don't know because you *choose* not to know," I bite out. "You're happy to bury your head in the sand, aren't you? Just like you did when your father held me against my will for days, and you did nothing. Have you conveniently forgotten that?"

"I apologized for that, Megan."

Her voice trembles slightly, but I don't care.

"You *apologized?*" I repeat, my voice rising with disbelief. "You think saying sorry is enough for what that man put me through?"

"No," she admits, a hint of shame in her tone. "But it's a start. And I can't explain myself without sounding like a complete spineless bitch, but... my father has a power over me that I'm still trying to break free from."

I roll my eyes, even though she can't see me.

"And *how's* that going?" I ask, my voice laced with suspicion. "Because last I heard, you were *still* living under his damn roof."

"I'm not," she blurts out. "As of yesterday."

I sigh, rubbing my temple. "Not interested, Naomi."

"Megan, wait—I got married."

That gives me pause.

For the first time since I answered the call, real surprise flickers through me.

"To the gangster?" I ask, my voice blank.

"That's a very cliché way to describe Gabriel."

"I'm just going off what *you* told me about him." I shake my head. "You swore up and down that you'd never marry him, that your father was forcing you into it, and now you're saying you *chose* to go through with it?"

She exhales heavily. "He cares about me."

"So?"

"And..." she hesitates. "I care about him, too. I mean, when I think back on it, Gabriel's the only person who's ever really *listened* to me, the only one who's protected me. Even my own family never cared what I wanted."

I narrow my eyes, gripping the phone tighter.

"I thought Gabriel didn't want to marry you either."

"He... changed his mind."

"Or maybe he didn't have a choice."

Naomi sighs. "Gabriel has different views about his *family obligations* than I do. He wants to rebuild his family's reputation, and I... I'm supporting him in that."

"Let me get this straight," I say, my tone sharp. "You hated him. You resented your father for forcing this arrangement. And now, *out of nowhere,* you're suddenly all in on supporting his *mission?*"

"You wouldn't understand."

"No, I don't understand." I press my free hand against the counter, grounding myself. "Because the woman I knew, the friend I thought I had, would have never let herself be manipulated like this."

"I was pretending to be someone else back then."

"Or maybe you're pretending to be someone else now."

There's a long, heavy silence.

I hear her breathing on the other end, the soft, shaky sound of someone trying to hold it together. But I am the one who should be struggling to keep my emotions in check —not her.

"I don't expect you to understand everything today, Megan," she finally says. "I just wanted to apologize again and tell you my news."

I shake my head, disgust curling in my stomach.

"After all this time? After *everything*?" I let out a dry laugh. "So what, you've had some kind of epiphany that you suddenly want to mend fences? *Now* you want to fix our so-called friendship?"

"I never stopped wanting to fix it."

I scoff. "Oh yeah? Then how come this is the first time I've heard from you in months? You called me about your weird-ass mafia wedding, but you never once picked up the phone to ask about my son."

She inhales sharply. "I... I didn't think I had the right to."

"You don't."

Another silence.

Then—her voice cracks.

"You truly hate me, don't you?" she whispers.

I stare at the wall, my throat tightening.

Do I?

Sometimes, I think I really do.

She was the only person I thought I could trust. The one person I believed would never betray me.

And like everyone else in my life—except Hunter—she failed me.

I don't answer her.

Because maybe, just maybe, silence is the most honest response I can give.

"I'll say one final thing before I let you go, Megan."

Naomi's voice carries an edge of urgency, but I don't know if it's because she's afraid of losing me for good or if she's just trying to soothe her own guilt.

"I need you to remember that you're not the only one who comes from a fucked-up family."

I scoff. "And how exactly would I know that, Naomi? When did you ever tell me?"

For years, I thought she was just like me. An ordinary girl from nowhere California trying to find her place in the world.

An aspiring stylist to the stars. A party girl. Someone running toward fame and fortune, not away from something darker.

But that wasn't Naomi at all, was it?

She was a liar.

A mafia princess from New Orleans, running from an arranged marriage, hiding behind the persona of a carefree LA girl.

I shake my head. "When exactly was I supposed to figure that out? When you were texting your 'mystery guy'? When we used to window shop for designer clothes, you pretended you'd never owned some of those brands?" My voice hardens. "Or was it when you stood by and said nothing while your father held me captive?"

Naomi sighs, and for a moment, she sounds exhausted.

"I misspoke," she admits. "What I meant to say is... I hope you'll take into account that I come from a complicated family. And I need some grace here."

"Grace?" I let out a short, bitter laugh.

Naomi has always been good at making excuses. She hides behind them like armor, shielding herself from blame, from consequence.

"Sometimes, people do better once they know better," she continues. "And I won't sit idly by and allow my father to hurt you again."

I hesitate, my pulse spiking just slightly.

"That's a strong promise," I say carefully.

"I mean it."

"Forgive me if I don't exactly trust your word these days."

She lets out a slow breath. "I know. I don't blame you for that. But I have an ally now—Gabriel."

I roll my eyes. "Oh, so now you're using your brand-new mafia husband as proof that I should trust you?"

"He's not just my husband," Naomi insists. "He knows how much I've missed our friendship, and he encouraged me to try again with you."

That stops me for a second.

Gabriel encouraged her?

I don't know much about him—only that he was forced into a marriage he didn't want just as much as Naomi was—that he's ruthless when it comes to protecting his family name.

And now, suddenly, he's invested in Naomi and me making amends?

"What's in it for him?" I ask skeptically.

"Nothing," she says quickly. Too quickly. She's hiding something.

I narrow my eyes. "I don't believe that for a second."

Naomi sighs. "He sees the toll my father has taken on me. He knows how much I regret what happened between us."

"Does he also know that you stood by while your father held me hostage?"

Her sharp inhale tells me that cut deep.

I don't regret saying it.

I refuse to let her gloss over what happened to me—what she allowed to happen.

"I think about that moment every single day," she whispers.

I don't answer.

I don't give her the comfort of pretending it's okay.

Because it's not.

She clears her throat, shifting gears. "Gabriel wants me to be stronger, Megan. He wants me to stop being my father's puppet."

"That's great," I say, flat and emotionless. "Do that. But it doesn't mean we can just go back to how things were."

"I'm not expecting that."

"Good."

She hesitates. "But I'd like for us to try. I'd love to meet your son."

A silence stretches between us.

I glance out the massive floor-to-ceiling windows of my new studio, sunlight casting long golden shadows across the unfinished canvas in front of me.

This place should feel like a fresh start.

Instead, it feels like a battleground.

A war between the person I used to be and the person I'm becoming.

"You once told me that I was the only friend you ever had," Naomi says softly. "That we were like sisters."

I close my eyes, pressing my fingertips against my temple. I did say that once.

And I meant it.

But that was before.

Before I realized Naomi's loyalty was never mine to have.

Before I learned that friendship can be just as much of a lie as love.

Before she betrayed me.

"I have to go," I say, my voice devoid of warmth.

"Megan, please—"

"No." I cut her off, exhaling sharply. "You want grace? Work for it. You want forgiveness? Earn it."

A shaky breath leaves her.

I don't wait for her to respond.

I hang up.

My hands tremble as I set my phone down on the table.

For a moment, I just stand there, the weight of the conversation pressing against my chest like a heavy stone.

Then, with slow precision, I grab a paintbrush, dip it into a deep, inky black, and drag the bristles across the blank canvas in one long, defiant stroke.

Because I am not the same girl Naomi left behind.

And I never will be again.

Chapter 40

Half Hunter, 100% Perfect

MEGAN

I step into the penthouse as the silver elevator doors slide shut behind me, my thoughts a tangled mess, knotted and frayed from the conversation I just had. The weight of Naomi's words presses against my skull like a headache I can't shake.

Hunter glances up from the couch, his storm-gray eyes lifting, his mouth curving into a small smile as I drop my bags onto the floor with an unceremonious thud.

"Hey, how'd it go today?" he asks, his deep voice laced with curiosity.

"Fine." The word comes out sharper than I intend as I kick off my shoes, the force of it echoing the frustration bubbling beneath my skin.

His brow quirks slightly. "Just 'fine'?"

I don't answer. I can't. My mind is too tangled in Naomi's voice, in the excuses, the apologies, the tangled web of guilt and regret that I don't know how to untangle.

Instead, I walk to the kitchen, reaching for the bottle of

cabernet on the counter. The deep ruby liquid swirls in my glass as I pour myself a generous serving.

The scent of simmering tomato sauce and fresh basil fills the air—warm, rich, comforting. It should soothe me.

But it doesn't.

Not when my thoughts are a storm I can't escape.

When I turn, Hunter is standing in the doorway, arms crossed, watching me carefully.

"You hungry?" he asks. "Lena made us something."

"That was nice of her." I take a slow sip of my wine, letting it burn its way down. "Where's Deuce?"

"Asleep. He just had a bottle."

I peek into our son's room, my heart clenching as I take in the tiny, perfect boy lying peacefully in his crib.

It's a cruel irony—how something so pure and whole came from someone as messed up as me.

Then, as if reading my thoughts, I remember.

Deuce is half Hunter.

That's why he's so perfect.

"Want to talk about it?" Hunter's voice is gentle, but the weight behind it is heavy.

I close my eyes, grip the edge of the crib for grounding, then let out a slow breath before turning back to him.

"No." My voice is quieter this time, softer. But when I see the flicker of hurt in his expression, I reach for him, needing him to understand. "Not now."

He nods slowly, his gaze searching mine, always so damn patient with me— something no one else in my life has ever been.

Hunter doesn't push. He never does. Instead, he steps forward and wraps his arms around me, pulling me into his solid chest.

Even through the tangled mess in my head, his warmth

seeps into my skin. I let out a shaky breath, letting him hold me together when I feel like I might fall apart.

"I just need you," I whisper against his neck.

His hands flex around my waist, his breath catching slightly at the urgency in my voice.

In one swift motion, he lifts me onto the counter, the wine glass forgotten as it clatters beside us.

His mouth captures mine in a deep, searing kiss, and I kiss him back with a desperation that surprises even me— like I need to drown in him, like I need to erase everything else.

I don't want tenderness.

I don't want soft words or whispered reassurances.

I want Hunter.

I want this.

Raw. Consuming. Something that burns away everything else.

And he understands.

His hands grip my thighs, pulling me flush against him, matching my intensity, feeding my hunger.

In one motion, he hoists me up, lightly patting my ass before carrying me toward our bedroom. Each step he takes is a heartbeat pounding out all the words I can't say—to Naomi, to my father, to his wife, to my sister.

I don't need words.

I need him.

We crash onto the bed, a tangle of limbs and heat, a desperate collision of need and escape. My fingers claw at his shirt, at my clothes, until there's nothing between us but bare skin and urgency.

I lose myself in the sensation—the press of his body against mine, the weight of him anchoring me to the present, keeping me from drowning in the past.

His breath is hot against my ear, his voice husky as he whispers my name.

"Megan?"

I know what he's asking.

"I'm okay," I whisper back. Even though it's only half true.

But he doesn't push.

He never does.

When we finish, I press myself against him, burying myself in the comfort of his warmth, desperate for the contact to last longer than it ever does.

If I could crawl inside him, I would.

I always feel safest when our bodies are intertwined, when there's nowhere else to run but into his arms.

Hunter strokes my back, his touch gentler now, grounding.

The quiet aftermath is filled only with our mingled breath, the steady rhythm of his heartbeat beneath my cheek.

After a long silence, he speaks.

"You sure you don't want to talk?" His voice is low, careful.

My throat tightens.

"Not yet."

I rest my head against his chest, his steady rise and fall lulling me into something that almost feels like peace.

"Whatever it is," he murmurs, pressing a kiss into my hair, "I'm here."

I cling to those words like a lifeline.

Hunter is the one constant in my life.

I can't wait to marry him, to make our bond legal.

I've been dragging my feet with planning, too focused on finishing my piece for the exhibit—but I need to fix that.

My relationship is just as important as my art.

Maybe more.

Hunter doesn't normally offer words of comfort when we make love. We both prefer dirty talk, teasing smirks and breathless laughter.

But this is different.

This is him, worried about me.

I decide to change the mood—to deflect. It's the coward's way out... but it works.

"Why didn't you tell me Lars had a daughter?" I whisper.

His chest rises and falls before he answers.

"It wasn't my news to share."

A pause. Then—"Is that what's wrong?"

I hesitate. "A little."

His fingers trace slow circles on my back. "Why?"

I swallow. "If you can keep something like that from me... what else can you hide away in that head of yours?"

Hunter shifts slightly, tilting my chin so our eyes meet. His expression is unreadable. Deep. Knowing. Unshaken.

"Let's make one thing clear," he says, his voice dark with certainty. "You are mine to love and protect until the day I die. But there will always be things I don't tell you because of that."

My stomach tightens.

"Everyone has secrets, Megan." His thumb brushes over my cheek. "And getting yourself all upset over things that don't concern you isn't a productive way to spend your time."

"Is that right?" I bite back.

His lips curl slightly. "I get that having someone love you is scary, baby, but if you keep running from it... you'll never know just how good it can be."

"And you know this how?"

His gaze darkens. "Because since I let you in, I've never been this happy in my fucking life."

The tears spill before I even feel them coming.

And for the first time, I let myself believe that I deserve this.

I deserve him.

Chapter 41

The Starlight Showdown

MEGAN

The moment I step into the space, I feel it.

The weight of this moment.

The energy of the Starlight Exhibit hums around me—the polished marble floors, the soft murmur of conversations, the clinking of champagne glasses. My piece, the one I nearly let fear keep me from finishing, hangs proudly on the far wall. Illuminated, commanding attention.

For the first time in my life, I don't feel like a scholarship student in an art school.

I feel like an artist.

A real one.

Hunter's hand rests at the small of my back, his touch warm and grounding. He hasn't left my side all evening, though he's been content to let me soak it all in.

"This is your night," he murmurs, his voice filled with quiet pride. "Take it in, baby."

And I do.

I scan the crowd, taking in the sight of art critics, collectors, and fellow artists, all moving through the gallery with appreciation. Some stop in front of my painting, tilting their heads in quiet study, discussing what the dark, moody strokes mean to them.

I did that.

That's my work. My vision. Hanging in a gallery, not just confined to a classroom or an unfinished sketchpad.

I belong here.

"Excuse me—are you the artist?"

I turn, startled, to see a middle-aged woman in a sleek black dress and thick-rimmed glasses, a Starlight Foundation badge pinned to her lapel.

"I—yes," I say, a little breathless. "I'm Megan Taylor."

The artist.

She beams. "Your piece is one of the most talked-about of the evening."

My heart pounds. "Really?"

"Absolutely. Your use of color, the emotional depth—it's phenomenal. I overheard a few collectors asking about your work." She hands me a sleek card. "If you haven't already, I strongly suggest you start thinking about representation. You're going to need it."

I take the card with trembling fingers. A gallery representative. Offering me advice about my future.

This is real.

This is happening.

I open my mouth to thank her, but before I can, an all-too-familiar mocking laugh cuts through the conversation.

"Oh my God, is that really you, Megan?"

My stomach twists.

I turn toward the voice, already bracing myself.

And there they are—three familiar faces from school.

Ashley and her flunkies, Rachel and Maya.

I exhale slowly, steadying myself as they saunter closer. "It was nice meeting you," I tell the gallery rep, being sure to shake her hand, then step away, hoping she doesn't overhear whatever is about to go down.

"Wow," Ashley says, looking around dramatically. "I guess some people really can just fuck their way into success."

"Too bad it didn't work out for you," I snap back.

Maya smirks, her arms crossed. "It must be nice to have a rich fiancé who can buy you a spot in an exhibit like this."

"And a half-decent outfit for once," Rachel adds her two cents.

There it is.

I should have known this was coming.

I glance at Hunter out of the corner of my eye, knowing his first instinct is to step in. To shut them up with one sharp look.

But I don't need that.

Not tonight.

This is my night.

I lift my chin, facing them head-on.

"Funny," I say smoothly, swirling the champagne in my glass. "I don't recall any of you being invited to show here."

Ashley snorts. "Oh, please. We all know how this works, Megan. Some of us will spend years refining our technique, networking, grinding to make a name for ourselves—"

"And some of us just have actual talent," I cut in, voice razor-sharp. "Which is why my work is hanging in this exhibit, and yours isn't."

Ashley visibly stiffens, her face twisting into an ugly sneer.

Rachel nudges her, whispering something under her

breath, but I catch the tail end of it—something about me being 'hood trash' who got lucky.

"You know what's really sad?" I let out a short laugh, shaking my head. "I actually used to think you all had something I didn't—some secret advantage. But now I see it."

I step closer, pointing my finger at them but lowering my voice just enough to make sure they hang onto every word.

"You're all just bitter as hell that I made it here before you."

The tension crackles between us, thick and hot.

Ashley opens her mouth to respond but suddenly hesitates.

Her gaze flickers —to my hand.

To my engagement ring.

A flawless diamond, catching the soft gallery light.

Rachel's eyes widen slightly, too. "Shit," she murmurs under her breath. "That's actually stunning."

Before I can respond, Ashley whips her head toward Rachel, eyes blazing.

"Are you serious right now?" she snaps. "Are you actually complimenting *her*?"

Rachel shrinks slightly, caught between her own admiration and Ashley's disapproval. "I mean... I'm just saying. It's a gorgeous ring."

Ashley glares daggers at her, her lips twisting with fury. "Yeah, it's stunning—because it cost a damn fortune, and she probably worked super hard on her hands and knees for it."

A few months ago, a sexual dig like that would have gutted me, but instead, I simply tilt my head with a smirk and watch the bitch unravel.

Ashley hates this.

She hates that I'm not intimidated.

She hates that I made it here first.

But most of all, she hates that she's losing control of the narrative.

She spent so long pretending she was better than me. And now?

Now, she has to face the truth.

I give her a slow, satisfied smile. "Jealousy isn't a great look on you, Ashley. In fact, you've never looked uglier."

Ashley clenches her jaw, her nostrils flaring, but she has nothing left to say.

Rachel shifts uncomfortably. Maya mutters something under her breath, and just like that, they retreat, their heels clicking sharply against the marble floor as they disappear into the crowd.

I watch them go, my pulse still pounding, but it's not from fear.

It's from victory.

A slow smirk tugs at my lips.

Hunter suddenly steps beside me, slipping an arm around my waist. "I could've handled that for you, you know."

I tilt my head, looking up at him. "I know."

His lips brush against my temple, his pride in me as clear as the stars in his steel-gray eyes.

"But I didn't need you to."

I did this.

I fought for this.

I deserve this.

And for the first time, I truly believe it.

He grins, nodding. "No, you didn't, and it was sexy as hell. If you weren't the star of this show tonight, I'd take you to the bathroom and fuck you properly."

"Later, Mr. Middleton." I wink.

I turn back toward my painting, taking it in—every brushstroke, every choice, every piece of me embedded into the canvas.

It's not just a painting.

It's proof.

Proof that I belong.

That I'm not just a student.

I am an artist.

And this?

This is just the beginning.

Chapter 42

Keeping The Peace

HUNTER

Power is about perception.

And tonight, I need every motherfucker in this room to perceive me exactly the way I want them to.

As a man who is unshaken.

As a man who is still standing.

As a man who—despite the attempt on my life, despite that my woman was kidnapped, despite the newborn son waiting for me at home, despite the fact that my enemies might think I'm distracted—I'm still the deadliest son of a bitch they've ever sat across from.

That's why I make them wait.

Vaughn, Christian, and I arrive twenty-two minutes late to the meeting, strolling through the double doors of Tuscan Trattoria, a high-end Italian restaurant in West Hollywood that serves as neutral ground for these kinds of conversations when I don't host at the Blue Whiskey.

I don't rush.

I don't apologize.

I let them feel my absence before they feel my presence.

And when I finally sit, I don't even acknowledge their impatience. I simply lean back, take in the room, and let the silence do the heavy lifting.

Two groups.

Two men sitting across from me—Santos Ortega and Vincent Morelli.

Santos is old-school Mexican cartel, an old lion with graying hair, a sharp suit, and sharper eyes. He's been running things in his corner of the city for decades, and though he's ruthless as hell, he's also a businessman first.

Vincent Morelli, on the other hand, is young, brash, and barely controlling the Italian operations left behind by his recently deceased uncle from Las Vegas. He's still learning, still fighting for respect. Which means he's unpredictable and the problem I'm here to neutralize.

The tension in the air is thick. The smell of garlic and charred meat drifts through the room, but no one is here for the fucking food.

Vincent leans forward first, his gold-ringed fingers drumming against the table. In fact, his whole outfit is a throwback to the early 90's. He must have a thing for nostalgia.

"Glad you could make it, Middleton," he says, voice slick with sarcasm.

I just stare at him. Unblinking. Silent. Letting him feel the weight of his own words.

A lesser man would try to fill the space, try to justify his annoyance.

Vincent shifts slightly, his confidence cracking just a fraction.

Santos chuckles under his breath, sipping from a glass of red wine.

"You're late," Vincent mutters again, clearly unable to let it go.

I finally lean forward, slow and deliberate, folding my hands together on the table.

"You're still breathing," I say, my voice even. "I'd say we're even."

Christian exhales sharply through his nose—a quiet, restrained laugh. Vaughn smirks.

Santos leans back, amused, watching the young Morelli heir struggle to keep his composure.

Vincent's face darkens, but he knows better than to push.

Because I may have come to the table late, but I didn't come weak.

I came as the man who survived an assassination attempt.

I came as the man who most respect, and many still fear.

"Let's cut the bullshit," I say, my voice dropping an octave. "We're here because after Fabre's failed attempt to kill me, someone got bold and put a bullet in a car in front of my club last week. And while I don't mind sending a very public message about how bad of a fucking idea that was, my fiancée seems to think my energy is better spent at home with our son."

I let that sit for a second.

I don't flinch when I say it. I don't soften my voice. I don't let them think for one second that fatherhood has made me weak.

It's made me sharper. More dangerous.

Because now? I've got more to lose.

Santos gives me a slow, knowing nod. "The same thing happened at my body shop."

Of course, I already knew that. That's why we're here.

I shift my gaze to Vincent, and I see it immediately—the subtle tension in his jaw, the way his fingers tap just a little too fast against the table.

He's nervous.

Which means he knows something or he's guilty.

"You got something to say, Morelli?" I ask, my voice sharp enough to cut through the thick atmosphere.

Vincent scoffs, but it's weak. "I don't know what you or the old man are talking about. You asked me to come here. I'm here. But I didn't shoot anyone."

I nod slowly. "Right." I glance at Vaughn. "Remind me —how many men deny their participation in whatever stupid shit they've done?"

Vaughn smirks. "Too many."

Christian leans forward, his dark eyes cold. "But they always seem to find the truth toward the end."

Vincent exhales sharply, his fingers stilling against the table.

"Now, see," I continue, my voice calm, deadly, controlled. "I think you may need a brief lesson on how this works. Do you know Ben Pierre?"

"Of course, I know him. The Hatian hellraiser. Everyone in LA knows who he is."

"Then you should know that when people he does business with, such as myself and Mr. Santos, are being targeted, that makes him uneasy, and an uneasy Ben is like a powder keg."

"So?"

"That's where I come in. I'm here to make sure that shit doesn't blow up."

Vincent shifts in his seat, his bravado cracking just slightly.

I take another pause, letting silence press in on him.

Then, I sit back, my hands relaxed on the table, my posture easy—like this is nothing more than a casual conversation.

"You put a bullet in my car," I say, my voice low and measured. "That's a declaration of war. But you're young and dumb, and I'm in a generous fucking mood. So I'm going to give you a choice."

Vincent swallows. "Yeah?"

"Yeah." I nod toward Christian.

Christian reaches into his jacket, pulls out a thick, white envelope, and slides it across the table toward Vincent.

Vincent eyes it warily.

"Open it," I instruct.

He does, his brows furrowing as he pulls out the contents—ten thousand dollars in cash.

"You're out," I say simply. "No more moving weight through Santo's shop, no more backdoor deals at the Blue Whiskey, and no more stupid motherfuckers that work for you taking shots at us."

Vincent looks up, his face paling. "That's—"

"That's your only option," I cut in smoothly. "Take the money and go back to Las Vegas. It's not going to happen for you here. And if you make me deal with you another way, it's not going to be over drinks and pasta, Vincent. And I promise you—" I lean in, lowering my voice just for him, "I won't miss."

Santos chuckles under his breath, clearly entertained. He didn't really need to be at this meeting, but I felt like putting on a show. Everyone needs to know just how invested I am in keeping the peace.

Vincent's jaw flexes. His hand clenches the envelope, his pride struggling with his fear. Making his name in Los Angeles was important to him, but there are rules to this shit—with little room for error. Hell, I'm actually doing him a favor. Rumor had it that both Santos and Ben were thinking about killing him, which would have set off a whole new set of problems for me.

So here we are.

And in the end, with a guy like Vincent?

Fear wins.

He nods stiffly, holding the envelope of cash tightly. "Fine."

I let a slow smirk spread across my face.

"Good boy."

Then I stand, Christian and Vaughn rising beside me, and without another word, I walk out of the restaurant—still breathing, still untouchable, and still the motherfucker to who this city answers.

And I intend to keep it that way.

Chapter 43

Well, This Is What I Wanted

HUNTER

"That was fun," Christian laughs aloud, shaking his head.

"Fuck yeah, it was," Vaughn adds with a grin.

Bringing these two in full-time to Middleton Enterprises has been the best decision I've ever made. Well—if you let them tell it, they made the decision after someone tried to kill my ass. But however it happened, it feels good to have the only men I'd trust with my life watching my back daily.

I was always strong.

But the three of us together? Almost invincible.

Until we step inside the Blue Whiskey.

The moment we cross the threshold, the air between us changes. The easy laughter dies instantly, replaced by a tense, electric silence.

Because standing at the bar is Lena.

And standing real damn close to her is Oliver.

I don't miss the way she throws her head back, laughing at something he's just whispered in her ear. A laugh I've never seen from her before—light, unguarded, genuine.

And in the span of a breath, a barrage of conflicting feelings floods through me.

On one hand, this is what I wanted.

I purposely hired Oliver because I was hoping Lena would feel a spark with a guy I have no personal ties to, someone closer to her age and with similar interests. Because no matter how much Christian means to me, Lena's well-being will always come first.

I thought I lost her forever.

Now that she's back in my life, it's my duty to keep her safe, to make sure she's happy.

And yet...

Christian's fury is radiating off him like a damn heat wave.

A fury I know too well.

It's possessive.

It's territorial.

It's the same rage I'd feel if some random motherfucker even looked at Megan, much less made her laugh like that.

But this?

This is where Christian is making a mistake.

My sister is not his.

And never will be.

"They seem cozy," Vaughn comments, his voice tinged with amusement. "I wonder what they're talking about."

I shoot him a sharp look. He's fanning the flames, and I don't appreciate the shit.

Christian's eye twitches, his body wound so tight that I half expect him to snap and tear Oliver apart right here in the middle of the damn bar.

"I'm glad they're getting along," I say casually, hoping to ease Christian's frayed edges. "He's going to be a big help in showing Lena how to—"

"How to what?" Christian cuts in, his voice icy. "Can we cut the bullshit, please?"

I sigh heavily.

The conversation I was hoping to avoid is happening whether I want it to or not.

"Let's take this to my office," I say.

"There's nothing to talk about."

"Then let's talk about *nothing* in my office."

Vaughn excuses himself to take a phone call, leaving just the two of us.

As we make our way toward the stairs, we have to pass Lena and Oliver, who are too wrapped up in their conversation to even notice us at first.

That alone should tell Christian everything he needs to know.

Lena's eyes soften the second she sees us.

"Hi, big brother," she says, walking over and wrapping her arms around me—a habit she's picked up ever since we reunited.

"Hey," I say back, my eyes flicking toward Christian, whose jaw is tight enough to crack teeth.

"You two good?" I ask her.

She grins. "Oliver might have missed his calling. He should have been a comedian. He was just telling me—"

"We need to head to a meeting," Christian cuts her off.

Her smile vanishes. "Well, hello to you too, Christian."

He mutters something unintelligible.

Lena narrows her eyes. "What's your problem?"

"Hunt, you ready?" Christian ignores her completely, which only pisses her off more.

"I'm ready," I answer.

"You two want some dinner brought up?" Lena offers. "Oliver makes a delicious—"

"We already ate," Christian snaps.

Fuck me.

He's further gone than I thought.

How the hell did I let this happen?

By the time we're behind the closed doors of my office, Christian is already on edge, pacing.

"I know what you're going to say," he mutters, his voice low, frustrated.

I exhale sharply. "Then why put us in the position where I have to say it?"

"Nothing inappropriate has happened between us."

"And nothing ever will."

His fists clench. "I know that."

"So fix that attitude of yours and stop being shitty toward her just because she laughed at one of her coworker's jokes."

Christian runs a frustrated hand through his hair.

"Just because? You think I'm an idiot? I fucking know why you brought his overqualified ass here."

I fold my arms. "I hired Oliver so that my sister has the space to live out her dreams. He can run the kitchen while she experiments, creating new recipes or whatever her heart desires. The first twenty years of her life were hell. She deserves to live a soft life now."

"I realize that!"

I tilt my head. "Do you?"

He lets out a sharp breath, sinking onto the leather sofa. His posture shifts—less angry, more defeated.

"Yes, I know," he admits.

"And if this was the other way around?"

His eyes flick to mine. "I'd be saying the same thing to you."

We sit in tense silence.

Until the tension finally dissipates.

"So we're good?" I ask. "Do we understand each other?"

Christian nods once, firmly. "Perfectly."

I've known Christian for most of my adult life.

And there's a tone to his voice that lets me know that he hears me now.

Nothing has happened yet that can't be forgotten or forgiven.

Attraction is normal.

Acting on it?

That's something else entirely.

And after tonight?

Christian knows precisely where the line is.

And friend or no friend, he'd better not fucking cross it.

Chapter 44

The Family I Chose

MEGAN

The afternoon air is warm but crisp, the kind of rare, perfect Los Angeles day where the sun isn't oppressive but gently filters through the palm trees that line the park's pathway.

I push Deuce's stroller at an easy pace, his tiny body snug beneath the light muslin blanket I tucked around him before we left. The faint sound of his soft breathing assures me that he's still fast asleep, completely oblivious to the world beyond his dreams.

Lena walks beside me, hands tucked into the pockets of her cropped hoodie, her sneakers scuffing the pavement as she kicks at a stray pebble.

It's been a while since we had time like this—just us.

No club business.

No security details lurking in the background.

No Hunter, Lars, Vaughn, or Christian watching over us like we're helpless.

Just two women, a baby, and a perfect day.

"So," Lena says, tilting her head toward me, a playful smirk tugging at her lips. "Are we ever going to talk about the fact that you're getting married to my brother in, like, two months?"

I let out a breathy laugh. "Try six weeks."

Her eyes widen. "Jesus. That soon?"

"Yep."

"And you're just...what? Casually walking in the park like you don't have a million things to plan?"

I glance at her, brows raised. "Did you just meet me? Have I ever been the 'bridezilla' type?"

Lena scoffs. "You haven't had time to be. You've been too busy running a nightclub, having a baby, painting a masterpiece, and surviving a kidnapping."

"Yeah, well," I sigh, adjusting my grip on the stroller handle, "those things tend to keep a girl distracted."

"So what's the plan?" she presses, her voice lighter now. "Are we talking about a big fancy wedding or something small and intimate?"

"I think we're past the point of a big wedding."

"Well, how can I help? I've been begging you for an assignment for weeks."

"I want something elegant but simple," I tell her. "I don't need a giant ballroom with two hundred guests because first of all — I don't know two hundred people. But I do want it to feel...special. Like a night neither of us will forget."

Lena nods, clearly approving. "Where are you thinking?"

"The Middleton estate."

Her eyebrows shoot up. "Wait, you mean the massive mansion in the Hollywood Hills that almost broke you and Hunter up?"

"The very one," I smirk.

"You want to live there now?"

"I didn't say I wanted to live there, but he bought the damn place already. And now it's just sitting there doing nothing, which is a sin because it has the most beautiful courtyard. I think it'd be perfect for the ceremony."

"You visited it?"

"No, I looked it up online on one of those real estate listing sites. There were a lot of pictures. I have to give it to him. It's gorgeous."

Lena twirls a loose thread on her hoodie. "That actually sounds amazing. And very...you and Hunter. Classy, but not over-the-top."

"Exactly."

"Have you told Hunter about your idea?"

"Not yet."

We walk a little further, the sounds of birds chirping and palm leaves rustling filling the space between us.

"So what else?" she asks. "Colors? Dress? Do you have a theme?"

"God, you sound like a wedding planner," I tease.

She grins. "Hey, I take my role as Maid of Honor very seriously."

I glance at her warmly.

It still floors me sometimes—how far we've come.

How a girl who was once just a quiet presence in the background of my life has become family.

Lena is the closest thing I have to a sister.

And maybe that's why what she says next hits me harder than I expected.

"So," she starts, a little hesitantly. "How are you feeling about... you know, not having any family from your side at the wedding?"

The question sinks into my chest like a stone.

I don't answer right away.

Instead, I focus on the sound of the stroller wheels rolling over the pavement. I should have expected the question, but hearing it out loud makes it feel more real.

More...final.

When I marry Hunter, the only real family that will be there for me is Deuce. My father, stepmother, and sister won't be there, and I don't want them to be, but it also would be nice to have someone on my side of the pews.

She offers a sheepish smile. "Sorry. I just—I mean, I know you and Hunter have his whole family presence covered, but... does it ever bother you?"

I exhale slowly, adjusting Deuce's blanket even though it doesn't need adjusting.

"It's not like I ever imagined my parents walking me down the aisle," I admit. "And my sister? Yeah, that's a hard no."

My chest tightens.

Lena is quiet for a moment. Then she gently nudges me with her elbow. "You know, you don't have to go through this alone, right?"

I meet her gaze.

And I see it—the genuine care, the unwavering loyalty.

I let out a breathy laugh. "What, are you offering to be my long-lost sister now?"

She smirks. "Hey, Billy basically dumped me on your doorstep, and you've been nothing short of a mentor to me."

I roll my eyes, but my heart feels a little lighter.

"A mentor? That's a bit of an exaggeration."

Lena stops walking for a moment and turns toward me. "Look, all I'm saying is, family isn't just about blood. It's about who shows up for you. And I don't know if you noticed, Megan, but you've got a whole damn army behind you. Hunter. Me. Christian. Vaughn. Even Lars, in his grumpy-ass way."

I smile because now I understand why she brought it up.

She's right.

I might not have the family I was born into, but I have the family I chose.

And maybe that's even better.

Lena goes quiet for a few beats, staring at the paved path ahead of us. Something about her body language shifts. I know her well enough now to recognize when she's debating whether or not to say something.

I wait.

And then—

"So," she finally says, clearing her throat. "About Christian."

I bite back a grin.

There it is.

"What about him?"

She exhales, rolling her shoulders. "He's...acting weird."

I give her a pointed look. "How do you mean?"

I already know exactly what she means. Hunter gave me an earful about it the last three days. While he claims he's handled things—it seems to be eating him up inside for some reason.

"I mean, the other night, he barely looked at me. And when he did, he was either mumbling crap under his breath or pissed off. Now, he hasn't been in the club for two nights straight. Vaughn said he's been working from his old office."

I tilt my head, feigning innocence. "I don't know, Lena. Maybe it has something to do with the way you were practically drooling over Oliver."

Lena gapes at me. "I was not drooling."

"Oh, babe. You were giggling all over him like a lovesick schoolgirl ."

She groans dramatically, covering her face. "I was just talking to him! He's funny, okay?"

"Okay."

"And nice."

"Okay."

"And maybe a little...hot."

I smirk. "And now we're getting somewhere because Oliver is like Hollywood hot."

"Whatever he looks like," Lena sighs. "Christian has no reason to be mad. Who I may or may not be flirting with has nothing to do with him. He's my brother's best friend."

"I think you and I know that there's something there, whether either of you wants to admit it or not."

We're both resigned to silence as we round the corner of the path. Both of us mulling over what's going on in our lives.

I have six weeks until I'm Mrs. Middleton.

And there's a storm brewing between Christian and Lena,

But something tells me?

It's all going to work out as it should.

I'm a little more optimistic these days.

Chapter 45

Is This A Negotiaton?

HUNTER

Weddings are just another kind of negotiation.

At least, that's how I'm approaching this conversation as I sit across from Megan at the kitchen island, our wedding guest list spread out between us like a battlefield. Deuce is downstairs at Lena's place, so we have plenty of time to hash this out.

Megan is armed with a pink highlighter and a glint in her eye that tells me I'm about to go toe-to-toe with my favorite opponent.

And me?

I'm just trying to keep some of my more questionable business associates from being blacklisted.

The reality is that there's a certain cache in being an invited guest to anything I'm hosting, and a lot of people want to be seen at our wedding—most of them unsavory.

"This is ridiculous," Megan mutters, crossing out another name with zero remorse.

I glance at the latest casualty. "Ben Pierre? Really? He sent a gift for Deuce when he was born."

Megan snorts. "Hunter, he sent a hand-embroidered bulletproof vest for a newborn. That's not a gift—that's a threat wrapped in cashmere."

I smirk. "It's called being practical."

"It's called being insane."

"It was a joke, Megan."

She gives me a look. "There's nothing funny about that shit."

I take a slow sip of my favorite whiskey, leaning back in my chair. "I'm just saying, cutting him from the list might come off as...disrespectful."

Megan narrows her eyes. "Is this a business negotiation or my wedding day?"

"The sooner that you understand that it needs to be a perfect balance of both, we'll both be able to get some sleep tonight."

She lets out an exaggerated sigh, rubbing her temple. "Is this up for negotiation?"

I grin.

There it is...that word.

"You know there's nothing more that turns me on than negotiating with you, baby."

"Is that right?"

She twirls her highlighter, chewing on the end of it for a moment before speaking again.

"Okay then, I have a request. Well, actually, two of them. If you accept my terms, then you can add whoever you want to the guest list."

"Whoever I want?" I raise a brow. "Uh-oh, do I need to be worried about these requests?"

She hesitates, and that alone tells me I should be.

Then she meets my gaze, voice softer. "I want to invite Lars's daughter."

I sit up straighter, my amusement fading slightly.

"Elsa?"

Megan nods. "Yes."

I take a measured breath.

I can already see where this is going.

"Megan," I say slowly, choosing my words carefully. "Lars and his daughter don't exactly have a good relationship. We'd be sticking our noses in where they don't belong."

Megan folds her arms, her expression stubborn. "Exactly. And I know Lars—he won't reach out himself. He won't want to make her feel obligated. But if we invite her? Maybe it's an opening."

I tap my fingers against the counter, thinking.

Lars rarely talks about Elsa, but when he does? There's regret there. A deep, aching kind.

I'm not against the idea. But...

"You're assuming she'll come."

"I'm assuming she'll at least have a choice," Megan counters. "Especially if you send a private plane for her."

I lean forward, studying her.

She's so damn sure.

So determined.

And that's one of the things I love about her—how fiercely she cares.

But still...

"She lives in London," I remind her. "That's a long way to travel for a man she barely speaks to. A man she barely knows."

Megan shrugs. "Then she'll say no. But at least she'll know Lars wants her there."

"But he doesn't want her there, you do."

"You don't know that he doesn't want her to come."

I sigh, rubbing the back of my neck. "You really want this?"

Her eyes soften. "I do."

I run a hand down my face, then point at the list.

"Fine, then Pierre stays."

Megan groans. "I can't believe we're negotiating wedding guests like it's a damn business deal."

"You started it." I grin. "I guess I taught you well."

She leans forward, propping her chin on her palm, studying me.

"You taught me a lot of good things."

My dick immediately hardens.

I want to get this damn negotiation over with so I can get her pretty ass underneath me pronto.

"What's the second part of the deal?" I ask so we can get this over with and get to more important things that involve zero clothes.

"Naomi's father."

I take another swallow of whiskey because it sounds like I'm going to need it.

"What about him?"

"I can't even say that I completely understand your business, so this might be a hard ask, but if you were considering hurting Naomi's father in any way as retribution for what he did, I don't want you to do it."

"That is not something that can be negotiated." My hard-on quickly deflates.

"Why not? You've taught me that everything is up for negotiation."

"Not this."

"Explain."

"Do I really need to, Megan?"

"Yes."

"He kidnapped you, and he tried to kill me. To many in my circle, it's already a mistake that I've allowed him to continue breathing this long, but I have my reasons."

"And I can't imagine what those reasons are, but you're not a cold-blooded murderer, Hunter."

I love the way Megan sees me, although it's highly inaccurate.

"I don't have to be the one to slit his throat in order for him to be gone," I tell her, although a part of me knows that I'd rather be the one holding the knife if and when it happens.

"He's Naomi's father."

"And?"

"And, if I have any hope of Naomi and I reconciling one day, I can't be the one responsible for the murder of her father."

"And you won't be responsible."

"If you're involved, I would be."

"Megan, that fat fucker is the head of a major crime organization. It's a miracle he's lived this long. His elimination would be about business, not personal."

"I'm asking you not to make it your business. It's my second request, and it's what I want. Hell, we can even call it a wedding gift. Give me that, and you can invite whoever you want."

"Sorry, baby, but that's not enough of an incentive for me. I'll marry you butt-ass naked with no fucking guests before I agree to those terms."

She sighs with exasperation.

"Let me change the terms then."

"New terms?" I raise an eyebrow. "What are they?"

"I'll agree to us moving to the Middleton Estate."

"You'll move in the house?" I ask skeptically.

"Yep."

We sit in comfortable silence for a moment, but I can feel it.

There's a power one feels when you have the upper hand in a negotiation, and that power is oozing out of her damn pores right now. Damn, the student has surpassed the master.

And it's sexy as fuck.

Megan's still watching me, but now there's something else in her eyes.

Something dangerous.

Something tempting.

I arch a brow. "What now?"

She shrugs one shoulder, eyes dancing. "Just thinking."

"About?"

She grins. "About how attractive you are as you consider how to counter my offer."

I smirk, standing from my chair and rounding the counter, moving toward her at an unhurried pace.

"Oh yeah?"

Megan tilts her head up, still seated but completely unfazed by the predatory way I'm closing in.

"Yeah."

I place my hands on either side of her, trapping her between me and the counter. "You like it when we negotiate?"

Her breath catches slightly. "Mm-hmm."

I drag my lips along the curve of her jaw, letting my hands skim down her arms before resting on her hips.

"What else do you like, baby?" I murmur against her skin.

She exhales, her hands sliding under my shirt, nails dragging lightly over my stomach.

"I like it when you listen to me."

I chuckle. "I always listen."

Megan hums. "And I like it when you let me win."

I pull back, grinning. "You didn't win, though."

Her eyes flash, challenging. "Didn't I?"

And just like that, I scoop her up off the chair, making her yelp in surprise before she laughs, wrapping her arms around my neck.

I carry her toward the bedroom, her laughter dissolving into something softer, heavier.

Something charged.

I set her down, pinning her beneath me, pressing my weight against her dampened core as her flowy blue skirt pools around her waist.

"You like winning, huh?" I murmur, tracing the neckline of her tank top with my fingers.

She gasps slightly, arching into my touch.

"I love winning."

I smirk. "Then let me make you feel like a fucking champion, baby."

Megan doesn't argue when I take one of her nipples into my mouth.

Not this time.

The only sounds from her now are gasps of pure pleasure until she bends one of her legs underneath me, pushing a knee into my chest.

"Wait," she says in a breathy voice.

"What is it?" I ask as I press my lips to the skin of her thigh.

"Do you accept my terms?"

"I should bring you to all my meetings," I smirk proudly.

"Do. You. Accept. My. Terms?"

Pussy is a wild motivator, and I can see I'm not going to get any until I agree to these insane terms of hers.

"You're entirely too soft for this life you're about to marry into."

"Yeah," she grins. "But it's too late to turn back now."

Her leg relaxes.

Then, she spreads open for me.

And the only answer I could ever give flies out of my mouth.

"Terms accepted, baby."

Chapter 46

My Cross To Bear

HUNTER

Today has been a shit show.

On top of the fact that I may have a mild, completely manageable, not-at-all-concerning case of wedding jitters (*who the hell even am I?*), everyone in my life is being difficult and getting on my last damn nerve.

Starting with Vaughn.

"So let me get this straight," Vaughn says, crossing his arms as he leans against my desk. "We're not putting Fabre in the dirt now?"

"No."

"Because your fiancée asked you nicely not to?"

"That is correct."

Vaughn lets out a harsh, disbelieving laugh. He turns to Christian, shaking his head. "Are you listening to this crap? Back me up here, man."

Christian, who has been noticeably quiet since our little come-to-Jesus conversation, only shrugs.

"It's Hunter's decision," he says coolly.

Vaughn lets out another incredulous snort and stares at him like he doesn't know who Christian is.

"So Big Daddy over here gives you a punch in the chest, and now you're just rolling over like a good little boy?"

In less than two seconds, Christian is in Vaughn's face, jaw tight, voice low and sharp.

"Watch yourself, motherfucker."

I slam my palm against my desk, the sharp crack vibrating through the room.

"Both of you need to shut the fuck up." My voice is deadly calm, but they both know me well enough to hear the warning beneath it. "Don't make me regret bringing you both into my business."

Vaughn scoffs. "While it's true that your name is the legendary one in the streets, let's be clear, Hunt—both Christian and I have helped you build this empire. You didn't do us any favors by bringing us into the fold." He leans in, his tone dropping. "You need us."

I rub a hand over my jaw. I get it. He's pissed. But he needs to calm his emotional ass down.

Fabre is my cross to bear, not his.

"I never said you two weren't valuable to my success," I say, voice even. "That's why I gave you both a piece of ownership, not a salary. But let *me* be clear Vaughn—you two are partners in my legitimate holdings, not the work I do as a consultant. Fabre is my business, not yours."

"Wow," Vaughn scoffs, shaking his head. "You hear this shit, Christian?"

Christian doesn't answer. Just watches me, his face unreadable.

Which, honestly? Is worse.

A quiet Christian is a problem I'm going to have to deal with later.

But after the wedding.

After Megan is officially mine.

"We were just with you on one of those *consultant* calls last week," Vaughn continues. "We're with you on a lot of those damn consults. We know where the bodies are buried, or have you forgotten that?"

"No," I say, leveling him with a look, "but the whole point of our new arrangement was to free you both of that."

Vaughn's eyes darken. "If you're not free, we're not free."

"Exactly," Christian mutters.

I let out a long, slow exhale. "I don't want to discuss this anymore."

But Vaughn won't let this go. "So we just wait for Fabre to take another shot at you?"

"He won't do that."

Vaughn laughs, but there's no humor in it. "And how the fuck do you know that, you arrogant bastard? You are not safe."

I lean back, expression cool. "Last time I checked, I put you in charge of a whole-ass security company that's going to make sure I stay safe."

Vaughn's jaw flexes. "Or you could simply tell the lovely Miss Taylor that you can't oblige her this one thing."

"I will not," I smirk. "And maybe if you learned the fine art of couples negotiation, you'd still be married."

The moment the words are out, the temperature in the room drops.

Vaughn goes completely still.

Christian winces.

And I know.

I fucked up.

Vaughn's ex was a pure bitch, but he loved her, and I just hit a nerve.

Before I can say anything—before I can do the rare thing and apologize—Vaughn shakes his head, pushing off the desk.

"I'll see you at the altar, fucker."

His voice is flat, detached.

And then he's gone.

I rub my temples, letting out another slow breath.

The door swings open five minutes later, and I don't even bother looking up.

"If you're here to bitch at me too, Lena, I swear to—"

"Relax, big brother," she says, flopping into the now-empty chair leather sofa. "I come in peace."

I finally look at her, noticing the way she's studying me.

"You look like shit."

"Gee, thanks."

She shrugs. "Just an observation."

I sigh, rubbing my face. "You here for a reason?"

Lena leans forward, propping her chin in her palm. "Yeah. To remind you that you're about to marry the love of your life and the mother of your child in, oh, I don't know—two days?"

I grunt.

She smirks. "Wow. You sound *so* excited."

I roll my eyes. "It's not that."

"No?" She tilts her head. "Then what? Because it sounds like you're letting your partners and whatever other stress is going on in your business get in the way of what actually matters—Megan and Deuce."

I don't answer.

Lena sighs. "Hunter, I know you have one million things going on, but can you just—take a second?"

I drag a hand over my face.

Lena waits.

Finally, I exhale sharply. "I don't get nervous."

She raises a brow. "But?"

I look at her. "But I don't want to fuck this up."

Something in her face softens.

"You won't."

I scoff. "You don't know that. If you had asked me eighteen months ago if I'd be getting married, I would have looked at you like you were crazy."

"Maybe, but if you'd have told me that I had an older brother out in the world eighteen months ago, I wouldn't have believed it either." She leans in, voice softer now. "You won't fuck this up, Hunter, because I see the way she looks at you. And the way you look at her. You adore each other in a way that is beautiful to watch."

I let out a breath, staring at my desk.

Lena smirks again. "Besides, you already made her manager of the Blue Whiskey, threatened her college bullies, flew her to Paris in a private jet, helped with her art career, and put a baby in her. I think you're set."

I chuckle under my breath. "I see she's briefed you on our entire courtship."

"Go home to your fiancée." She nudges my arm. "Stop overthinking things. And maybe—just maybe—try to enjoy getting married. It's the one time you'll do it."

I shake my head.

But as I watch my little sister walk out, I can't help but feel like she's right.

Because at the end of the day?

It's not about Fabre. Or Vaughn. Or Christian. Or whatever new crisis pops up in my world.

It's about Megan.

The woman I'm marrying in two days.

The woman who loves me and all of my shit.

At the end of the day, it's going to be a beautiful life.

Chapter 47

I Do, I Do, I Do

MEGAN

The sun is setting over the Hollywood Hills, casting a golden glow across our new home. A light breeze sways the white rose petals that line the stone pathway leading to the altar, where Hunter is waiting for me.

I take a deep breath, gripping my bouquet of cream-colored peonies and roses as I stand at the end of the aisle.

Lars is at my side, his broad frame steady, protective. The gruffness in his eyes softens as he looks at me. His reaction when I asked him to walk me down the aisle almost moved me to tears. When Parker disappeared from my life, I thought my one ally in this made family of ours was gone, but it turns out that Lars was always the true ally, and I'm so fortunate he agreed to be part of our big day.

"You ready?" he asks.

I nod, but my heart is pounding.

Because this is it.

This is the moment where I promise forever to a man

who has already given me everything—his loyalty, his love, and the family I never thought I'd have.

As I step forward, the small crowd of guests (most of whom I don't know) quietly rises.

My eyes find Hunter's immediately.

And suddenly, there is nothing else.

Not the quiet murmurs of our guests. Not the soft notes of the acoustic guitar playing in the background.

Just him.

Hunter stands at the altar, tall and imposing in his black-tailored tux, the sunlight catching in his stormy gray eyes.

Lord, he's sexy.

He doesn't smile—not yet. But his jaw tenses, and his fingers flex at his sides like he's restraining himself from coming down the aisle and carrying me the rest of the way.

Deuce lets out a soft baby noise from Lena's arms, and it makes Hunter's lips twitch slightly. Deuce is wearing a onesie that looks like a tuxedo with cute little satin black booties to match. It was Lena's idea to hold him at the altar so that he'd be a part of the ceremony, and then Ruby would take him upstairs to bed when it was time for the cocktail reception.

I finally reach Hunter, *my man*, placing my hand in his warm, calloused one.

Lars nods at Hunter before stepping aside, and unknown silent words are exchanged between them with just a look.

"I told you I'd get her here," Lars eventually says with a rare smile.

Hunter smirks. "Appreciate it."

Lars takes a seat next to his daughter Elsa, who Hunter flew into Los Angeles the day before yesterday. She's a beautiful woman, and I can see genetic traces of Lars in her smile and expressive eyes.

Lena rocks Deuce gently, whispering something to him.

"He's staring at you, Megan," she says softly, looking down at my son. "Like he knows what's happening."

I blink back tears.

Because he *is* watching me.

Like he understands that this moment means something important.

Like he knows he came from love.

The officiant smiles, stepping forward. "We gather here today, under this beautiful sunset, to witness and celebrate the union of Hunter Middleton and Megan Taylor..."

I barely hear her words.

I'm too focused on Hunter.

On the way his thumb brushes over my knuckles, the way his eyes never leave mine.

And then, the officiant turns to me.

"Megan, your vows?"

I take a deep breath, gripping Hunter's hands tighter.

"Hunter," I begin, my voice steady but my heart racing.

"I never thought a love like this was possible for me. That I could find someone who sees me for everything I am and everything I'm not—and chooses me anyway."

Hunter's grip tightens.

I smile softly.

"You have changed my life in every way imaginable. You taught me what real love looks like—Not a love that hurts but a love that nurtures. And not the kind that fades or bends when things get hard, but the kind that stays and fights. "

Hunter exhales sharply.

I swallow, emotion thick in my throat.

"I promise to love you fiercely, to stand beside you, to challenge you, and to protect what we've built together. I promise to be your partner in every sense of the word."

Then I smirk slightly.

"And I promise to always pretend that you run the Blue Whiskey when everyone here knows that I'm the real boss of that place."

A few guests chuckle. Some others clap.

Hunter lets out a small huff of amusement.

Then, the officiant nods toward him.

"Hunter, your vows?"

He doesn't hesitate.

"Megan," he says, his voice low, steady.

"I was never supposed to love like this. Never supposed to let anyone in. And then you wrecked every single belief I had."

A soft laugh escapes me.

His eyes darken with emotion.

"I have spent my entire life building walls. Walls offer protection. Walls are safe. But you tore them down without even trying, and now—I've never felt more protected."

I feel a single tear slip down my cheek.

Hunter catches it with his thumb.

"You are the most infuriating, stubborn, breathtaking woman I have ever met. And I will spend the rest of my life making sure you know just how much I fucking love you."

There's not a dry eye in the crowd.

Especially mine.

The officiant clears her throat, trying to collect herself.

"May we have the rings?"

Vaughn hands Hunter my engagement ring, Christian hands him my diamond band, and Lena gives me his. I slide the platinum band onto his finger, feeling the weight of what this means.

"With this ring, I thee wed."

Hunter does the same, his touch lingering.

"With this ring, I thee wed."

Then the officiant grins.

"You may now kiss the bride."

Hunter doesn't wait.

He cups my face and kisses me deeply, sealing his vow with a promise only we understand. The kiss isn't tasteful like we practiced but somewhat lewd, considering it's a sacred ceremony, but my guess is that everyone understands because when we're finished, the crowd erupts in a loud cheer.

Deuce lets out a pleasant gurgle, and we both kiss him on the forehead, sealing our bond as a family even more.

***

The celebration moves to the terrace, string lights twinkling above us as our friends and family raise their glasses.

Vaughn is the first to toast.

"To Megan," he says, lifting his glass. "For taming a fucking beast."

Laughter fills the space.

Christian stands next, glancing at Lena briefly before speaking. "To Hunter, for finally accepting that love doesn't make you weak—it makes you powerful."

I squeeze Hunter's hand, my chest tightening at his words.

Lena goes last, her eyes warm. "To my big brother and my best friend. May your love always be as powerful and exciting as it is now."

Hunter smirks, pulling me closer. "Oh, don't worry. It will be."

Everyone laughs.

Several people come to our table and introduce themselves to me, but I realize I'll never remember all their names except for one, Ben Pierre, since we spent a lot of time discussing his invitation during our prewedding negotiation.

"Congratulations, Mrs. Middleton. Thank you for including me in your celebration," he says with a heavy Haitian accent.

"It's very nice to meet you, Mr. Pierre. I'm glad you could join us."

"May your union be blessed with many more sons."

Or daughters, I think to myself, but I dare not correct him and thank him politely anyway.

After a moment, I look around, soaking in the moment—and then I see her.

Naomi.

She's standing near the back, looking unsure, hesitant.

She looks good.

She has long goddess braids in her hair and is wearing a sparkly gold dress that complements her skin tone. I remember how she's big on dressing for her undertones—she has warm ones, and mine are neutral. I remember because she taught me that.

I glance at Hunter, who is watching me carefully.

"You... invited her?" I whisper.

Hunter nods. "Figured it was time for you to decide how you wanted to handle it."

I inhale deeply, trying to figure out what the hell I feel. Our last conversation wasn't the best. I told her the ball was in her court, but now it's in mine whether I wanted it to be or not.

I swallow, my fingers tightening around my champagne flute. A million emotions war inside me.

Anger.

Hurt.

Confusion.

Hope.

How dare she just pop up on the most important day of my life. I don't care who flew her here. But then I think about Deuce, upstairs sleeping peacefully as his parents celebrate the second most important day of their lives (his birth being the first).

I have everything I've ever wanted now.

A home. A family. A man who loves me unconditionally.

And maybe... maybe that means I can afford to be a little bigger than my pain.

I let out a slow, measured breath. "I should probably go talk to her."

Hunter arches a brow. "It can wait if you want."

"Did you tell her that I asked you not to hurt her father?"

"No, she doesn't know anything about that."

I nod, setting my glass down. "Then, I think I want to talk to her."

He presses a soft kiss to my temple, a silent reassurance, before releasing my hand.

I make my way toward her, weaving through the guests as I fight back the tightness in my chest. The moment Naomi sees me coming, she straightens, her big brown eyes wary but hopeful.

Neither of us speaks at first.

It's... awkward as hell.

Finally, I sigh. "You came."

Her lips press together for a beat; then, she gives a small nod. "I did."

"You look good."

"And you look great."

I study her carefully, trying to read her. Trying to understand. I notice the subtle way her hands tremble. She's nervous. Uncertain.

She's never looked like this before.

Naomi has always been the bold one. The one who could walk into any room and own it.

But right now?

Right now, she looks like she's waiting for me to tell her to leave.

And I realize...

She expects that I will.

"Hunter called you?" I ask after a moment.

A small, guilty smile tugs at the corner of her lips. "Yeah. He did. And that plane he sent was something else."

"Did he make you come?"

"Of course not, Megan. I wanted to."

I exhale, my eyes flicking toward my husband—my husband—who is watching us from a distance, talking to Christian and Vaughn but keeping an eye on me like he always does.

He knows I'm a fighter.

But he also knows that I don't need to keep fighting forever.

I turn back to Naomi, crossing my arms. "What do you want from me?"

She winces slightly at my bluntness. "I don't know," she admits. "I just... I wanted to be here. For you."

I raise an eyebrow. "Now?"

She lets out a small, breathy laugh. "Yeah. A little late, I know."

I nod slowly. "Yeah."

She bites her lip, her expression serious now. "I was scared, Megan."

I tilt my head. "Of what?"

She exhales heavily. "Of what it would mean to choose you over my father. There are serious consequences when you betray someone like him."

A beat of silence.

Then—

"But I did it," she says quietly. "I left."

My breath catches.

"You... left?"

She nods. "Gabriel—my husband—helped me. We, well, *I*... cut ties with my father. His relationship with him is a little more complicated."

My chest tightens.

I don't know what I expected from this conversation, but it wasn't this.

I swallow the lump in my throat.

"That's... that's big for you."

She gives me a weak smile. "Yeah. It is."

Another pause.

And then she whispers, "I'm sorry, Megan."

For the first time tonight, my vision blurs.

I shouldn't let this get to me. I should be stronger than this. But hearing her say it—finally, truly say it—it cracks something in me.

The anger starts to fade.

Not completely.

Not yet.

But a little.

Because I look at her and for the first time in a long, long time... I don't see the girl who betrayed me. I see the girl I cried with, partied with, and sometimes prayed with. The girl who, despite everything, is still standing here, in front of me, trying to find a way back into my life.

And maybe...

Maybe I can finally let her.

"Okay," I murmur.

Her brows knit together. "Okay?"

I nod.

"You're here. And I guess that's a start."

Her breath shudders out of her like she wasn't expecting that.

Like she's been preparing herself for rejection.

I reach forward, hesitating for only a second before I touch her hand, squeezing it briefly.

And for the first time in a long time, I feel hopeful that I'll get my friend back.

I walk back toward Hunter, my emotions a tangled mess.

He tilts his head, waiting.

"Well?" he asks as I step up to him.

I let out a slow breath. Then, finally—I smile.

"Thank you for not killing her father."

His lips curve slightly. "You're welcome."

I roll my eyes. "Don't be smug about it."

He pulls me against him, pressing a kiss to my forehead. "Wouldn't dream of it, wifey."

I smile against his chest.

"Come dance with me," I say, pulling at his waist

toward the temporary dance floor installed specifically for the reception.

"I don't dance."

"Everybody dances on their wedding day."

"You're going to be the death of me, Megan Middleton. You know I can't tell you no."

"Exactly," I laugh with reckless abandon. "So why bother trying?"

Epilogue

MEGAN

I lay under the sunkissed sky in my birthday suit with the sexiest man alive between my thighs—my new husband.

"That's it, Mr. Middleton. I'm almost there," I cry, and my back arches as I come closer to my sweet release. Birds are flying above us at the private beachfront we're staying at on our honeymoon, compliments of one Mr. Ben Pierre.

It's utter bliss.

Hunter growls as my body shudders from my orgasm, running his hand down the center of my chest and then taking one of my nipples into his mouth.

"Fuck, you're beautiful when you come, Mrs. Middleton," he growls possessively, and I run my hands through his hair and grip it at the roots, letting him know just how much I approve of every single thing he is doing to my body.

We roll together off the chaise lounge, and my head falls back against the warm sand as more pleasure washes over me. Hunter's skilled mouth and fingers work in tandem, teasing and pleasuring every sensitive spot until my body is trembling beneath him again. I gasp and moan shamelessly, lost in the overwhelming ecstasy.

"So damn close," I pant, my fingernails raking down his muscular back. "Please, Hunter, I need *you* inside me, not your fingers."

He lifts his head, his grey eyes dark with lust. "In a moment, my love. Let me taste you again. I'm hungry for you."

Before I can protest, his mouth lowers between my thighs, and his tongue delves deep, lapping at my slick folds with long, languid strokes. My hips buck involuntarily as he suckles my aching clit, driving me to new heights of arousal.

It's a sweet kind of torture.

"Yes!" I hiss, fisting the sand beneath me. "I'm coming again."

Hunter brings me to the brink of climax again with his wicked tongue before pulling back with a satisfied smirk.

"That's not nice," I say to him.

"You said you wanted this dick, so I'm going to give it to you, baby."

I bite the corner of my lip as he positions himself above me and positions the thick head of his dick at the entrance of my aching pussy.

"Are you ready for me, Mrs. Middleton?" he asks huskily.

"Yes," I breathe shallow breaths. "Stop playing around and fuck me hard."

With one powerful thrust, he shoves himself balls deep inside me, and we both groan at the exquisite sensation. Our connection has always been electric, but now that we're married, our need for each other almost feels insatiable.

He sets a relentless pace, pounding into me with deep

strokes that make me cry out and pleasure as sand flies everywhere.

"Yes, just like that," I urge him on, wrapping my legs tightly around his waist to pull him impossibly deeper.

Our bodies are in perfect sync, hips meeting with each thrust as we move together in what feels like an almost spiritual dance. I can feel every hard inch of him stretching every soft part of me, filling me so completely. Pleasure coils tighter and tighter in my core with each exquisite stroke.

"Are you close?" Hunter pants, his voice strained.

"Absolutely not, old man," I tease. "Are you tired?"

"You're going to pay for that," he growls.

My head thrashes from side to side as the tension inside me builds to an almost unbearable level. I need to get control of the rhythm between us, so I push at Hunter's chest so that he's on his back, and I straddle my legs on top of him.

"No, you're going to pay," I tell him as I lower myself down the length of him.

"That's it, baby. Work that magical pussy on me."

"I'm going to put you to bed, Mr. Middleton," I say, feeling powerfully sexy as I work my hips up and down and side to side.

"Fuck!" he groans as his upward thrusts grow more erratic.

He's getting close.

And so am I.

"Come for me, Megan," he growls fiercely as he holds my bouncing breasts with his hands. "Let go and give yourself to me completely."

Silly man.

I've already given myself to him completely.

His hand slips between my slick pussy to where we're

joined, and he rubs tight circles over my aching clit. That's all it takes to send me hurtling over the edge into an orgasm that has me seeing bright white lights.

"Um, YES!" I scream my release, my pussy clamping down around Hunter like a vice as wave after wave of intense pleasure crashes through me.

Hunter lets out a hoarse shout as he pulls down at my hips while burying himself to the hilt one final time, finding his own climax. I can feel him pulsing inside me as he comes deep within my walls.

We remain locked together as we ride out the after-shocks of our passion, panting harshly into each other's necks, covered in sand and sweat. My heart feels like it might burst with how much I love this man.

"That was incredible," Hunter murmurs, pressing tender kisses to my neck and collarbone as he slowly with-draws from my still vibrating core. He lifts us back on the chaise, spooning me protectively from behind. "I bet we just made a brother or sister for Deuce."

I hum in contentment, snuggling back against his strong chest. The warm sun bathes our sated bodies as the sounds of the ocean lull us into a peaceful state. I could happily stay like this forever.

"I bet we did."

"You are absolutely perfect, Mrs. Middleton," he praises, running a possessive hand over the curves of my hip and thigh. "I'm the luckiest man alive to call you my wife."

"You're right — you are lucky."

He playfully slaps one of my ass cheeks.

"That mouth of yours is getting slicker every day."

I offer a gentle kiss on his lips. "Is it?"

"We should rectify that," he says, and I feel his dick hardening again against my ass. My pulse quickens with excitement as I turn myself around and slide down Hunter's body so that my mouth meets my favorite part of his body.

"Oh, we will."

I slide Hunter's beautiful dick inside my mouth and try not to choke as I greedily suck him off.

"Damn, that feels so good," he hisses with pleasure.

I enjoy giving Hunter head, and it turns me on even more than I already was, priming me with wetness that begs for more.

"Come here, baby," he begs as if he's a mind reader. "I don't want to come in your mouth. I need to be inside of you."

This time, our lovemaking is more deliberate. He takes his time worshipping every inch of me with slow, purposeful strokes designed to drive me wild.

"My beautiful artist," Hunter murmurs reverently as he lavishes attention on my sensitive breasts with his wicked mouth. "I'm going to make love to you for hours until the sun goes down so that you remember who you belong to now," he promises darkly.

"Yes, please," I whimper shamelessly, spreading my legs wider in blatant invitation. "I am yours. I will always be yours."

"God, Megan," he rasps, nuzzling into the crook of my neck and inhaling the scent of my arousal mingling with his own. "You feel exactly like you were made just for me."

"I was," I pant softly, rocking my hips encouragingly.

Hunter draws back slowly before surging forward again with a grunt of satisfaction as he bottoms out inside me. "This sweet little cunt belongs to me now and forever," he declares fiercely, setting a deep, driving rhythm that quickly has me climbing back toward release.

"Forever," I moan through my sweet release.

We spend the next five days wrapped in each other's arms, sharing delicious meals, long walks on our private island, and hours of lovemaking.

It's absolute paradise.

"Only someone like you could find us a private island for our honeymoon."

"I have to admit, Ben came through."

We're walking together, wading our feet in the soft waves of the Atlantic Ocean.

Hunter laces his fingers through mine, his grip strong, steady—unchanging. The waves lap gently at our ankles, the water warm and soothing, as if the entire ocean is blessing us in its embrace.

"Did you ever imagine when you started working at the Blue Whiskey that you'd end up here...with me?" he asks, his deep voice gravelly, softened by the ocean breeze.

I chuckle. "Never."

"You happy?"

I glance up at him, my heart swelling at the sight of this man—my husband—my forever. His lips twitch like he's trying not to smirk because he already knows the answer.

"I am," I whisper.

His thumb brushes my palm. "Good answer."

I exhale, watching the horizon, the endless stretch of blue that reminds me of everything ahead of us.

A lifetime.

A family.

A love that will never break, never waver.

"What about you?" I ask softly, turning toward him. "Are you happy?"

Hunter doesn't hesitate.

He stops walking, pulling me into him, pressing his forehead to mine.

"Never been happier in my fucking life," he murmurs.

My lips curve into a smile.

The waves kiss our feet, the breeze wraps around us, and in this perfect, stolen moment, I know—

This is our forever.

The beginning of everything.

And I wouldn't change a damn thing.

THE END

We've come to the end of our love story, and I want to thank you SO much for joining me during this wild ride with Hunter and Megan. I love them so much that I'm writing a few novellas featuring side characters.

First up is Megan's bestie, Noemi. Read her arranged marriage story completely free (for a limited time) in The Runaway Bride.

Bonus Epilogue

Do you still want more of our favorite couple, Hunter and Megan Middleton? Then be sure to read the upcoming bonus epilogue of The Middleton Series over in my reader community, where I share works-in-progress and give my readers early access to all my new romances. Membership is free.

https://lisalangblakeney.com/community

Acknowledgments

This trilogy features one of my new favorite couples, Hunter and Megan, and was first written exclusively for my phenomenal Romance Ninja Insiders over on Patreon.

Ladies, without your support, I would not have been able to indulge my muse and write stories outside of my usual series. I love y'all!

NINJA ADDICTS
Beejay Johnson
Breaking The Epigraph
Carmenita Rogers
Cheryl Cutaia
Junita Spann
Lisa Adams
Lisa Lopez
Marguerite G
Melissa A Pratt
Pat Chrisp-Langston
Susan Williams
Tahkeiya White
Victoria Nogales

NINJA GROUPIES
Aline Lewis-Pack

Dorothy Morris
Lolita Palmer
Martha
Toni McConnell

NINJA SUPPORTERS
Amy Mikelson
Angie Lauridsen
C Kennedy
Cheryl Artmann
Dawn Gilmore
Dee Puffer
Dolores Shortt Mawhinney
Donna Bellaire
Edana Walker
Erin Marshall
Fran K
Jamie J
Johanne Levesque Murray
Karen
Karen Niles
LadyMack24
Michele Handal
Nikki Afetian
Norma
Randi Vincent
Serena Fritz

MASTERSON

Meet Alpha Roman Masterson
Free For A Limited Time!

"Our passion is incredibly intense. The connection between us borders on the possessive. Our feelings are absolutely forbidden. The question now is…what the fuck are we going to do about it?"

DOWNLOAD NOW
Available exclusively through this link.

Also From Lisa Lang Blakeney

****Discounted Book Bundles****
Ultimate Masterson Book Bundle
Ultimate King Brothers Book Bundle
Ultimate Nighthawks Book Bundle
Ultimate Alpha Book One Bundle

The Masterson Series
Devour this addictive series about the possessive bad boy,
Roman Masterson, who falls hard and fast for the girl he's
promised his family to protect.
Masterson
Masterson Unleashed
Masterson In Love
Masterson Made
Joseph Loves Juliette

Masterson Next Generation Series
The crazy hot fruit doesn't fall far from the tree. Dive into
this second generation of Masterson men!
Knox - Knox & Gigi

Bronx - Bronx & Karma
Seven - Seven & Sasha

The King Brothers Series
Dive into this series of interconnected standalones featuring 3 alpha hot brothers and the women they lay claim to without apology.
Claimed - Camden & Jade
Indebted - Cutter & Sloan
Broken - Stone & Tiny
Promised - All King Brothers

The Nighthawk Series
Sexy & sweet sports romances set in the professional world of football. All standalones.
Saint - Saint & Sabrina
Wolf - Cooper & Ursula
Diesel - Mason & Olivia
Jett - Jett & Adrienne
Rush - Rush & Mia
Freak - Freak & Willow
Brick - Brick & Kaya
Dak - Dak & Katrina

Valencia Ice Mafia Series
Hot hockey romances set on the college campus of Valencia City University.
Neo - Neo & Violet
Shane - Shane & Kennedy
Bass - Coming Soon!

The Middleton Series
(Club Blue Whiskey)

Dark, age-gap, romantic suspense trilogy, set in the underbelly of Los Angeles featuring dangerous billionaire Hunter Middleton and the object of his obsession, Megan.

Obsession
Submission
Possession

Where You Can Find Me

MY VIP LIST (Get the nitty gritty)
I have a VIP Reader mailing list. I only send free books, new release, sales or special giveaway information to this group. No spam. You can join here:
http://LisaLangBlakeney.com/VIP

MY READERS GROUP (Casual fun)
Join my online Readers Group on Facebook also known as my "Romance Ninja Warriors" where I share all things new going on, celebrate birthdays, post teasers, yummy pics, giveaways and just chit chat.
http://LisaLangBlakeney.com/community

ROMANCE NINJA INSIDER (Early access!)
For exclusive serials, early access to all my releases, and more goodies become a romance ninja insider over at my Patreon community.
Get started with this 7 day free trial!

About the Author

Lisa Lang Blakeney is a USA Today Bestselling author of contemporary romance sold in more than 28 countries. Worried that her fellow PTO moms might disapprove, she wrote and published her steamy debut novel Masterson under a different title and pen name in August of 2015.

Thanks to strong reader support of her alpha male character, Roman Masterson, she was encouraged to continue with the series and published the entire Masterson Trilogy the following year. She hasn't looked back since and continues to write novels featuring strong alpha men and the smart women they seek to claim.

A romance junkie for sure, you can find Lisa watching a romantic comedy, reading a romance novel, or writing one of her own most days of the week. If she's not doing that, she's outside in the garden tending to her roses.

Lisa is the wife of one alpha (whom she met in college), mother to four girls, and two labradoodles. Get news on releases, sales and giveaways when you become one of Lisa's VIP readers at : http://LisaLangBlakeney.com/VIP

facebook.com/authorlisalangblakeney

x.com/LisaLangWrites

instagram.com/LisaLangBlakeney

amazon.com/author/lisalangblakeney

bookbub.com/authors/lisa-lang-blakeney

goodreads.com/Lisa_Lang_Blakeney

pinterest.com/lisalangwrites

tiktok.com/@lisalangblakeney

patreon.com/lisalangblakeney